# Poul Anderson
# Time and Stars

*A Panther Book*

**Time and Stars**

A Panther Book

First published in Great Britain
by Victor Gollancz Limited 1964

Panther edition published 1966

Copyright © Poul Anderson 1964

to
Anne Elisabeth Hertz ('*Fikke*')

*Printed in Great Britain by Cox & Wyman Ltd.,
London, Reading and Fakenham, and published
by Panther Books Ltd.,
108 Brompton Road, London, S.W.3*

Grateful acknowledgment is made to the following copyright holders for permission to reprint stories which appeared in magazines as noted:

No Truce with Kings, *The Magazine of Fantasy and Science Fiction*, June 1963. Copyright © 1963 by Mercury Press, Inc.

Turning Point, *Worlds of If Science Fiction*, May 1963. Copyright © 1963 by Digest Productions Corporation.

Escape from Orbit, *Amazing Stories*, October 1962. Copyright © 1962 by Ziff-Davis Publishing Company.

Epilogue, *Analog Science Fact* – Science Fiction, March 1962. Copyright © 1962 by The Conde Nast Publications, Inc.

The Critique of Impure Reason, *Worlds of If Science Fiction*. November 1962. Copyright © 1962 by Digest Productions Corporation.

# Contents

No Truce with Kings 9

Turning Point 67

Escape from Orbit 81

Epilogue 101

The Critique of
Impure Reason 149

'SONG, Charlie! Give's a song!'

'Yay, Charlie!'

The whole mess was drunk, and the junior officers at the far end of the table were only somewhat noisier than their seniors near the colonel. Rugs and hangings could not much muffle the racket, shouts, stamping boots, thump of fists on oak and clash of cups raised aloft, that rang from wall to stony wall. High up among shadows that hid the rafters they hung from, the regimental banners stirred in a draft, as if to join the chaos. Below, the light of bracketed lanterns and bellowing fireplace winked on trophies and weapons.

Autumn comes early on Echo Summit, and it was storming outside, wind-hoot past the watchtowers and rain-rush in the courtyards, an undertone that walked through the buildings and down all corridors, as if the story were true that the unit's dead came out of the cemetery each September Nineteenth night and tried to join the celebration but had forgotten how. No one let it bother him, here or in the enlisted barracks, except maybe the hex major. The Third Division, the Catamounts, was known as the most riotous gang in the Army of the Pacific States of America, and of its regiments the Rolling Stones who held Fort Nakamura were the wildest.

'Go on, boy! Lead off. You've got the closest thing to a voice in the whole goddamn Sierra,' Colonel Mackenzie called. He loosened the collar of his black dress tunic and lounged back, legs asprawl, pipe in one hand beaker of whisky in the other: a thickset man with blue wrinkle-meshed eyes in a battered face, his cropped hair turning gray but his mustache still arrogantly red.

'Charlie is my darlin', my darlin', my darlin',' sang Captain Hulse. He stopped as the noise abated a little. Young Lieutenant Amadeo got up, grinned, and launched into one they well knew.

*'I am a Catamountain, I guard a border pass.*
*And every time I venture out, the cold will freeze m—'*

9

'Colonel, sir. Begging your pardon.'

Mackenzie twisted around and looked into the face of Sergeant Irwin. The man's expression shocked him. 'Yes?'

*'I am a bloody hero, a decorated vet:*
*The Order of the Purple Shaft, with pineapple clusters yet!'*

'Message just come in, sir. Major Speyer asks to see you right away.'

Speyer, who didn't like being drunk, had volunteered for duty tonight; otherwise men drew lots for it on a holiday. Remembering the last word from San Francisco, Mackenzie grew chill.

The mess bawled forth the chorus, not noticing when the colonel knocked out his pipe and rose.

> *'The guns go boom! Hey, tiddley boom!*
> *The rockets vroom, the arrows zoom.*
> *From slug to slug is damn small room.*
> *Get me out of here and back to the good old womb!*
> *(Hey, doodle dee day!)'*

All right-thinking Catamounts maintained that they could operate better with the booze sloshing up to their eardrums than any other outfit cold sober. Mackenzie ignored the tingle in his veins; forgot it. He walked a straight line to the door, automatically taking his sidearm off the rack as he passed by. The song pursued him into the hall.

*'For maggots in the rations, we hardly ever lack.*
> *You bite into a sandwich and the sandwich bites right back.*
*The coffee is the finest grade of Sacramento mud.*
*The ketchup's good in combat, though, for simulating blood.*
*(Cho-orus!)*

> *The drums go bump! A-tumpty-tump!*
> *The bugles make like Gabrïl's trump—'*

Lanterns were far apart in the passage. Portraits of former commanders watched the colonel and the sergeant from eyes that were hidden in grotesque darknesses. Footfalls clattered too loudly here.

> *'I've got an arrow in my rump.*
> *Right about and rearward, heroes, on the jump!*
> *(Hey, doodle dee day!)'*

Mackenzie went between a pair of fieldpieces flanking a stairway – they had been captured at Rock Springs during the Wyoming War, a generation ago – and upward. There was more distance between places in this keep than his legs liked at their present age. But it was old, had been added to decade by decade; and it needed to be massive, chiseled and mortared from Sierra granite, for it guarded a key to the nation. More than one army had broken against its revetments, before the Nevada marches were pacified, and more young men than Mackenzie wished to think about had gone from this base to die among angry strangers.

*But she's never been attacked from the west. God, or whatever you are, you can spare her that, can't you?*

The command office was lonesome at this hour. The room where Sergeant Irwin had his desk lay so silent: no clerks pushing pens, no messengers going in or out, no wives making a splash of color with their dresses as they waited to see the colonel about some problem down in the Village. When he opened the door to the inner room, though, Mackenzie heard the wind shriek around the angle of the wall. Rain slashed at the black windowpane and ran down in streams which the lanterns turned molten.

'Here the colonel is, sir,' Irwin said in an uneven voice. He gulped and closed the door behind Mackenzie.

Speyer stood by the commander's desk. It was a beat-up old object with little upon it: an inkwell, a letter basket, an interphone, a photograph of Nora, faded in these dozen years since her death. The major was a tall and gaunt man, hook-nosed, going bald on top. His uniform always looked unpressed, somehow. But he had the sharpest brain in the Cats, Mackenzie thought; and Christ, how could any man read as many books as Phil did! Officially he was the adjutant, in practice the chief adviser.

'Well?' Mackenzie said. The alcohol did not seem to numb him, rather make him too acutely aware of things: how the lanterns smelled hot (when would they get a big enough generator to run electric lights?), and the floor was hard under his feet, and a crack went through the plaster of the north wall, and the stove wasn't driving out much of the chill. He forced bravado, stuck thumbs in belt and rocked back on his heels. 'Well, Phil, what's wrong now?'

'Wire from Frisco,' Speyer said. He had been folding and

unfolding a piece of paper, which he handed over.

'Huh? Why not a radio call?'

'Telegram's less likely to be intercepted. This one's in code, at that. Irwin decoded it for me.'

'What the hell kind of nonsense is this?'

'Have a look, Jimbo, and you'll find out. It's for you, anyway. Direct from GHQ.'

Mackenzie focused on Irwin's scrawl. The usual formalities of an order; then:

You are hereby notified that the Pacific States Senate has passed a bill of impeachment against Owen Brodsky, formerly Judge of the Pacific States of America, and deprived him of office. As of 2000 hours this date, former Vice Humphrey Fallon is Judge of the PSA in accordance with the Law of Succession. The existence of dissident elements constituting a public danger has made it necessary for Judge Fallon to put the entire nation under martial law, effective at 2100 hours this date. You are therefore issued the following instructions:

1. The above intelligence is to be held strictly confidential until an official proclamation is made. No person who has received knowledge in the course of transmitting this message shall divulge same to any other person whatsoever. Violators of this section and anyone thereby receiving information shall be placed immediately in solitary confinement to await court-martial.

2. You will sequestrate all arms and ammunition except for ten percent of available stock, and keep same under heavy guard.

3. You will keep all men in the Fort Nakamura area until you are relieved. Your relief is Colonel Simon Hollis, who will start from San Francisco tomorrow morning with one battalion. They are expected to arrive at Fort Nakamura in five days, at which time you will surrender your command to him. Colonel Hollis will designate those officers and enlisted men who are to be replaced by members of his battalion, which will be integrated into the regiment. You will lead the men replaced back to San Francisco and report to Brigadier General Mendoza at New Fort Baker. To avoid provocations, these men will be disarmed except for officers' sidearms.

4. For your private information, Captain Thomas Danielis

has been appointed senior aide to Colonel Hollis.

5. You are again reminded that the Pacific States of America are under martial law because of a national emergency. Complete loyalty to the legal government is required. Any mutinous talk must be severely punished. Anyone giving aid or comfort to the Brodsky faction is guilty of treason and will be dealt with accordingly.

Gerald O'Donnell, Gen. APSA, CINC

Thunder went off in the mountains like artillery. It was a while before Mackenzie stirred, and then merely to lay the paper on his desk. He could only summon feeling slowly, up into a hollowness that filled his skin.

'They dared,' Speyer said without tone. 'They really did.'

'Huh?' Mackenzie swiveled eyes around to the major's face. Speyer didn't meet that stare. He was concentrating his own gaze on his hands, which were now rolling a cigarette. But the words jerked from him, harsh and quick:

'I can guess what happened. The warhawks have been hollering for impeachment ever since Brodsky compromised the border dispute with West Canada. And Fallon, yeah, he's got ambitions of his own. But his partisans are a minority and he knows it. Electing him Vice helped soothe the warhawks some, but he'd never make Judge the regular way, because Brodsky isn't going to die of old age before Fallon does, and anyhow more than fifty percent of the Senate are sober, satisfied bossmen who don't agree that the PSA has a divine mandate to reunify the continent. I don't see how an impeachment could get through an honestly convened Senate. More likely they'd vote out Fallon.'

'But a Senate had been called,' Mackenzie said. The words sounded to him like someone else talking. 'The newscasts told us.'

'Sure. Called for yesterday, "to debate ratification of the treaty with West Canada." But the bossmen are scattered up and down the country, each at his own Station. They have to *get* to San Francisco. A couple of arranged delays – hell, if a bridge just happened to be blown on the Boise railroad, a round dozen of Brodsky's staunchest supporters wouldn't arrive on time – so the Senate has a quorum, all right, but every one of Fallon's supporters are there, and so many of the rest are missing that the warhawks have a clear majority. Then they meet on a holiday,

when no cityman is paying attention. Presto, impeachment and
a new Judge!' Speyer finished his cigarette and stuck it between
his lips while he fumbled for a match. A muscle twitched in his
jaw.

'You sure?' Mackenzie mumbled. He thought dimly that this
moment was like one time he'd visited Puget City and been invited for a sail on the Guardian's yacht, and a fog had closed in.
Everything was cold and blind, with nothing you could catch in
your hands.

'Of course I'm not sure!' Speyer snarled. 'Nobody will be sure
till it's too late.' The matchbox shook in his grasp.

'They, uh, they got a new Cinc too, I noticed.'

'Uh-huh. They'd want to replace everybody they can't trust,
as fast as possible, and De Barros was a Brodsky appointee.' The
match flared with a hellish *scrit*. Speyer inhaled till his cheeks
collapsed. 'You and me included, naturally. The regiment reduced to minimum armament so that nobody will get ideas about
resistance when the new colonel arrives. You'll note he's coming
with a battalion at his heels just the same, just in case. Otherwise he could take a plane and be here tomorrow.'

'Why not a train?' Mackenzie caught a whiff of smoke and
felt for his pipe. The bowl was hot in his tunic pocket.

'Probably all rolling stock has to head north. Get troops
among the bossmen there to forestall a revolt. The valleys are
safe enough, peaceful ranchers and Esper colonies. None of
them'll pot-shot Fallonite soldiers marching to garrison Echo
and Donner outposts.' A dreadful scorn weighted Speyer's
words.

'What are we going to do?'

'I assume Fallon's take-over followed legal forms; that there
was a quorum,' Speyer said. 'Nobody will ever agree whether it
was really Constitutional. ... I've been reading this damned
message over and over since Irwin decoded it. There's a lot between the lines. I think Brodsky's at large, for instance. If he
were under arrest this would've said as much, and there'd have
been less worry about rebellion. Maybe some of his household
troops smuggled him away in time. He'll be hunted like a jack-
rabbit, of course.'

Mackenzie took out his pipe but forgot he had done so. 'Tom's
coming with our replacements,' he said thinly.

'Yeah. Your son-in-law. That was a smart touch, wasn't it?

A kind of hostage for your good behavior, but also a backhand promise that you and yours won't suffer if you report in as ordered. Tom's a good kid. He'll stand by his own.

'This is his regiment too,' Mackenzie said. He squared his shoulders. 'He wanted to fight West Canada, sure. Young and . . . and a lot of Pacificans did get killed in the Idaho Panhandle during the skirmishes. Women and kids among 'em.'

'Well,' Speyer said, 'you're the colonel, Jimbo. What should we do?'

'Oh, Jesus, I don't know. I'm nothing but a soldier.' The pipe-stem broke in Mackenzie's fingers. 'But we're not some bossman's personal militia here. We swore to support the Constitution.'

'*I* can't see where Brosdky's yielding some of our claims in Idaho is grounds for impeachment. I think he was right.'

'Well—'

'A *coup d'état* by any other name would stink as bad. You may not be much of a student of current events, Jimbo, but you know as well as I do what Fallon's Judgeship will mean. War with West Canada is almost the least of it. Fallon also stands for a strong central government. He'll find ways to grind down the old bossman families. A lot of their heads and scions will die in the front lines; that stunt goes back to David and Uriah. Others will be accused of collusion with the Brodsky people – not altogether falsely – and impoverished by fines. Esper communities will get nice big land grants, so their economic competition can bankrupt still other estates. Later wars will keep bossmen away for years at a time, unable to supervise their own affairs, which will therefore go to the devil. And thus we march toward the glorious goal of Reunification.'

'If Esper Central favors him, what can we do? I've heard enough about psi blasts. I can't ask my men to face them.'

'You could ask your men to face the Hellbomb itself, Jimbo, and they would. A Mackenzie has commanded the Rolling Stones for over fifty years.'

'Yes. I thought Tom, someday—'

'We've watched this brewing for a long time. Remember the talk we had about it last week?'

'Uh-huh.'

'I might also remind you that the Constitution was written explicitly "to confirm the separate regions in their ancient liberties." '

'Let me alone!' Mackenzie shouted. 'I don't know what's right or wrong, I tell you! Let me alone!'

Speyer fell silent, watching him through a screen of foul smoke. Mackenzie walked back and forth a while, boots slamming the floor like drumbeats. Finally he threw the broken pipe across the room so it shattered.

'Okay.' He must ram each word past the tension in his throat. 'Irwin's a good man who can keep his lip buttoned. Send him out to cut the telegraph line a few miles downhill. Make it look as if the storm did it. The wire breaks often enough, heaven knows. Officially, then, we never got GHQ's message. That gives us a few days to contact Sierra Command HQ. I won't go against General Cruikshank . . . but I'm pretty sure which way he'll go if he sees a chance. Tomorrow we prepare for action. It'll be no trick to throw back Hollis' battalion, and they'll need a while to bring some real strength against us. Before then the first snow should be along, and we'll be shut off for the winter. Only we can use skis and snowshoes, ourselves, to keep in touch with the other units and organize something. By spring – we'll see what happens.'

'Thanks, Jimbo.' The wind almost drowned Speyer's words. 'I'd . . . I'd better go tell Laura.'

'Yeah.' Speyer squeezed Mackenzie's shoulder. There were tears in the major's eyes.

Mackenzie went out with parade-ground steps, ignoring Irwin: down the hall, down a stairway at its other end, past guarded doors where he returned salutes without really noticing, and so to his own quarters in the south wing.

His daughter had gone to sleep already. He took a lantern off its hook in his bleak little parlor, and entered her room. She had come back here while her husband was in San Francisco.

For a moment Mackenzie couldn't quite remember why he had sent Tom there. He passed a hand over his stubbly scalp, as if to squeeze something out . . . oh, yes, ostensibly to arrange for a new issue of uniforms; actually to get the boy out of the way until the political crisis had blown over. Tom was too honest for his own good, an admirer of Fallon and the Esper movement. His outspokenness had led to friction with his brother officers They were mostly of bossman stock or from well-to-do protectee families. The existing social order had been good to them. But Tom Danielis began as a fisher lad in a poverty-stricken village on the Mendocino coast. In spare moments he'd learned the three R's from a local Esper; once literate, he joined the Army and earned a commission by sheer guts and brains. He had never forgotten that the Espers helped the poor and that Fallon promised to help the Espers. ... Then, too, battle, glory, Reunification, Federal Democracy, those were heady dreams when you were young.

Laura's room was little changed since she left it to get married last year. And she had only been seventeen then. Objects survived which had belonged to a small person with pigtails and starched frocks — a teddy bear loved to shapelessness, a doll house her father had built, her mother's picture drawn by a corporal who stopped a bullet at Salt Lake. Oh, God, how much she had come to look like her mother.

Dark hair streamed over a pillow turned gold by the light. Mackenzie shook her as gently as he was able. She awoke instantly, and he saw the terror within her.

'Dad! Anything about Tom?'

'He's okay.' Mackenzie set the lantern on the floor and himself on the edge of the bed. Her fingers were cold where they caught at his hand.

'He isn't,' she said. 'I know you too well.'

'He's not been hurt yet. I hope he won't be.'

Mackenzie braced himself. Because she was a soldier's daughter, he told her the truth in a few words; but he was not strong enough to look at her while he did. When he had finished, he sat dully listening to the rain.

'You're going to revolt,' she whispered.

'I'm going to consult with SCHQ and follow my commanding officer's orders,' Mackenzie said.

'You know what they'll be ... once he knows you'll back him.'

Mackenzie shrugged. His head had begun to ache. Hang-over started already? He'd need a good deal more booze before he could sleep tonight. No, no time for sleep — yes, there would be. Tomorrow would do to assemble the regiment in the courtyard and address them from the breech of Black Hepzibah, as a Mackenzie of the Rolling Stones always addressed his men, and—. He found himself ludicrously recalling a day when he and Nora and this girl here had gone rowing on Lake Tahoe. The water was the color of Nora's eyes, green and blue and with sunlight flimmering across the surface, but so clear you could see the rocks on the bottom; and Laura's own little bottom had stuck straight in the air as she trailed her hands astern.

She sat thinking for a space before saying flatly: 'I suppose you can't be talked out of it.' He shook his head. 'Well, can I leave tomorrow early, then?'

'Yes. I'll get you a coach.'

'T-t-to hell with that. I'm better in the saddle than you are.'

'Okay. A couple of men to escort you, though.' Mackenzie drew a long breath. 'Maybe you can persuade Tom—'

'No. I can't. Please don't ask me to, Dad.'

He gave her the last gift he could: 'I wouldn't want you to stay. That'd be shirking your own duty. Tell Tom I still think he's the right man for you. Goodnight, duck.' It came out too fast, but he dared not delay. When she began to cry he must unfold her arms from his neck and depart the room.

*But I had not expected so much killing!'*

*'Nor I . . . at this stage of things. There will be more yet, I am afraid, before the immediate purpose is achieved.'*

*'You told me—'*

*'I told you our hopes, Mwyr. You know as well as I that the Great Science is only exact on the broadest scale of history. Individual events are subject to statistical fluctuation.'*

*'That is an easy way, is it not, to describe sentient beings dying in the mud?'*

*'You are new here. Theory is one thing, adjustment to practical necessities is another. Do you think it does not hurt me to see that happen which I myself have helped plan?'*

*'Oh, I know, I know. Which makes it no easier to live with my guilt.'*

*'To live with your responsibilities, you mean.'*

*'Your phrase.'*

*'No, this is not semantic trickery. The distinction is real. You have read reports and seen films, but I was here with the first expedition. And here I have been for more than two centuries. Their agony is no abstraction to me.'*

*'But it was different when we first discovered them. The Aftermath of their nuclear wars was still so horribly present. That was when they needed us – the poor starveling anarchs – and we, we did nothing but observe.'*

*Now you are hysterical. Could we come in blindly, ignorant of every last fact about them, and expect to be anything but one more disruptive element? An element whose effects we ourselves would not have been able to predict. That would have been criminal indeed, like a surgeon who started to operate as soon as he met the patient, without so much as taking a case history. We had to let them go their own way while we studied in secret. You have no idea how desperately hard we worked to gain information and understanding. That work goes on. It was only seventy years ago that we felt enough assurance to introduce the first new factor into this one selected society. As we continue to learn more, the plan will be adjusted. It maybe take us a thousand years to complete our mission.'*

*'But meanwhile they have pulled themselves back out of the wreckage. They are finding their own answers to their problems. What right have we to—'*

*'I begin to wonder, Mwyr, what right you have to claim even the title of apprentice psychodyamician. Consider what their "answers" actually amount to. Most of the planet is still in a state of barbarism. This continent has come farthest toward recovery, because of having the widest distribution of technical skills and equipment before the destruction. But what social structure has evolved? A jumble of quarrelsome successor states. A feudalism where the balance of political, military, and economic power lies with a landed aristocracy, of all archaic things. A score of languages and subcultures developing along their own incompatible lines. A blind technology worship inherited from the ancestral society that, unchecked, will lead them in the end back to a machine civilization as demoniac as the one that tore itself apart three centuries ago. Are you distressed that a few hundred men have been killed because our agents promoted a revolution which did not come off quite so smoothly as we hoped? Well, you have the word of the Great Science itself that, without our guidance, the totaled misery of this race through the next five thousand years would outweigh by three orders of magnitude whatever pain we are forced to inflict.'*

*'—Yes. Of course. I realize I am being emotional. It is difficult not to be at first, I suppose.'*

*'You should be thankful that your initial exposure to the hard necessities of the plan was so mild. There is worse to come.'*

'*So I have been told.*'

'*In abstract terms. But consider the reality. A government ambitious to restore the old nation will act aggressively, thus embroiling itself in prolonged wars with powerful neighbors. Both directly and indirectly, through the operation of economic factors they are too naïve to control, the aristocrats and freeholders will be eroded away by those wars. Anomic democracy will replace their system, first dominated by a corrupt capitalism and later by sheer force of whoever holds the central government. But there will be no place for the vast displaced proletariat, the one-time landowners and the foreigners incorporated by conquest. They will offer fertile soil to any demagogue. The empire will undergo endless upheaval, civil strife, despotism, decay, and outside invasion. Oh, we will have much to answer for before we are done!*'

'*Do you think . . . when we see the final result . . . will the blood wash off us?*'

'*No. We pay the heaviest price of all.*'

Spring in the high Sierra is cold, wet, snowbanks melting away from forest floor and giant rocks, rivers in spate until their canyons clang, a breeze ruffling puddles in the road. The first green breath across the aspen seems infinitely tender against pine and spruce, which gloom into a brilliant sky. A raven swoops low, gruk, gruk, look out for that damn hawk! But then you cross timber line and the world becomes tumbled blue-gray immensity, with the sun ablaze on what snows remain and the wind sounding hollow in your ears.

Captain Thomas Danielis, Field Artillery, Loyalist Army of the Pacific States, turned his horse aside. He was a dark young man, slender and snub-nosed. Behind him a squad slipped and cursed, dripping mud from feet to helmets, trying to get a gun carrier unstuck. Its alcohol motor was too feeble to do more than spin the wheels. The infantry squelched on past, stoop-shouldered, worn down by altitude and a wet bivouac and pounds of mire on each boot. Their line snaked from around a prowlike crag, up the twisted road and over the ridge ahead. A gust brought the smell of sweat to Danielis.

But they were good joes, he thought. Dirty, dogged, they did their profane best. His own company, at least, was going to get hot food tonight, if he had to cook the quartermaster sergeant.

The horse's hoofs banged on a block of ancient concrete jutting from the muck. If this had been the old days . . . but wishes weren't bullets. Beyond this part of the range lay lands mostly desert, claimed by the Saints, who were no longer a menace but with whom there was scant commerce. So the mountain highways had never been considered worth repaving, and the railroad ended at Hangtown. Therefore the expeditionary force to the Tahoe area must slog through unpeopled forests and icy uplands, God help the poor bastards.

*God help them in Nakamura, too,* Danielis thought. His mouth drew taut, he slapped his hands together and spurred the horse with needless violence. Sparks shot from iron shoes as the beast clattered off the road toward the highest point of the ridge. The man's saber banged his leg.

Reining in, he unlimbered his field glasses. From here he could look across a jumbled sweep of mountainscape, where cloud shadows sailed over cliffs and boulders, down into the gloom of a canyon and across to the other side. A few tufts of grass thrust out beneath him, mummy brown, and a marmot wakened early from winter sleep whistled somewhere in the stone confusion. He still couldn't see the castle. Nor had he expected to, as yet. He knew this country . . . how well he did!

There might be a glimpse of hostile activity, though. It had been eerie to march this far with no sign of the enemy, of anyone else whatsoever; to send out patrols in search of rebel units that could not be found; to ride with shoulder muscles tense against the sniper's arrow that never came. Old Jimbo Mackenzie was not one to sit passive behind walls, and the Rolling Stones had not been given their nickname in jest.

*If Jimbo is alive. How do I know he is? That buzzard yonder may be the very one which hacked out his eyes.*

Danielis bit his lip and made himself look steadily through the glasses. Don't think about Mackenzie, how he outroared and outdrank and outlaughed you and you never minded, how he sat knotting his brows over the chessboard where you could mop him up ten times out of ten and *he* never cared, how proud and happy he stood at the wedding . . . Nor think about Laura, who tried to keep you from knowing how often she wept at night, who now bore a grandchild beneath her heart and woke alone in the San Francisco house from the evil dreams of pregnancy.

Every one of those dogfaces plodding toward the castle which has killed every army ever sent against it – every one of them has somebody at home and hell rejoices at how many have somebody on the rebel side. Better look for hostile spoor and let it go at that.

Wait! Daniels stiffened. A rider— he focused. *One of our own.* Fallon's army added a blue band to the uniform. *Returning scout.* A tingle went along his spine. He decided to hear the report firsthand. But the fellow was still a mile off, perforce riding slowly over the hugger-mugger terrain. There was no hurry about intercepting him. Danielis continued to survey the land.

A reconnaissance plane appeared, an ungainly dragonfly with sunlight flashing off a propeller head. Its drone bumbled among rock walls, where echoes threw the noise back and forth. Doubtless an auxiliary to the scouts, employing two-way radio communication. Later the plane would work as a spotter for artillery. There was no use making a bomber of it; Fort Nakamura was proof against anything that today's puny aircraft could drop, and might well shoot the thing down.

A shoe scraped behind Danielis. Horse and man whirled as one. His pistol jumped into his hand.

It lowered. 'Oh. Excuse me, Philosopher.'

The man in the blue robe nodded. A smile softened his stern face. He must be around sixty years old, hair white and skin lined, but he walked these heights like a wild goat. The Yang and Yin symbol burned gold on his breast.

'You're needlessly on edge, son,' he said. A trace of Texas accent stretched out his words. The Espers obeyed the laws wherever they lived, but acknowledge no country their own: nothing less than mankind, perhaps ultimately all life through the space-time universe. Nevertheless, the Pacific States had gained enormously in prestige and influence when the Order's unenterable Central was established in San Francisco at the time when the city was being rebuilt in earnest. There had been no objection – on the contrary – to the Grand Seeker's desire that Philosopher Woodworth accompany the expedition as an observer. Not even from the chaplains; the churches had finally gotten it straight that the Esper teachings were neutral with respect to religion.

Danielis managed a grin. 'Can you blame me?'

'No blame. But advice. Your attitude isn't useful. Does nothin' but wear you out. You've been fightin' a battle for weeks before it began.'

Danielis remembered the apostle who had visited his home in San Francisco — by invitation, in the hope that Laura might learn some peace. His simile had been still homelier: 'You only need to wash one dish at a time.' The memory brought a smart to Danielis' eyes, so that he said roughly:

'I might relax if you'd use your powers to tell me what's waiting for us.'

'I'm no adept, son. Too much in the material world, I'm afraid. Somebody's got to do the practical work of the Order, and someday I'll get the chance to retire and explore the frontier inside me. But you need to start early, and stick to it a lifetime, to develop your full powers.' Woodworth looked across the peaks, seemed almost to merge himself with their loneliness.

Danielis hesitated to break into that meditation. He wondered what practical purpose the Philosopher was serving on this trip. To bring back a report, more accurate than untrained senses and undisciplined emotions could prepare? Yes, that must be it. The Espers might yet decide to take a hand in this war. However reluctantly, Central had allowed the awesome psi powers to be released now and again, when the Order was seriously threatened; and Judge Fallon was a better friend to them than Brodsky or the earlier Senate of Bossmen and House of People's Deputies had been.

The horse stamped and blew out its breath in a snort. Woodworth glanced back at the rider. 'If you ask me, though,' he said, 'I don't reckon you'll find much doin' around here. I was in the Rangers myself, back home, before I saw the Way. This country feels empty.'

'If we could know!' Danielis exploded. 'They've had the whole winter to do what they liked in the mountains, while the snow kept us out. What scouts we could get in reported a beehive — as late as two weeks ago. What have they planned?'

Woodworth made no reply.

It flooded from Danielis, he couldn't stop, he had to cover the recollection of Laura bidding him good-by on his second expedition against her father, six months after the first one came home in bloody fragments:

'If we had the resources! A few wretched little railroads and motor cars; a handful of aircraft; most of our supply trains drawn by mules – what kind of mobility does that give us? And what really drives me crazy ... we know how to make what they had in the old days. We've got the books, the information. More, maybe, than the ancestors. I've watched the electrosmith at Fort Nakamura turn out transistor units with enough bandwidth to carry television, no bigger than my fist. I've seen the scientific journals, the research labs, biology, chemistry, astronomy, mathematics. And all useless!'

'Not so,' Woodworth answered mildly. 'Like my own Order, the community of scholarship's becomin' supranational. Printin' presses, radiophones, telescribes—'

'I say useless. Useless to stop men killing each other because there's no authority strong enough to make them behave. Useless to take a farmer's hands off a horse-drawn plow and put them on the wheel of a tractor. We've got the knowledge, but we can't apply it.'

'You do apply it, son, where too much power and industrial plant isn't required. Remember, the world's a lot poorer in natural resources than it was before the Hellbombs. I've seen the Black Lands myself, where the firestorm passed over the Texas oilfields.' Woodworth's serenity cracked a little. He turned his eyes back to the peaks.

'There's oil elsewhere,' Danielis insisted. 'And coal, iron, uranium, everything we need. But the world hasn't got the organization to get at it. Not in any quantity. So we fill the Central Valley with crops that'll yield alcohol, to keep a few motors turning; and we import a dribble of other stuff along an unbelievably inefficient chain of middlemen; and most of it's eaten by the armies.' He jerked his head toward that part of the sky which the handmade airplane had crossed. 'That's one reason we've got to have Reunification. So we can rebuild.'

'And the other?' Woodworth asked softly.

'Democracy – universal suffrage—' Danielis swallowed. 'And so fathers and sons won't have to fight each other again.'

'Those are better reasons,' Woodworth said. 'Good enough for the Espers to support. But as for that machinery you want—' He shook his head. 'No, you're wrong there. That's no way for men to live.'

'Maybe not,' Danielis said. 'Though my own father wouldn't have been crippled by overwork if he'd had some machines to help him. ... Oh, I don't know. First things first. Let's get this war over with and argue later.' He remembered the scout, now gone from view. 'Pardon me, Philosopher, I've got an errand.'

The Esper raised his hand in token of peace. Danielis cantered off.

Splashing along the roadside, he saw the man he wanted, halted by Major Jacobsen. The latter, who must have sent him out, sat mounted near the infantry line. The scout was a Klamath Indian, stocky in buckskins, a bow on his shoulder. Arrows were favored over guns by many of the men from the northern districts: cheaper than bullets, no noise, less range but as much firepower as a bolt-action rifle. In the bad old days before the Pacific States had formed their union, archers along forest trails had saved many a town from conquest; they still helped keep that union loose.

'Ah, Captain Danielis,' Jacobsen hailed. 'You're just in time. Lieutenant Smith was about to report what his detachment found out.'

'And the plane,' said Smith imperturbably. 'What the pilot told us he'd seen from the air gave us the guts to go there and check for ourselves.'

'Well?'

'Nobody around.'

'What?'

'Fort's been evacuated. So's the settlement. Not a soul.'

'But – but—' Jacobsen collected himself. 'Go on.'

'We studied the signs as best's we could. Looks like non-combatants left some time ago. By sledge and ski, I'd guess, maybe north to some strong point. I suppose the men shifted their own stuff at the same time, gradual-like, what they couldn't carry with 'em at the last. Because the regiment and its support units, even field artillery, pulled out just three-four days ago. Ground's all tore up. They headed downslope, sort of west by northwest far's we could tell from what we saw.'

Jacobsen choked. 'Where are they bound?'

A flaw of wind struck Danielis in the face and ruffled the horses' manes. At his back he heard the slow plop and squish of boots, groan of wheels, chuff of motors, rattle of wood and metal, yells and whipcracks of muleskinners. But it seemed very remote. A map grew before him, blotting out the world.

The Loyalist Army had had savage fighting the whole winter, from the Trinity Alps to Puget Sound – for Brodsky had managed to reach Mount Rainier, whose lord had furnished broadcasting facilities, and Rainier was too well fortified to take at once. The bossmen and the autonomous tribes rose in arms, persuaded that a usurper threatened their damned little local privileges. Their protectees fought beside them, if only because no rustic had been taught any higher loyalty than to his patron. West Canada, fearful of what Fallon might do when he got the chance, lent the rebels aid that was scarcely even clandestine.

Nonetheless, the national army was stronger: more matériel, better organization, above everything an ideal of the future. Cinc O'Donnell had outlined a strategy – concentrate the loyal forces at a few points, overwhelm resistance, restore order and establish bases in the region, then proceed to the next place – which worked. The government now controlled the entire coast, with naval units to keep an eye on the Canadians in Vancouver and guard the important Hawaii trade routes; the northern half of Washington almost to the Idaho line; the Columbia Valley; central California as far north as Redding. The remaining rebellious Stations and towns were isolated from each other in mountains, forests, deserts. Bossdom after bossdom fell as the loyalists pressed on, defeating the enemy in detail, cutting him off from supplies and hope. The only real worry had been Cruikshank's Sierra Command, an army in its own right rather than a levy of yokels and citymen, big and tough and expertly led. This expedition against Fort Nakamura was only a small part of what had looked like a difficult campaign.

But now the Rolling Stones had pulled out. Offered no fight whatsoever. Which meant that their brother Catamounts must also have evacuated. You don't give up one anchor of a line you intend to hold. So?

'Down into the valleys,' Danielis said; and there sounded in his ears, crazily, the voice of Laura as she used to sing. *Down in the valley, valley so low.*

'Judas!' the major exclaimed. Even the Indian grunted as if he had taken a belly blow. 'No, they couldn't. We've have known.'

*Hang your head over, hear the wind blow.* It hooted across cold rocks.

'There are plenty of forest trails,' Danielis said. 'Infantry and cavalry could use them, if they're accustomed to such country. And the Cats are. Vehicles, wagons, big guns, that's slower and harder. But they only need to outflank us, then they can get back onto Forty and Fifty – and cut us to pieces if we attempt pursuit. I'm afraid they've got us boxed.'

'The eastern slope—,' said Jacobsen helplessly.

'What for? Want to occupy a lot of sagebrush? No, we're trapped here till they deploy in the flatlands.' Danielis closed a hand on his saddlehorn so that the knuckles went bloodless. 'I miss my guess if this isn't Colonel Mackenzie's idea. It's his style, for sure.'

'But then they're between us and Frisco! With damn near our whole strength in the north—'

*Between me and Laura,* Danielis thought.

He said aloud: 'I suggest, Major, we get hold of the C.O. at once. And then we better get on the radio.' From some well he drew the power to raise his head. The wind lashed his eyes. 'This needn't be a disaster. They'll be easier to beat out in the open, actually, once we come to grips.'

*Roses love sunshine, violets love dew,*
*Angels in heaven know I love you.*

The rains which fill the winter of the California lowlands were about ended. Northward along a highway whose pavement clopped under hoofs, Mackenzie rode through a tremendous greenness. Eucalyptus and live oak, flanking the road, exploded with new leaves. Beyond them on either side stretched a checkerboard of fields and vineyards, intricately hued, until the distant hills on the right and the higher, nearer ones on the left made walls. The freeholder houses that had been scattered across the land a ways back were no longer to be seen. This end of the Napa Valley belonged to the Esper community at St. Helena. Clouds banked like white mountains over the western ridge. The breeze bore to Mackenzie a smell of growth and turned earth.

Behind him it rumbled with men. The Rolling Stones were on the move. The regiment proper kept to the highway, three thousand boots slamming down at once with an earthquake noise, and so did the guns and wagons. There was no immediate danger of attack. But the cavalrymen attached to the force must needs spread out. The sun flashed off their helmets and lance heads.

Mackenzie's attention was directed forward. Amber walls and red tile roofs could be seen among plum trees that were a surf of pink and white blossoms. The community was big, several thousand people. The muscles tightened in his abdomen. 'Think we can trust them?' he asked, not for the first time. 'We've only got a radio agreement to a parley.'

Speyer, riding beside him, nodded. 'I expect they'll be honest. Particularly with our boys right outside. Espers believe in non-violence anyway.'

'Yeah, but if it did come to fighting – I know there aren't very many adepts so far. The Order hasn't been around long enough for that. But when you get this many Espers together, there's bound to be a few who've gotten somewhere with their damned psionics. I don't want my men blasted, or lifted in the air and dropped, or any such nasty thing.'

Speyer threw him a sidelong glance. 'Are you scared of them, Jimbo?' he murmured.

'Hell, no!' Mackenzie wondered if he was a liar or not. 'But I don't like 'em.'

'They do a lot of good. Among the poor, especially.'

'Sure, sure. Though any decent bossman looks after his own protectees, and we've got things like churches and hospices as well. I don't see where just being charitable – and they can afford it, with the profits they make on their holdings – I don't see where that gives any right to raise the orphans and pauper kids they take in, the way they do: so's to make the poor tikes unfit for life anywhere outside.'

'The object of that, as you well know, is to orient them toward the so-called interior frontier. Which American civilization as a whole is not much interested in. Frankly, quite apart from the remarkable powers some Espers have developed, I often envy them.'

'You, Phil?' Mackenzie goggled at his friend.

The lines drew deep in Speyer's face. 'This winter I've helped shoot a lot of my fellow countrymen,' he said low. 'My mother and wife and kids are crowded with the rest of the Village in the Mount Lassen fort, and when we said good-by we knew it was quite possibly permanent. And in the past I've helped shoot a lot of other men who never did me any personal harm.' He sighed. 'I've often wondered what it's like to know peace, inside as well as outside.'

Mackenzie sent Laura and Tom out of his head.

'Of course,' Speyer went on, 'the fundamental reason you – and I, for that matter – distrust the Espers is that they do represent something alien to us. Something that may eventually choke out the whole concept of life that we grew up with. You know, a couple weeks back in Sacramento I dropped in at the University research lab to see what was going on. Incredible! The ordinary soldier would swear it was witchwork. It was certainly more weird than ... than simply reading minds or moving objects by thinking at them. But to you or me it's a shiny new marvel. We'll wallow in it.

'Now why's that? Because the lab is scientific. Those men work with chemicals, electronics, subviral particles. That fits into the educated American's world-view. But the mystic unity of creation ... no, not our cup of tea. The only way we can hope to achieve Oneness is to renounce everything we've ever believed in. At your age or mine, Jimbo, a man is seldom ready to tear down his whole life and start from scratch.'

'Maybe so.' Mackenzie lost interest. The settlement was quite near now.

He turned around to Captain Hulse, riding a few paces behind. 'Here we go,' he said. 'Give my compliments to Lieutenant Colonel Yamaguchi and tell him he's in charge till we get back. If anything seems suspicious, he's to act at his own discretion.'

'Yes, sir.' Hulse saluted and wheeled smartly about. There had been no practical need for Mackenzie to repeat what had long been agreed on; but he knew the value of ritual. He clicked his big sorrel gelding into a trot. At his back he heard bugles sound orders and sergeants howl at their platoons.

Speyer kept pace. Mackenzie had insisted on bringing an extra man to the discussion. His own wits were probably no match for a high-level Esper, but Phil's might be.

*Not that there's any question of diplomacy or whatever. I hope.* To ease himself, he concentrated on what was real and present – hoofbeats, the rise and fall of the saddle beneath him, the horse's muscles rippling between his thighs, the creak and jingle of his saber belt, the clean odor of the animal – and suddenly remembered this was the sort of trick the Espers recommended.

None of their communities was walled, as most towns and every bossman's Station was. The officers turned off the highway and went down a street between colonnaded buildings. Side streets ran off in both directions. The settlement covered no great area, though, being composed of groups that lived together, sodalities or superfamilies or whatever you wanted to call them.

Some hostility toward the Order and a great many dirty jokes stemmed from that practice. But Speyer, who should know, said there was no more sexual swapping around than in the outside world. The idea was simply to get away from possessiveness, thee versus me, and to raise children as part of a whole rather than an insular clan.

The kids were out, staring round-eyed from the porticoes, hundreds of them. They looked healthy and, underneath a natural fear of the invaders, happy enough. But pretty solemn, Mackenzie thought; and all in the same blue garb. Adults stood among them, expressionless. Everybody had come in from the fields as the regiment neared. The silence was like barricades. Mackenzie felt sweat begin to trickle down his ribs. When he emerged on the central square, he let out his breath in a near gasp.

A fountain, the basin carved into a lotus, tinkled in the middle of the plaza. Flowering trees stood around it. The square was defined on three sides by massive buildings that must be for storage. On the fourth side rose a smaller temple-like structure with a graceful cupola, obviously headquarters and meeting house. On its lowest step were ranked half a dozen blue-robed men, five of them husky youths. The sixth was middle-aged, the Yang and Yin on his breast. His features, ordinary in themselves, held an implacable calm.

Mackenzie and Speyer drew rein. The colonel flipped a soft salute. 'Philosopher Gaines? I'm Mackenzie, here's Major Speyer.' He swore at himself for being so awkward about it and wondered what to do with his hands. The young fellows he understood, more or less; they watched him with badly concealed hostility. But he had some trouble meeting Gaines' eyes.

The settlement leader inclined his head. 'Welcome, gentlemen. Won't you come in?'

Mackenzie dismounted, hitched his horse to a post and removed his helmet. His worn reddish-brown uniform felt shabbier yet in these surroundings. 'Thanks. Uh, I'll have to make this quick.'

'To be sure. Follow me, please.'

Stiff-backed, the young men trailed after their elders, through an entry chamber and down a short hall. Speyer looked around at the mosaics. 'Why, this is lovely,' he murmured.

'Thank you,' said Gaines. 'Here's my office.' He opened a door of superbly grained walnut and gestured the visitors through.

When he closed it behind himself, the acolytes waited outside.

The room was austere, whitewashed walls enclosing little more than desk, a shelf of books, and some backless chairs. A window opened on a garden. Gaines sat down. Mackenzie and Speyer followed suit, uncomfortable on this furniture.

'We'd better get right to business,' the colonel blurted.

Gaines said nothing. At last Mackenzie must plow ahead: 'Here's the situation. Our force is to occupy Calistoga, with detachments on either side of the hills. That way we'll control both the Napa Valley and the Valley of the Moon ... from the northern ends, at least. The best place to station our eastern wing is here. We plan to establish a fortified camp in the field yonder. I'm sorry about the damage to your crops, but you'll be compensated once the proper government has been restored. And food, medicine – you understand this army has to requisition such items, but we won't let anybody suffer undue hardship and we'll give receipts. Uh, as a precaution we'll need to quarter a few men in this community, to sort of keep an eye on things. They'll interfere as little as possible. Okay?'

'The charter of the Order guarantees exemption from military requirements,' Gaines answered evenly. 'In fact, no armed man is supposed to cross the boundary of any land held by an Esper settlement. I cannot be party to a violation of the law, Colonel.'

'If you want to split legal hairs, Philosopher,' Speyer said, 'then I'll remind you that both Fallon and Judge Brodsky have declared martial law. Ordinary rules are suspended.'

Gaines smiled. 'Since only one government can be legitimate,' he said, 'the proclamations of the other are necessarily null and void. To a disinterested observer, it would appear that Judge Fallon's title is the stronger, especially when his side controls a large continuous area rather than some scattered bossdoms.'

'Not any more, it doesn't,' Mackenzie snapped.

Speyer gestured him back. 'Perhaps you haven't followed the developments of the last few weeks, Philosopher,' he said. 'Allow me to recapitulate. The Sierra Command stole a march on the Fallonites and came down out of the mountains. There was almost nothing left in the middle part of California to oppose us, so we took over rapidly. By occupying Sacramento, we control river and rail traffic. Our bases extend south below Bakersfield, with Yosemite and King's Canyon not far away to provide sites for extremely strong positions. When we've consolidated this northern end of our gains, the Fallonite forces around Redding will be trapped between us and the powerful bossmen who still hold out in the Trinity, Shasta, and Lassen regions. The very fact of our being here has forced the enemy to evacuate the Columbia Valley, so that San Francisco may be defended. It's an open question which side today has the last word in the larger territory.'

'What about the army that went into the Sierra against you?' Gaines inquired shrewdly. 'Have you contained them?'

Mackenzie scowled. 'No. That's no secret. They got out through the Mother Lode country and went around us. They're down in Los Angeles and San Diego now.'

'A formidable host. Do you expect to stand them off indefinitely?'

'We're going to make a hell of a good try,' Mackenzie said. 'Where we are, we've got the advantage of interior communications. And most of the freeholders are glad to slip us word about whatever they observe. We can concentrate at any point the enemy starts to attack.'

'Pity that this rich land must also be torn apart by war.'

'Yeah. Isn't it?'

'Our strategic objective is obvious enough,' Speyer said. 'We have cut enemy communications across the middle, except by sea, which is not very satisfactory for troops operating far inland. We deny him access to a good part of his food and manufactured supplies, and most especially to the bulk of his fuel alcohol. The backbone of our own side is the bossdoms, which are almost self-contained economic and social units. Before long they'll be in better shape than the rootless army they face. I think Judge Brodsky will be back in San Francisco before fall.'

'If your plans succeed,' Gaines said.

'That's our worry.' Mackenzie leaned forward, one fist doubled on his knee. 'Okay, Philosopher. I know you'd rather see Fallon come out on top, but I expect you've got more sense than to sign up in a lost cause. Will you cooperate with us?'

'The Order takes no part in political affairs, Colonel, except when its own existence is endangered.'

'Oh, pipe down. By "cooperate" I don't mean anything but keeping out from under our feet.'

'I am afraid that would still count as cooperation. We cannot have military establishments on our lands.'

Mackenzie stared at Gaines' face, which had set into granite lines, and wondered if he had heard aright. 'Are you ordering us off?' a stranger asked with his voice.

'Yes,' the Philosopher said.

'With our artillery zeroed in on your town?'

'Would you really shell women and children, Colonel?'

*O Nora*— 'We don't need to. Our men can walk right in.'

'Against psi blasts? I beg you not to have those poor boys destroyed.' Gaines paused, then : 'I might also point out that by losing your regiment you imperil your whole cause. You are free to march around our holdings and proceed to Calistoga.'

*Leaving a Fallonite nest at my back, spang across my communications southward.* The teeth grated together in Mackenzie's mouth.

Gaines rose. 'The discussion is at an end, gentlemen,' he said. 'You have one hour to get off our lands.'

Mackenzie and Speyer stood up too. 'We're not done yet,' the major said. Sweat studded his forehead and the long nose. 'I want to make some further explanations.'

Gaines crossed the room and opened the door. 'Show these gentlemen out,' he said to the five acolytes.

'No, by God!' Mackenzie shouted. He clapped a hand to his sidearm.

'Inform the adepts,' Gaines said.

One of the young men turned. Mackenzie heard the slap-slap of his sandals, running down the hall. Gaines nodded. 'I think you had better go,' he said.

Speyer grew rigid. His eyes shut. They flew open and he breathed, '*Inform* the adepts?'

Mackenzie saw the stiffness break in Gaines' countenance. There was no time for more than a second's bewilderment. His body acted for him. The gun clanked from his holster simultaneously with Speyer's.

'Get that messenger, Jimbo,' the major rapped. 'I'll keep these birds covered.'

As he plunged forward, Mackenzie found himself worrying about the regimental honor. Was it right to open hostilities when you had come on a parley? But Gaines had cut the talk off himself—

'Stop him!' Gaines yelled.

The four remaining acolytes sprang into motion. Two of them

T—B

barred the doorway, the other two moved in on either side. 'Hold it or I'll shoot!' Speyer cried, and was ignored.

Mackenzie couldn't bring himself to fire on unarmed men. He gave the youngster before him the pistol barrel in his teeth. Bloody-faced, the Esper lurched back. Mackenzie stiff-armed the one coming in from the left. The third tried to fill the doorway. Mackenzie put a foot behind his ankles and pushed. As he went down, Mackenzie kicked him in the temple, hard enough to stun, and jumped over him.

The fourth was on his back. Mackenzie writhed about to face the man. Those arms that hugged him, pinioning his gun, were bear strong. Mackenzie put the butt of his free left hand under the fellow's nose, and pushed. The acolyte must let go. Mackenzie gave him a knee in the stomach, whirled, and ran.

There was not much further commotion behind him. Phil must have them under control. Mackenzie pelted along the hall, into the entry chamber. Where had that goddamn runner gone? He looked out the open entrance, onto the square. Sunlight hurt his eyes. His breath came in painful gulps, there was a stitch in his side, yeah, he was getting old.

Blue robes fluttered from a street. Mackenzie recognized the messenger. The youth pointed at this building. A gabble of his words drifted faintly through Mackenzie's pulse. There were seven or eight men with him – older men, nothing to mark their clothes ... but Mackenzie knew a high-ranking officer when he saw one. The acolyte was dismissed. Those whom he had summoned crossed the square with long strides.

Terror knotted Mackenzie's bowels. He put it down. A Catamount didn't stampede, even from somebody who could turn him inside out with a look. He could do nothing about the wretchedness that followed, though. *If they clobber me, so much the better. I won't lie awake night wondering how Laura is.*

The adepts were almost to the steps. Mackenzie trod forth. He swept his revolver in an arc. 'Halt!' His voice sounded tiny in the stillness that brooded over the town.

They jarred to a stop and stood there in a group. He saw them enforce a catlike relaxation, and their faces became blank visors. None spoke. Finally Mackenzie was unable to keep silent.

'This place is hereby occupied under the laws of war,' he said. 'Go back to your quarters.'

'What have you done with our leader?' asked a tall man. His

voice was even but deeply resonant.

'Read my mind and find out,' Mackenzie gibed. *No, you're being childish.* 'He's okay, long's he keeps his nose clean. You too. Beat it.'

'We do not wish to pervert psionics to violence,' said the tall man. 'Please do not force us.'

'Your chief sent for you before we'd done anything,' Mackenzie retorted. 'Looks like violence was what he had in mind. On your way.'

The Espers exchanged glances. The tall man nodded. His companions walked slowly off. 'I would like to see Philosopher Gaines,' the tall man said.

'You will pretty soon.'

'Am I to understand that he is being held a prisoner?'

'Understand what you like.' The other Espers were rounding the corner of the building. 'I don't want to shoot. Go on back before I have to.'

'An impasse of sorts,' the tall man said. 'Neither of us wishes to injure one whom he considers defenseless. Allow me to conduct you off these grounds.'

Mackenzie wet his lips. Weather had chapped them rough. 'If you can put a hex on me, go ahead,' he challenged. 'Otherwise scram.'

'Well, I shall not hinder you from rejoining your men. It seems the easiest way of getting you to leave. But I most solemnly warn that any armed force which tries to enter will be annihilated.'

*Guess I had better go get the boys, at that. Phil can't mount guard on those guys forever.*

The tall man went over to the hitching post. 'Which of these horses is yours?' he asked blandly.

*Almighty eager to get rid of me, isn't he— Holy hellfire! There must be a rear door!*

Mackenzie spun on his heel. The Esper shouted. Mackenzie dashed back through the entry chamber. His boots threw echoes at him. No, not to the left, there's only the office that way. Right . . . around this corner—

A long hall stretched before him. A stairway curved from the middle. The other Espers were already on it.

'Halt!' Mackenzie called. 'Stop or I'll shoot!'

The two men in the lead sped onward. The rest turned and headed down again, toward him.

He fired with care, to disable rather than kill. The hall reverberated with the explosions. One after another they dropped, a bullet in leg or hip or shoulder. With such small targets, Mackenzie missed some shots. As the tall man, the last of them, closed in from behind, the hammer clicked on an empty chamber.

Mackenzie drew his saber and gave him the flat of it alongside the head. The Esper lurched. Mackenzie got past and bounded up the stair. It wound like something in a nightmare. He thought his heart was going to go to pieces.

At the end, an iron door opened on a landing. One man was fumbling with the lock. The other blue-robe attacked.

Mackenzie stuck his sword between the Esper's legs. As his opponent stumbled, the colonel threw a left hook to the jaw. The man sagged against the wall. Mackenzie grabbed the robe of the other and hurled him to the floor. 'Get out,' he rattled.

They pulled themselves together and glared at him. He thrust air with his blade. 'From now on I aim to kill,' he said.

'Get help, Dave,' said the one who had been opening the door. 'I'll watch him.' The other went unevenly down the stairs. The first man stood out of saber reach. 'Do you want to be destroyed?' he asked.

Mackenzie turned the knob at his back, but the door was still locked. 'I don't think you can do it,' he said. 'Not without what's here.'

The Esper struggled for self-control. They waited through minutes that stretched. Then a noise began below. The Esper pointed. 'We have nothing but agricultural implements,' he said, 'but you have only that blade. Will you surrender?'

Mackenzie spat on the floor. The Esper went on down.

Presently the attackers came into view. There might be a hundred, judging from the hubbub behind them, but because of the curve Mackenzie could see no more than ten or fifteen – burly fieldhands, their robes tucked high and sharp tools aloft. The landing was too wide for defense. He advanced to the stairway, where they could only come at him two at a time.

A couple of sawtoothed hay knives led the assault. Mackenzie parried one blow and chopped. His edge went into meat and struck bone. Blood ran out, impossibly red, even in the dim light here. The man fell to all fours with a shriek. Mackenzie dodged a cut from the companion. Metal clashed on metal. The weapons locked. Mackenzie's arm was forced back. He looked into a broad suntanned face. The side of his hand smote the young man's larynx. The Esper fell against the one behind and they went down together. It took a while to clear the tangle and resume action.

A pitchfork thrust for the colonel's belly. He managed to grab it with his left hand, divert the tines, and chop at the fingers on the shaft. A scythe gashed his right side. He saw his own blood but wasn't aware of pain. A flesh wound, no more. He swept his saber back and forth. The forefront retreated from its whistling menace. *But God, my knees are like rubber, I can't hold out another five minutes.*

A bugle sounded. There was a spatter of gunfire. The mob on the staircase congealed. Someone screamed.

Hoofs banged across the ground floor. A voice rasped: 'Hold everything, there! Drop those weapons and come on down. First man tries anything gets shot.'

Mackenzie leaned on his saber and fought for air. He hardly noticed the Espers melt away.

When he felt a little better, he went to one of the small windows and looked out. Horsemen were in the plaza. Not yet in sight, but nearing, he heard infantry.

Speyer arrived, followed by a sergeant of engineers and several privates. The major hurried to Mackenzie. 'You okay, Jimbo? You been hurt!'

'A scratch,' Mackenzie said. He was getting back his strength, though no sense of victory accompanied it, only the knowledge of aloneness. The injury began to sting. 'Not worth a fuss. Look.'

'Yes, I suppose you'll live. Okay, men, get that door open.'

The engineers took forth their tools and assailed the lock with a vigor that must spring half from fear. 'How'd you guys show up so soon?' Mackenzie asked.

'I thought there'd be trouble,' Speyer said, 'so when I heard shots I jumped through the window and ran around to my horse. That was just before those clodhoppers attacked you; I saw them gathering as I rode out. Our cavalry got in almost at once, of course, and the dogfaces weren't far behind.'

'Any resistance?'

'No, not after we fired a few rounds in the air.' Speyer glanced outside. 'We're in full possession now.'

Mackenzie regarded the door. 'Well,' he said, 'I feel better about our having pulled guns on them in the office. Looks like their adepts really depend on plain old weapons, huh? And Esper communities aren't supposed to have arms. Their charters say so. ... That was a damn good guess of yours, Phil. How'd you do it?'

'I sort of wondered why the chief had to send a runner to fetch guys that claim to be telepaths. There we go!'

The lock jingled apart. The sergeant opened the door. Mackenzie and Speyer went into the great room under the dome.

They walked around for a long time, wordless, among shapes of metal and less identifiable substances. Nothing was familiar. Mackenzie paused at last before a helix which projected from a transparent cube. Formless darknesses swirled within the box, sparked as if with tiny stars.

'I figured maybe the Espers had found a cache of old-time stuff, from just before the Hellbombs,' he said in a muffled voice. 'Ultra-secret weapons that never got a chance to be used. But this doesn't look like it. Think so?'

'No,' Speyer said. 'It doesn't look to me as if these things were made by human beings at all.'

*'But do you not understand? They occupied a settlement! That proves to the world that Espers are not invulnerable. And to complete the catastrophe, they seized its arsenal.'*

*'Have no fears about that. No untrained person can activate those instruments. The circuits are locked except in the presence of certain encephalic rhythms which result from conditioning. That same conditioning makes it impossible for the so-called adepts to reveal any of their knowledge to the uninitiated, no matter what may be done to them.'*

*'Yes, I know that much. But it is not what I had in mind. What frightens me is the fact that the revelation will spread. Everyone will know the Esper adepts do not plumb unknown depths of the psyche after all, but merely have access to an advanced physical science. Not only will this lift rebel spirits, but worse, it will cause many, perhaps most of the Order's members to break away in disillusionment.'*

*'Not at once. News travels slowly under present conditions. Also, Mwyr, you underestimate the ability of the human mind to ignore data which conflict with cherished beliefs.'*

*'But—'*

*'Well, let us assume the worst. Let us suppose that faith is*

lost and the Order disintegrates. That will be a serious setback to the plan, but not a fatal one. Psionics was merely one
bit of folklore we found potent enough to serve as the moti-
vator of a new orientation toward life. There are others, for
example the widespread belief in magic among the less educated classes. We can begin again on a different basis, if we
must. The exact form of the creed is not important. It is only
scaffolding for the real structure: a communal anti-material-
istic social group, to which more and more people will turn
for sheer lack of anything else, as the coming empire breaks up.
In the end, the new culture can and will discard whatever
superstitions gave it the initial impetus.'

'A hundred-year setback, at least.'

'True. It would be much more difficult to introduce a radical
alien element now, when the autochthonous society has developed strong institutions of its own, than it was in the past.
I merely wish to reassure you that the task is not impossible.
I do not actually propose to let matters go that far. The Espers
can be salvaged.'

'How?'

'We must intervene directly.'

'Has that been computed as being unavoidable?'

'Yes. The matrix yields an unambiguous answer. I do not
like it any better than you. But direct action occurs oftener
than we tell neophytes in the schools. The most elegant pro-
cedure would of course be to establish such initial conditions
in a society that its evolution along desired lines becomes auto-
matic. Furthermore, that would let us close our minds to
the distressing fact of our own blood guilt. Unfortunately,
the Great Science does not extend down to the details of day-
to-day practicality.

'In the present instance, we shall help to smash the reac-
tionaries. The government will then proceed so harshly against
its conquered opponents that many of those who accept the
story about what was found at St. Helena will not live to
spread the tale. The rest ... well, they will be discredited by
their own defeat. Admittedly, the story will linger for life-
times, whispered here and there. But what of that? Those who
believe in the Way will, as a rule, simply be strengthened in
their faith, by the very process of denying such ugly rumors.
As more and more persons, common citizens as well as Espers,

*reject materialism, the legend will seem more and more fan-
tastic. It will seem obvious that certain ancients invented the
tale to account for a fact that they in their ignorance were
unable to comprehend.'*

*'I see. . . .'*

*'You are not happy here, are you, Mwyr?'*

*'I cannot quite say. Everything is so distorted.'*

*'Be glad you were not sent to one of the really alien planets.'*

*'I might almost prefer that. There would be a hostile en-
vironment to think about. One could forget how far it is to
home.'*

*'Three years' travel.'*

*'You say that so glibly. As if three shipboard years were
not equal to fifty in cosmic time. As if we could expect a relief vessel daily, not once in a century. And . . . as if the
region that our ships have explored amounts to one chip out
of this one galaxy!'*

*'That region will grow until someday it engulfs the galaxy.'*

*'Yes, yes, yes. I know. Why do you think I chose to become
a psychodynamician? Why am I here, learning how to meddle
with the destiny of a world where I do not belong? "To create
the union of sentient beings, each member species a step toward life's mastery of the universe." Brave slogan! But in
practice, it seems, only a chosen few races are to be allowed
the freedom of that universe.'*

*'Not so, Mwyr. Consider these ones with whom we are, as
you say, meddling. Consider what use they made of nuclear
energy when they had it. At the rate they are going, they will
have it again within a century or two. Not long after that they
will be building spaceships. Even granted that time lag atten-
uates the effects of interstellar contact, those effects are cumula-
tive. So do you wish such a band of carnivores turned loose on
the galaxy?*

*'No, let them become inwardly civilized first; then we shall
see if they can be trusted. If not, they will at least be happy on
their own planet, in a mode of life designed for them by the
Great Science. Remember, they have an immemorial aspira-
tion toward peace on earth; but that is something they will
never achieve by themselves. I do not pretend to be a very
good person, Mwyr. Yet this work that we are doing makes me
feel not altogether useless in the cosmos.'*

Promotion was fast that year, casualties being so high. Captain Thomas Danielis was raised to major for his conspicuous part in putting down the revolt of the Los Angeles citymen. Soon after occurred the Battle of Maricopa, when the loyalists failed bloodily to break the stranglehold of the Sierran rebels on the San Joaquin Valley, and he was breveted lieutenant colonel. The army was ordered northward and moved warily under the coast ranges, half expecting attack from the east. But the Brodskyites seemed too busy consolidating their latest gains. The trouble came from guerrillas and the hedgehog resistance of bossman Stations. After one particularly stiff clash, they stopped near Pinnacles for a breather.

Danielis made his way through camp, where tents stood in tight rows between the guns and men lay about dozing, talking, gambling, staring at the blank blue sky. The air was hot, pungent with cookfire smoke, horses, mules, dung, sweat, boot oil; the green of the hills that lifted around the site was dulling toward summer brown. He was idle until time for the conference the general had called, but restlessness drove him. *By now I'm a father*, he thought, *and I've never seen my kid.*

*At that, I'm lucky*, he reminded himself. *I've got my life and limbs.* He remembered Jacobsen dying in his arms at Maricopa. You wouldn't have thought the human body could hold so much blood. Though maybe one was no longer human, when the pain was so great that one could do nothing but shriek until the darkness came.

*And I used to think war was glamorous. Hunger, thirst, exhaustion, terror, mutilation, death, and forever the sameness, boredom grinding you down to an ox. . . . I've had it. I'm going into business after the war. Economic integration, as the bossman system breaks up, yes, there'll be a lot of ways for a man to get ahead, but decently without a weapon in his hand—* Danielis realized he was repeating thoughts that were months old. What the hell else was there to think about, though?

The large tent where prisoners were interrogated lay near his path. A couple of privates were conducting a man inside. The fellow was blond, burly, and sullen. He wore a sergeant's stripes, but otherwise his only item of uniform was the badge of Warden Echevarry, bossman in this part of the coastal mountains. A lumberjack in peacetime, Danielis guessed from the look of him; a soldier in a private army whenever the interests of Echevarry were threatened; captured in yesterday's engagement.

On impulse, Danielis followed. He got into the tent as Captain Lambert, chubby behind a portable desk, finished the preliminaries, and blinked in the sudden gloom.

'Oh.' The intelligence officer started to rise. 'Yes, sir?'

'At ease,' Danielis said. 'Just thought I'd listen in.'

'Well, I'll try to put on a good show for you.' Lambert reseated himself and looked at the prisoner, who stood with hunched shoulders and widespread legs between his guards. 'Now, sergeant, we'd like to know a few things.'

'I don't have to say nothing except name, rank, and home town,' the man growled. 'You got those.'

'Um-m-m, that's questionable. You aren't a foreign soldier, you're in rebellion against the government of your own country.'

'The hell I am! I'm an Echevarry man.'

'So what?'

'So my Judge is whoever Echevarry says. He says Brodsky. That makes you the rebel.'

'The law's been changed.'

'Your mucking Fallon got no right to change any laws. Especially part of the Constitution. I'm no hillrunner, Captain. I went to school some. And every year our Warden reads his people the Constitution.'

'Times have changed since it was drawn,' Lambert said. His tone sharpened. 'But I'm not going to argue with you. How many riflemen and how many archers in your company?'

Silence.

'We can make things a lot easier for you,' Lambert said. 'I'm not asking you to do anything treasonable. All I want is to confirm some information I've already got.'

The man shook his head angrily.

Lambert gestured. One of the privates stepped behind the captive, took his arm, and twisted a little.

'Echevarry wouldn't do that to me,' he said through white lips.

'Of course not,' Lambert said. 'You're his man.'

'Think I wanna be just a number on some list in Frisco? Damn right I'm my bossman's man!'

Lambert gestured again. The private twisted harder.

'Hold on, there,' Danielis barked. 'Stop that!'

The private let go, looking surprised. The prisoner drew a sobbing breath.

'I'm amazed at you, Captain Lambert,' Danielis said. He felt his own face reddening. 'If this has been your usual practice, there's going to be a court-martial.'

'No, sir,' Lambert said in a small voice. 'Honest. Only . . . they don't talk. Hardly any of them. What'm I supposed to do?'

'Follow the rules of war.'

'With rebels?'

'Take that man away,' Danielis ordered. The privates made haste to do so.

'Sorry, sir,' Lambert muttered. 'I guess . . . I guess I've lost too many buddies. I hate to lose more, simply for lack of information.'

'Me too.' A compassion rose in Danielis. He sat down on the table edge and began to roll a cigarette. 'But you see, we aren't in a regular war. And so, by a curious paradox, we have to follow the conventions more carefully than ever before.'

'I don't quite understand, sir.'

Danielis finished the cigarette and gave it to Lambert: olive branch or something. He started another for himself. 'The rebels aren't rebels by their own lights,' he said. 'They're being loyal to a tradition that we're trying to curb, eventually to destroy. Let's face it, the average bossman is a fairly good leader. He may be descended from some thug who grabbed power by strong-arm methods during the chaos, but by now his family's integrated itself with the region he rules. He knows it, and its people inside out. He's there in the flesh, a symbol of the community and its achievements, its folkways and essential independence. If you're in trouble, you don't have to work through some impersonal bureaucracy, you go direct to your bossman. His duties are as clearly defined as your own, and a good deal more demanding, to balance his privileges. He leads you in battle and in the ceremonies that give color and meaning to life. Your fathers and his have worked and played together for two or three hundred years. The land is alive with the memories of them. You and he *belong*.

'Well, that has to be swept away, so we can go on to a higher level. But we won't reach that level by alienating everyone. We're not a conquering army; we're more like the Householder Guard putting down a riot in some city. The opposition is part and parcel of our own society.'

Lambert struck a match for him. He inhaled and finished: 'On a practical plane, I might also remind you, Captain, that

the federal armed forces, Fallonite and Brodskyite together, are
none too large. Little more than a cadre, in fact. We're a bunch
of younger sons, countrymen who failed, poor citymen, adven-
turers, people who look to their regiment for that sense of whole-
ness they've grown up to expect and can't find in civilian life.'

'You're too deep for me, sir, I'm afraid,' Lambert said.

'Never mind,' Danielis sighed. 'Just bear in mind, there are
a good many more fighting men outside the opposing armies than
in. If the bossmen could establish a unified command, that'd be
the end of the Fallon government. Luckily, there's too much
provincial pride and too much geography between them for this
to happen – unless we outrage them beyond endurance. What
we want the ordinary freeholder, and even the ordinary bossman, to think is: "Well, those Fallonites aren't such bad guys,
and if I keep on the right side of them I don't stand to lose
much, and should even be able to gain something at the expense
of those who fight them to a finish." You see?'

'Y-yes. I guess so.'

'You're a smart fellow, Lambert. You don't have to beat information out of prisoners. Trick it out.'

'I'll try, sir.'

'Good.' Danielis glanced at the watch that had been given him
as per tradition, together with a sidearm, when he was first com-
missioned. (Such items were much too expensive for the common man. They had not been so in the age of mass production;
and perhaps in the coming age—) 'I have to go. See you around.'

He left the tent feeling somewhat more cheerful than before.
*No doubt I am a natural-born preacher,* he admitted, *and I
never could quite join in the horseplay at mess, and a lot of jokes
go completely by me; but if I can get even a few ideas across
where they count, that's pleasure enough.* A strain of music
came to him, some men and a banjo under a tree, and he found
himself whistling along. It was good that this much morale remained, after Maricopa and a northward march whose purpose
had not been divulged to anybody.

The conference tent was big enough to be called a pavilion.
Two sentries stood at the entrance. Danielis was nearly the last
to arrive, and found himself at the end of the table, opposite
Brigadier General Perez. Smoke hazed the air and there was a
muted buzz of conversation, but faces were taut.

When the blue-robed figure with a Yang and Yin on the breast entered, silence fell like a curtain. Danielis was astonished to recognize Philosopher Woodworth. He'd last seen the man in Los Angeles, and assumed he would stay at the Esper center there. Must have come here by special conveyance, under special orders. . . .

Perez introduced him. Both remained standing, under the eyes of the officers. 'I have some important news for you, gentlemen,' Perez said most quietly. 'You may consider it an honor to be here. It means that in my judgment you can be trusted, first, to keep absolute silence about what you are going to hear, and second, to execute a vital operation of extreme difficulty.' Danielis was made shockingly aware that several men were not present whose rank indicated they should be.

'I repeat,' Perez said, 'any breach of secrecy and the whole plan is ruined. In that case, the war will drag on for months or years. You know how bad our position is. You also know it will grow still worse as our stocks of those supplies the enemy now denies us are consumed. We could even be beaten. I'm not defeatist to say that, only realistic. We could lose the war.

'On the other hand, if this new scheme pans out, we may break the enemy's back this very month.'

He paused to let that sink in before continuing :

'The plan was worked out by GHQ in conjunction with Esper Central in San Francisco some weeks ago. It's the reason we are headed north—' He let the gasp subside that ran through the stifling air. 'Yes, you know that the Esper Order is neutral in political disputes. But you also know that it defends itself when attacked. And you probably know that an attack was made on it by the rebels. They seized the Napa Valley settlement and have been spreading malicious rumors about the Order since then. Would you like to comment on that, Philosopher Woodworth?'

The man in blue nodded and said coolly : 'We've our own ways of findin' out things – intelligence service, you might say – so I can give y'all a report of the facts. St. Helena was assaulted at a time when most of its adepts were away, helpin' a new community get started out in Montana.' *How did they travel so fast?* Danielis wondered. *Teleport, or what?* 'I don't know, myself, if the enemy knew about that or were just lucky. Anyhow, when the two or three adepts that were left came and warned them off, fightin' broke out and the adepts were killed before they could act.' He smiled. 'We don't claim to be immortal, except the way every livin' thing is immortal. Nor infallible, either. So now St. Helena's occupied. We don't figure to take any immediate steps about that, because a lot of people in the community might get hurt.

'As for the yarns the enemy command's been handin' out, well, I reckon I'd do the same, if I had a chance like that. Everybody knows an adept can do things that nobody else can. Troops that realize they've done wrong to the Order are goin' to be scared of supernatural revenge. You're educated men here, and know there's nothin' supernatural involved, just a way to use the powers latent in most of us. You also know the Order doesn't believe in revenge. But the ordinary foot soldier doesn't think your way. His officers have got to restore his spirit somehow. So they fake some equipment and tell him that's what the adepts were really usin' – an advanced technology, sure, but only a set of machines that can be put out of action if you're brave, same as any other machine. That's what happened.

'Still, it is a threat to the Order; and we can't let an attack on our people go unpunished, either. So Esper Central has decided to help out your side. The sooner this war's over, the better for everybody.'

A sigh gusted around the table, and a few exultant oaths. The hair stirred on Danielis' neck. Perez lifted a hand.

'Not too fast, please,' the general said. 'The adepts are not going to go around blasting your opponents for you. It was one hell of a tough decision for them to do as much as they agreed to. I, uh, understand that the, uh, personal development of every Esper will be set back many years by this much violence. They're making a big sacrifice.

'By their charter, they can use psionics to defend an establishments against attack. Okay . . . an assault on San Francisco will be construed as one on Central, their world headquarters.'

The realization of what was to come was blinding to Danielis. He scarcely heard Perez' carefully dry continuation:

'Let's review the strategic picture. By now the enemy holds more than half of California, all of Oregon and Idaho, and a good deal of Washington. We, this army, we're using the last land access to San Francisco that we've got. The enemy hasn't tried to pinch that off yet, because the troops we pulled out of the north – those that aren't in the field at present – make a strong city garrison that'd sally out. He's collecting too much profit elsewhere to accept the cost.

'Nor can he invest the city with any hope of success. We still hold Puget Sound and the southern California ports. Our ships bring in ample food and munitions. His own sea power is much inferior to ours: chiefly schooners donated by coastal bossmen, operating out of Portland. He might overwhelm an occasional convoy, but he hasn't tried that so far because it isn't worth his trouble; there would be others, more heavily escorted. And of course he can't enter the Bay, with artillery and rocket emplacements on both sides of the Golden Gate. No, about all he can do is maintain some water communication with Hawaii and Alaska.

'Nevertheless, his ultimate object is San Francisco. It has to be – the seat of government and industry, the heart of the nation.

'Well, then, here's the plan. Our army is to engage the Sierra Command and its militia auxiliaries again, striking out of San Jose. That's a perfectly logical maneuver. Successful, it would cut his California forces in two. We know, in fact, that he is already concentrating men in anticipation of precisely such an attempt.

'We aren't going to succeed. We'll give him a good stiff battle and be thrown back. That's the hardest part: to feign a serious defeat, even convincing our own troops, and still maintain good order. We'll have a lot of details to thresh out about that.

'We'll retreat northward, up the Peninsula toward Frisco. The enemy is bound to pursue. It will look like a God-given chance to destroy us and get to the city walls.

'When he is well into the Peninsula, with the ocean on his left and the Bay on his right, we will outflank him and attack from the rear. The Esper adepts will be there to help. Suddenly he'll be caught, between us and the capital's land defenses. What the adepts don't wipe out, we will. Nothing will remain of the Sierra Command but a few garrisons. The rest of the war will be a mopping-up operation.

'It's a brilliant piece of strategy. Like all such, it's damn difficult to execute. Are you prepared to do the job?'

Danielis didn't raise his voice with the others. He was thinking too hard of Laura.

Northward and to the right there was some fighting. Cannon spoke occasionally, or a drumfire of rifles; smoke lay thin over the grass and the wind-gnarled live oaks which covered those hills. But down along the seacoast was only surf, blowing air, a hiss of sand across the dunes.

Mackenzie rode on the beach, where the footing was easiest and the view widest. Most of his regiment were inland. But that was a wilderness: rough ground, woods, the snags of ancient homes, making travel slow and hard. Once this area had been densely peopled, but the firestorm after the Hellbomb scrubbed it clean and today's reduced population could not make a go on such infertile soil. There didn't even seem to be any foemen near this left wing of the army.

The Rolling Stones had certainly not been given it for that reason. They could have borne the brunt at the center as well as those outfits which actually were there, driving the enemy back toward San Francisco. They had been blooded often enough in this war, when they operated out of Calistoga to help expel the Fallonites from northern California. So thoroughly had that job been done that now only a skeleton force need remain in charge. Nearly the whole Sierra Command had gathered at Modesto, met the northward-moving opposition army that struck at them out of San Jose, and sent it in a shooting retreat. Another day or so, and the white city should appear before their eyes.

*And there the enemy will be sure to make a stand,* Mackenzie thought, *with the garrison to reinforce him. And his positions will have to be shelled; maybe we'll have to take the place street by street. Laura, kid, will you be alive at the end?*

*Of course, maybe it won't happen that way. Maybe my scheme'll work and we'll win easy— What a horrible word 'maybe' is!* He slapped his hands together with a pistol sound.

Speyer threw him a glance. The major's people were safe; he'd even been able to visit them at Mount Lassen, after the northern campaign was over. 'Rough,' he said.

'Rough on everybody,' Mackenzie said with a thick anger. 'This is a filthy war.'

Speyer shrugged. 'No different from most, except that this time Pacificans are on the receiving as well as the giving end.'

'You know damn well I never liked the business, anyplace.'

'What man in his right mind does?'

'When I want a sermon I'll ask for one.'

'Sorry,' said Speyer, and meant it.

'I'm sorry too,' said Mackenzie instantly contrite. 'Nerves on edge. Damnation! I could almost wish for some action.'

'Wouldn't be surprised if we got some. This whole affair smells wrong to me.'

Mackenzie looked around him. On the right the horizon was bounded by hills, beyond which the low but massive San Bruno range lifted. Here and there he spied one of his own squads, afoot or ahorse. Overhead sputtered a plane. But there was plenty of concealment for a redoubt. Hell could erupt at any minute ... though necessarily a small hell, quickly reduced by howitzer or bayonet, casualties light. (Huh! Every one of those light casualties was a man dead, with women and children to weep for him, or a man staring at the fragment of his arm, or a man with eyes and face gone in a burst of shot, and what kind of unsoldierly thoughts were these?)

Seeking comfort, Mackenzie glanced left. The ocean rolled greenish-gray, glittering far out, rising and breaking in a roar of white combers closer to land. He smelled salt and kelp. A few gulls mewed above dazzling sands. There was no sail or smoke-puff – only emptiness. The convoys from Puget Sound to San Francisco and the lean swift ships of the coastal bossmen were miles beyond the curve of the world.

Which was as it should be. Maybe things were working out okay on the high waters. One could only try, and hope. And ... it had been his suggestion, James Mackenzie speaking at the conference General Cruikshank held between the battles of Mariposa and San Jose; the same James Mackenzie who had first proposed that the Sierra Command come down out of the mountains, and who had exposed the gigantic fraud of Esperdom, and succeeded in playing down for his men the fact that behind the fraud lay a mystery one hardly dared think about. He would endure in the chronicles, that colonel, they would sing ballads about him for half a thousand years.

Only it didn't feel that way. James Mackenzie knew he was not much more than average bright under the best of conditions, now dull-minded with weariness and terrified of his daughter's fate. For himself he was haunted by the fear of certain crippling wounds. Often he had to drink himself to sleep. He was shaved, because an officer must maintain appearances, but realized very well that if he hadn't had an orderly to do the job for him he would be as shaggy as any buck private. His uniform was faded and threadbare, his body stank and itched, his mouth yearned for tobacco but there had been some trouble in the commissariat

and they were lucky to eat. His achievements amounted to patch-
work jobs carried out in utter confusion, or to slogging like this
and wishing only for an end to the whole mess. One day, win or
lose, his body would give out on him – he could feel the machinery wearing to pieces, arthritic twinges, shortness of breath,
dozing off in the middle of things – and the termination of himself would be as undignified and lonely as that of every other
human slob. Hero? What an all-time laugh!

He yanked his mind back to the immediate situation. Behind
him a core of the regiment accompanied the artillery along the
beach, a thousand men with motorized gun carriages, caissons,
mule-drawn wagons, a few trucks, one precious armored car.
They were a dun mass topped with helmets, in loose formation,
rifles or bows to hand. The sand deadened their footfalls, so that
only the surf and the wind could be heard. But whenever the
wind sank, Mackenzie caught the tune of the hex corps: a dozen
leathery older men, mostly Indians, carrying the wands of power
and whistling together the Song Against Witches. He took no
stock in magic himself, yet when that sound came to him the
skin crawled along his backbone.

*Everything's in good order,* he insisted. *We're doing fine.*

Then: *But Phil's right. This is a screwball business. The
enemy should have fought through to a southward line of retreat, not let themselves be boxed.*

Captain Hulse galloped close. Sand spurted when he checked
his horse. 'Patrol report, sir.'

'Well?' Mackenzie realized he had almost shouted. 'Go ahead.'

'Considerable activity observed about five miles northeast.
Looks like a troop headed our way.'

Mackenzie stiffened. 'Haven't you anything more definite
than that?'

'Not so far, with the ground so broken.'

'Get some aerial reconnaissance there, for Pete's sake!'

'Yes, sir. I'll throw out more scouts, too.'

'Carry on here, Phil.' Mackenzie headed toward the radio
truck. He carried a minicom in his saddlebag, of course, but
San Francisco had been continuously jamming on all bands
and you needed a powerful set to punch a signal even a few
miles. Patrols must communicate by messenger.

He noticed that the firing inland had slacked off. There were
decent roads in the interior Peninsula a ways further north,

where some resettlement had taken place. The enemy, still in possession of that area, could use them to effect rapid movements.

*If they withdrew their center and hit our flanks, where we're weakest—*

A voice from field HQ, barely audible through the squeals and buzzes, took his report and gave back what had been seen elsewhere. Large maneuvers right and left, yes, it did seem as if the Fallonites were going to try a breakthrough. Could be a feint, though. The main body of the Sierrans must remain where it was until the situation became clearer. The Rolling Stones must hold out a while on their own.

'Will do.' Mackenzie returned to the head of his columns. Speyer nodded grimly at the word.

'Better get prepared, hadn't we?'

'Uh-huh.' Mackenzie lost himself in a welter of commands, as officer after officer rode to him. The outlying sections were to be pulled in. The beach was to be defended, with the high ground immediately above.

Men scurried, horses neighed, guns trundled about. The scout plane returned, flying low enough to get a transmission through: yes, definitely an attack on the way; hard to tell how big a force, through the damned tree cover and down in the damned arroyos, but it might well be at brigade strength.

Mackenzie established himself on a hilltop with his staff and runners. A line of artillery stretched beneath him, across the strand. Cavalry waited behind them, lances agleam, an infantry company for support. Otherwise the foot soldiers had faded into the landscape. The sea boomed its own cannonade, and gulls began to gather as if they knew there would be meat before long.

'Think we can hold them?' Speyer asked.

'Sure,' Mackenzie said. 'If they come down the beach, we'll enfilade them, as well as shooting up their front. If they come higher, well, that's a textbook example of defensible terrain. 'Course, if another troop punches through the lines further inland, we'll be cut off, but that isn't our worry right now.'

'They must hope to get around our army and attack our rear.'

'Guess so. Not too smart of them, though. We can approach Frisco just as easily fighting backwards as forwards.'

'Unless the city garrison makes a sally.'

'Even then. Total numerical strengths are about equal, and we've got more ammo and alky. Also a lot of bossman militia for auxiliaries, who're used to disorganized warfare in hilly ground.'

'If we do whip them—' Speyer shut his lips together.

'Go on,' Mackenzie said.

'Nothing.'

'The hell it is. You were about to remind me of the next step: how do we take the city without too high a cost to both sides? Well, I happen to know we've got a hole card to play there, which might help.'

Speyer turned pitying eyes away from Mackenzie. Silence fell on the hilltop.

It was an unconscionably long time before the enemy came in view, first a few outriders far down the dunes, then the body of him, pouring from the ridges and gullies and woods. Reports flickered about Mackenzie – a powerful force, nearly twice as big as ours, but with little artillery; by now badly short of fuel, they must depend far more than we on animals to move their equipment. They were evidently going to charge, accept losses in order to get sabers and bayonets among the Rolling Stones' cannon. Mackenzie issued his directions accordingly.

The hostiles formed up, a mile or so distant. Through his field glasses Mackenzie recognized them, red sashes of the Madera Horse, green and gold pennon of the Dagos, fluttering in the iodine wind. He'd campaigned with both outfits in the past. It was treacherous to remember that Ives favored a blunt wedge formation and use the fact against him. . . . One enemy armored car and some fieldpieces, light horsedrawn ones, gleamed wickedly in the sunlight.

Bugles blew shrill. The Fallonite cavalry laid lance in rest and started trotting. They gathered speed as they went, a canter, a gallop, until the earth trembled with them. Then their infantry got going, flanked by its guns. The car rolled along between the first and second line of foot. Oddly, it had no rocket launcher on top or repeater barrels thrust from the fire slits. Those were good troops, Mackenzie thought, advancing in close order with that ripple down the ranks which bespoke veterans. He hated what must happen.

His defense waited immobile on the sand. Fire crackled from the hillsides, where mortar squads and riflemen crouched. A rider toppled, a dogface clutched his belly and went to his knees, their companions behind moved forward to close the lines again. Mackenzie looked to his howitzers. Men stood tensed at sights and lanyards. Let the foe get well in range— There! Yamaguchi, mounted just rearward of the gunners, drew his saber and flashed the blade downward. Cannon bellowed. Fire spurted through smoke, sand gouted up, shrapnel sleeted over the charging force. At once the gun crews fell into the rhythm of reloading, relaying, refiring, the steady three rounds per minute which conserved barrels and broke armies. Horses screamed in their own tangled red guts. But not many had been hit. The Madera cavalry continued in full gallop. Their lead was so close now that Mackenzie's glasses picked out a face, red, freckled, a ranch boy turned trooper, his mouth stretched out of shape as he yelled.

The archers behind the defending cannon let go. Arrows whistled skyward, flight after flight, curved past the gulls and down again. Flame and smoke ran ragged in the wiry hill grass, out of the ragged-leaved live oak copses. Men pitched to the sand, many still hideously astir, like insects that had been stepped on. The fieldpieces on the enemy left flank halted, swiveled about, and spat return fire. Futile . . . but God, their officer had courage! Mackenzie said the advancing lines waver. An attack by his own horse and foot, down the beach, ought to crumple them. 'Get ready to move,' he said into his minicom. He saw his men poise. The cannon belched anew.

The oncoming armored car slowed to a halt. Something within it chattered, loud enough to hear through the explosions.

A blue-white sheet ran over the nearest hill. Mackenzie shut half-blinded eyes. When he opened them again, he saw a grass fire through the crazy patterns of after-image. A Rolling Stone burst from cover, howling, his clothes ablaze. The man hit the sand and rolled over. That part of the beach lifted in one monster wave, crested twenty feet high, and smashed across the hill. The burning soldier vanished in the avalanche that buried his comrades.

'Psi blast!' someone screamed, thin and horrible, through chaos and ground-shudder. 'The Espers—'

Unbelievably, a bugle sounded and the Sierran cavalry lunged forward. Past their own guns, on against the scattering opposition . . . and horses and riders rose into the air, tumbled in a giant's invisible whirligig, crashed bone-breakingly to earth again. The second rank of lancers broke. Mounts reared, pawed the air, wheeled and fled in every direction.

A terrible deep hum filled the sky. Mackenzie saw the world as if through a haze, as if his brain were being dashed back and forth between the walls of his skull. Another glare ran across the hills, higher this time, burning men alive.

'They'll wipe us out,' Speyer called, a dim voice that rose and fell on the air tides. 'They'll re-form as we stampede—'

'No!' Mackenzie shouted. 'The adepts must be in that car. Come on!'

Most of his horse had recoiled on their own artillery, one squealing, trampling wreck. The infantry stood rigid, but about to bolt. A glance thrown to his right showed Mackenzie how the enemy themselves were in confusion, this had been a terrifying surprise to them too, but as soon as they got over the shock they'd advance and there'd be nothing left to stop them. . . . It was as if another man spurred his mount. The animal fought, foam-flecked with panic. He slugged its head around, brutally, and dug in spurs. They rushed down the hill toward the guns.

He needed all his strength to halt the gelding before the cannon mouths. A man slumped dead by his piece, though there was no mark on him. Mackenzie jumped to the ground. His steed bolted

He hadn't time to worry about that. Where was help? 'Come here!' His yell was lost in the riot. But suddenly another man was beside him, Speyer, snatching up a shell and slamming it into the breach. Mackenzie squinted through the telescope, took a bearing by guess and feel. He could see the Esper car where it squatted among dead and hurt. At this distance it looked too small to have blackened acres.

Speyer helped him lay the howitzer. He jerked the lanyard. The gun roared and sprang. The shell burst a few yards short of target, sand spurted and metal fragments whined.

Speyer had the next one loaded. Mackenzie aimed and fired. Overshot this time, but not by much. The car rocked. Concussion might have hurt the Espers inside; at least, the psi blasts had stopped. But it was necessary to strike before the foe got organized again.

He ran towards his own regimental car. The door gaped, the crew had fled. He threw himself into the driver's seat. Speyer clanged the door shut and stuck his face in the hood of the rocket-launcher periscope. Mackenzie raced the machine forward. The banner on its rooftop snapped in the wind.

Speyer aimed the launcher and pressed the firing button. The missile burned across intervening yards and exploded. The other car lurched on its wheels. A hole opened in its side.

*If the boys will only rally and advance— Well, if they don't, I'm done for anyway.* Mackenzie squealed to a stop, flung open the door and leaped out. Curled, blackened metal framed his entry. He wriggled through, into murk and stenches.

Two Espers lay there. The driver was dead, a chunk of steel through his breast. The other one, the adept, whimpered among his unhuman instruments. His face was hidden by blood. Mackenzie pitched the corpse on its side and pulled off the robe. He snatched a curving tube of metal and tumbled back out.

Speyer was still in the undamaged car, firing repeaters at those hostiles who ventured near. Mackenzie jumped onto the ladder of the disabled machine, climbed to its roof and stood erect. He waved the blue robe in one hand and the weapon he did not understand in the other. 'Come on, you sons!' he shouted, tiny against the sea wind. 'We've knocked 'em out for you! Want your breakfast in bed too?'

One bullet buzzed past his ear. Nothing else. Most of the enemy, horse and foot, stayed frozen. In that immense stillness he could not tell if he heard surf or the blood in his own veins.

Then a bugle called. The hex corps whistled triumphantly; their tomtoms thuttered. A ragged line of his infantry began to move toward him. More followed. The cavalry joined them, man by man and unit by unit, on their flanks. Soldiers ran down the smoking hillsides.

Mackenzie sprang to sand again and into his car. 'Let's get back,' he told Speyer. 'We got a battle to finish.'

'Shut up!' Tom Danielis said.

Philosopher Woodworth stared at him. Fog swirled and dripped in the forest, hiding the land and the brigade, gray nothingness through which came a muffled noise of men and horses and wheels, an isolated and infinitely weary sound. The air was cold, and clothing hung heavy on the skin.

'Sir,' protested Major Lescarbault. The eyes were wide and shocked in his gaunted face.

'I dare tell a ranking Esper to stop quacking about a subject of which he's totally ignorant?' Danielis answered. 'Well, it's past time that somebody did.'

Woodworth recovered his poise. 'All I said, son, was that we should consolidate our adepts and strike the Brodskyite center,' he reproved. 'What's wrong with that?'

Danielis clenched his fists. 'Nothing,' he said, 'except it invites a worse disaster than you've brought on us yet.'

'A setback or two,' Lescarbault argued. 'They did rout us on the west, but we turned their flank here by the Bay.'

'With the net result that their main body pivoted, attacked, and split us in half,' Danielis snapped. 'The Espers have been scant use since then . . . now the rebels know they need vehicles to transport their weapons, and can be killed. Artillery zeroes in on their position, or bands of woodsmen hit and run, leaving them dead, or the enemy simply goes around any spot where they're known to be. We haven't got enough adepts!'

'That's why I proposed gettin' them in one group, too big to withstand,' Woodworth said.

'And too cumbersome to be of any value,' Daniels replied. He felt more than a little sickened, knowing how the Order had cheated him his whole life; yes, he thought, that was the real bitterness, not the fact that the adepts had failed to defeat the rebels – by failing, essentially, to break their spirit – but the fact that the adepts were only someone else's cat's paws and every gentle, earnest soul in every Esper community was only someone's dupe.

Wildly he wanted to return to Laura – there'd be no chance thus far to see her – Laura and the kid, the last honest reality this fog-world had left him. He mastered himself and went on more evenly:

'The adepts, what few of them survive, will of course be helpful in defending San Francisco. An army free to move around in the field can deal with them, one way or another, but your . . . your weapons can repel an assault on the city walls. So that's where I'm going to take them.'

Probably the best he could do. There was no word from the northern half of the loyalist army. Doubtless they'd withdrawn to the capital, suffering heavy losses en route. Radio jamming continued, hampering friendly and hostile communications alike. He had to take action, either retreat southwards or fight his way through to the city. The latter course seemed wisest. He didn't believe that Laura had much to do with his choice.

'I'm no adept myself,' Woodworth said. 'I can't call them mind to mind.'

'You mean you can't use their equivalent of radio,' Danielis said brutally. 'Well, you've got an adept in attendance. Have him pass the word.'

Woodworth flinched. 'I hope,' he said, 'I hope you understand this came as a surprise to me too.'

'Oh, yes, certainly, Philosopher,' Lescarbault said unbidden.

Woodworth swallowed. 'I still hold with the Way and the Order,' he said harshly. 'There's nothin' else I can do. Is there? The Grand Seeker has promised a full explanation when this is over.' He shook his head. 'Okay, son, I'll do what I can.'

A certain compassion touched Danielis as the blue robe disappeared into the fog. He rapped his orders the more severely.

Slowly his command got going. He was with the Second Brigade; the rest were strewn over the Peninsula in the fragments into which the rebels had knocked them. He hoped the equally scattered adepts, joining him on his march through the San Bruno range, would guide some of those units to him. But most, wandering demoralized, were sure to surrender to the first rebels they came upon.

He rode near the front, on a muddy road that snaked over the highlands. His helmet was a monstrous weight. The horse stumbled beneath him, exhausted by – how many days? – of march, countermarch, battle, skirmish, thin rations or none, heat and cold and fear, in an empty land. Poor beast, he'd see that it got proper treatment when they reached the city. That all those poor beasts behind him did, after trudging and fighting and trudging until their eyes were filmed with fatigue.

*There'll be chance enough for rest in San Francisco. We're impregnable there, walls and cannon and the Esper machines to landward, the sea that feeds us at our backs. We can recover our strength, regroup our forces, bring fresh troops down from Washington and up from the south by water. The war isn't decided yet . . . God help us.*

*I wonder if it will ever be.*

*And then, will Jimbo Mackenzie come to see us, sit by the fire and swap yarns about what we did? Or talk about something else, anything else? If not, that's too high a price for victory.*

*Maybe not too high a price for what we've learned, though. Strangers on this planet ... what else could have forged those weapons? The adepts will talk if I myself have to torture them till they do.* But Danielis remembered tales muttered in the fisher huts of his boyhood, after dark, when ghosts walked in old men's minds. Before the holocaust there had been legends about the stars, and the legends lived on. He didn't know if he would be able to look again at the night sky without a shiver.

This damned fog—

Hoofs thudded. Danielis half drew his sidearm. But the rider was a scout of his own, who raised a drenched sleeve in salute. 'Colonel, an enemy force about ten miles ahead by road. Big.'

*So we'll have to fight now.* 'Do they seem aware of us?'

'No, sir. They're proceeding east along the ridge there.'

'Probably figure to occupy the Candlestick Park ruins,' Danielis murmured. His body was too tired for excitement. 'Good stronghold, that. Very well, Corporal.' He turned to Lescarbault and issued instructions.

The brigade formed itself in the formlessness. Patrols went out. Information began to flow back, and Danielis sketched a plan that ought to work. He didn't want to try for a decisive engagement, only brush the enemy aside and discourage them from pursuit. His men must be spared, as many as possible, for the city defense and the eventual counteroffensive.

Lescarbault came back. 'Sir! The radio jamming's ended!'

'What?' Danielis blinked, not quite comprehending.

'Yes, sir. I've been using a minicom—' Lescarbault lifted the wrist on which his tiny transceiver was strapped – 'for very short-range work, passing the battalion commanders their orders. The interference stopped a couple of minutes ago. Clear as daylight.'

Danielis pulled the wrist toward his own mouth. 'Hello, hello, radio wagon, this is the C.O. You read me?'

'Yes, sir,' said the voice.

'They turned off the jammer in the city for a reason. Get me the open military band.'

'Yes, sir.' Pause, while men mumbled and water runneled unseen in the arroyos. A wraith smoked past Danielis' eyes. Drops coursed off his helmet and down his collar. The horse's mane hung sodden.

Like the scream of an insect:

'—here at once! Every unit in the field, get to San Francisco at once! We're under attack by sea!'

Danielis let go Lescarbault's arm. He stared into emptiness while the voice wailed on and forever on.

'—bombarding Potrero Point. Decks jammed with troops. They must figure to make a landing there—'

Danielis' mind raced ahead of the words. It was as if Esp were no lie, as if he scanned the beloved city himself and felt her wounds in his own flesh. There was no fog around the Gate, of course, or so detailed a description could not have been given. Well, probably some streamers of it rolled in under the rusted remnants of the bridge, themselves like snowbanks against blue-green water and brilliant sky. But most of the Bay stood open to the sun. On the opposite shore lifted the Eastbay hills, green with gardens and agleam with villas; and Marin shouldered heavenward across the strait, looking to the roofs and walls and heights that were San Francisco. The convoy had gone between the coast defenses that could have smashed it, an unusually large convoy and not on time: but still the familiar big-bellied hulls, white sails, occasional fuming stacks, that kept the city fed. There had been an explanation about trouble with commerce raiders; and the fleet was passed on into the Bay, where San Francisco had no walls. Then the gun covers were taken off and the holds vomited armed men.

*Yes, they did seize a convoy, those piratical schooners. Used radio jamming of their own; together with ours, that choked off any cry of warning. They threw our supplies overboard and embarked the bossman militia. Some spy or traitor gave them the recognition signals. Now the capital lies open to them, her garrison stripped, hardly an adept left in Esper Central, the Sierrans thrusting against her southern gates, and Laura without me.*

'We're coming!' Danielis yelled. His brigade groaned into speed behind him. They struck with a desperate ferocity that carried them deep into enemy positions and then stranded them in separated groups. It became knife and saber in the fog. But Danielis, because he led the charge, had already taken a grenade on his breast.

East and south, in the harbor district and at the wreck of the Peninsula wall, there was still some fighting. As he rode higher,

Mackenzie saw how those parts were dimmed by smoke, which the wind scattered to show rubble that had been houses. The sound of firing drifted to him. But otherwise the city shone untouched, roofs and white walls in a web of streets, church spires raking the sky like masts, Federal House on Nob Hill and the Watchtower on Telegraph Hill as he remembered them from childhood visits. The Bay glittered insolently beautiful.

But he had no time for admiring the view, nor for wondering where Laura huddled. The attack on Twin Peaks must be swift, for surely Esper Central would defend itself.

On the avenue climbing the opposite side of those great humps, Speyer led half the Rolling Stones. (Yamaguchi lay dead on a pockmarked beach.) Mackenzie himself was taking this side. Horses clopped along. Portola, between blankly shuttered mansions; guns trundled and creaked, boots knocked on pavement, moccasins slithered, weapons rattled, men breathed heavily and the hex corps whistled against unknown demons. But silence overwhelmed the noise, echoes trapped it and let it die. Mackenzie recollected nightmares when he fled down a corridor which had no end. *Even if they don't cut loose at us,* he thought bleakly, *we've got to seize their place before our nerve gives out.*

Twin Peaks Boulevard turned off Portola and wound steeply to the right. The houses ended; wild grasses alone covered the quasi-sacred hills, up to the tops where stood the buildings forbidden to all but adepts. Those two soaring, iridescent, fountainlike skyscrapers had been raised by night, within a matter of weeks. Something like a moan stirred at Mackenzie's back.

'Bugler, sound the advance. On the double!'

A child's jeering, the notes lifted and were lost. Sweat stung Mackenzie's eyes. If he failed and was killed, that didn't matter too much . . . after everything which had happened . . . but the regiment, the regiment—

Flame shot across the street, the color of hell. There went a hiss and a roar. The pavement lay trenched, molten, smoking and reeking. Mackenzie wrestled his horse to a standstill. *A warning only. But if they had enough adepts to handle us, would they bother trying to scare us off?* Artillery, open fire!'

The field guns bellowed together, not only howitzers but motorized 75s taken along from Alemany Gate's emplacements.

Shells went overhead with a locomotive sound. They burst on the walls above and the racket thundered back down the wind.

Mackenzie tensed himself for an Esper blast, but none came. Had they knocked out the final defensive post in their own first barrage? Smoke cleared from the heights and he saw that the colors which played in the tower were dead and that wounds gaped across loveliness, showing unbelievably thin framework. It was like seeing the bones of a woman murdered by his hand.

Quick, though! He issued a string of commands and led the horse and foot on. The battery stayed where it was, firing and firing with hysterical fury. The dry brown grass started to burn, as red-hot fragments scattered across the slope. Through mushroom bursts, Mackenzie saw the building crumble. Whole sheets of facing broke and fell to earth. The skeleton vibrated, took a direct hit and sang in metal agony, slumped and twisted apart.

What was that which stood within?

There were no separate rooms, no floors, nothing but girders, enigmatic machines, here and there a globe still aglow like a minor sun. The structure had enclosed something nearly as tall as itself, a finned and shining column, almost like a rocket shell but impossibly huge and fair.

*Their spaceship*, Mackenzie thought in the clamor. *Yes, of course, the ancients had begun making spaceships, and we always figured we would again someday. This, though—!*

The archers lifted a tribal screech. The riflemen and cavalry took it up, crazy, jubilant, the howl of a beast of prey. By Satan, we've whipped the stars themselves! As they burst onto the hillcrest, the shelling stopped, and their yells overrode the wind. Smoke was acrid as blood smell in their nostrils.

A few dead blue-robes could be seen in the debris. Some halfdozen survivors milled toward the ship. A bowman let fly. His arrow glanced off the landing gear but brought the Espers to a halt. Troopers poured over the shards to capture them.

Mackenzie reined in. Something that was not human lay crushed near a machine. Its blood was deep violet color. *When the people have seen this, that's the end of the Order*. He felt no triumph. At St. Helena he had come to appreciate how fundamentally good the believers were.

But this was no moment for regret, or for wondering how harsh the future would be with man taken entirely off the leash. The building on the other peak was still intact. He had to consolidate his position here, then help Phil if need be.

However, the minicom said, 'Come on and join me, Jimbo. The fracas is over,' before he had completed his task. As he rode alone toward Speyer's place, he saw a Pacific States flag flutter up the mast on that skyscraper's top.

Guards stood awed and nervous at the portal. Mackenzie dismounted and walked inside. The entry chamber was a soaring, shimmering fantasy of colors and arches, through which men moved troll-like. A corporal led him down a hall. Evidently this building had been used for quarters, offices, storage, and less understandable purposes. ... There was a room whose door had been blown down with dynamite. The fluid abstract murals were stilled, scarred, and sooted. Four ragged troopers pointed guns at the two beings whom Speyer was questioning.

One slumped at something that might answer to a desk. The avian face was buried in seven-fingered hands and the rudimentary wings quivered with sobs. *Are they able to cry, then?* Mackenzie thought, astonished, and had a sudden wish to take the being in his arms and offer what comfort he was able.

The other one stood erect in a robe of woven metal. Great topaz eyes met Speyer's from a seven-foot height, and the voice turned accented English into music.

'—a G-type star some fifty light-years hence. It is barely visible to the naked eye, though not in this hemisphere.'

The major's fleshless, bristly countenance jutted forward as if to peck. 'When do you expect reinforcements?'

'There will be no other ship for almost a century, and it will only bring personnel. We are isolated by space and time; few can come to work here, to seek to build a bridge of minds across that gulf—'

'Yeah,' Speyer nodded prosaically. 'The light-speed limit. I thought so. If you're telling the truth.'

The being shuddered. 'Nothing is left for us but to speak truth, and pray that you will understand and help. Revenge, conquest, any form of mass violence is impossible when so much space and time lies between. Our labor has been done in the mind and heart. It is not too late, even now. The most crucial facts can still be kept hidden – oh, listen to me, for the sake of your unborn!'

Speyer nodded to Mackenzie. 'Everything okay?' he said. 'We got us a full bag here. About twenty left alive, this fellow the bossman. Seems like they're the only ones on Earth.'

'We guessed there couldn't be many,' the colonel said. His tone and his feelings were alike ashen. 'When we talked it over, you and me, and tried to figure what our clues meant. They'd have to be few, or they'd've operated more openly.'

'Listen, listen,' the being pleaded. 'We came in love. Our dream was to lead you – to make you lead yourselves – toward peace, fulfillment. ... Oh, yes, we would also gain, gain yet another race with whom we could someday converse as brothers. But there are many races in the universe. It was chiefly for your own tortured sakes that we wished to guide your future.'

'That controlled history notion isn't original with you,' Speyer grunted. 'We've invented it for ourselves now and then on Earth. The last time it led to the Hellbombs. No, thanks!'

'But we *know*! The Great Science predicts with absolute certainty—'

'Predicted this?' Speyer waved a hand at the blackened room.

'There are fluctuations. We are too few to control so many savages in every detail. But do you not wish an end to war, to all your ancient sufferings? I offer you that for your help today.'

'You succeeded in starting a pretty nasty war yourselves,' Speyer said.

The being twisted its fingers together. 'That was an error. The plan remains, the only way to lead your people toward peace. I, who have traveled between suns, will get down before your boots and beg you—'

'Stay put!' Speyer flung back. 'If you'd come openly, like honest folk, you'd have found some to listen to you. Maybe enough, even. But no, your do-gooding had to be subtle and crafty. You knew what was right for us. We weren't entitled to any say in the matter. God in heaven, I've never heard anything so arrogant!'

The being lifted its head. 'Do you tell children the whole truth?'

'As much as they're ready for.'

'Your child-culture is not ready to hear these truths.'

'Who qualified you to call us children – besides yourselves?'

'How do you know you are adult?'

'By trying adult jobs and finding out if I can handle them. Sure, we make some ghastly blunders, we humans. But they're our own. And we learn from them. You're the ones who won't learn, you and that damned psychological science you were bragging about, that wants to fit every living mind into the one frame it can understand.

'You wanted to re-establish the centralized state, didn't you? Did you ever stop to think that maybe feudalism is what suits man? Some one place to call our own, and belong to, and be part of; a community with traditions and honor; a chance for the individual to make decisions that count; a bulwark for liberty against the central overlords, who'll always want more and more power; a thousand different ways to live. We've always built supercountries, here on Earth, and we've always knocked them apart again. I think maybe the whole idea is wrong. And maybe this time we'll try something better. Why not a world of little states, too well rooted to dissolve in a nation, too small to do much harm – slowly rising above petty jealousies and spite, but keeping their identities – a thousand separate approaches to our problems. Maybe then we can solve a few of them . . . for ourselves!'

'You will never do so,' the being said. 'You will be torn in pieces all over again.'

'That's what you think. I think otherwise. But whichever is right – and I bet this is too big a universe for either of us to predict – we'll have made a free choice on Earth. I'd rather be dead than domesticated.

'The people are going to learn about you as soon as Judge Brodsky's been reinstated. No, sooner. The regiment will hear today, the city tomorrow, just to make sure no one gets ideas about suppressing the truth again. By the time your next spaceship comes, we'll be ready for it: in our own way, whatever that is.'

The being drew a fold of robe about his head. Speyer turned to Mackenzie. His face was wet. 'Anything . . . you want to say . . . Jimbo?'

'No,' Mackenzie mumbled. 'Can't think of anything. Let's get our command organized here. I don't expect we'll have to fight any more, though. It seems to be about ended down there.'

'Sure.' Speyer drew an uneven breath. 'The enemy troops elsewhere are bound to capitulate. They've got nothing left to fight for. We can start patching up pretty soon.'

There was a house with a patio whose wall was covered by

roses. The street outside had not yet come back to life, so that silence dwelt here under the yellow sunset. A maidservant showed Mackenzie through the back door and departed. He walked toward Laura, who sat on a bench beneath a willow. She watched him approach but did not rise. One hand rested on a cradle.

He stopped and knew not what to say. How thin she was!

Presently she told him, so low he could scarcely hear: 'Tom's dead.'

'Oh, no.' Darkness came and went before his eyes.

'I learned the day before yesterday, when a few of his men straggled home. He was killed in the San Bruno.'

Mackenzie did not dare join her, but his legs would not upbear him. He sat down on the flagstones and saw curious patterns in their arrangement. There was nothing else to look at.

Her voice ran on above him, toneless: 'Was it worth it? Not only Tom, but so many others, killed for a point of politics?'

'More than that was at stake,' he said.

'Yes, I heard on the radio. I still can't understand how it was worth it. I've tried very hard, but I can't.'

He had no strength left to defend himself. 'Maybe you're right, duck. I wouldn't know.'

'I'm not sorry for myself,' she said. 'I still have Jimmy. But Tom was cheated out of so much.'

He realized all at once that there was a baby, and he ought to take his grandchild to him and think thoughts about life going on into the future. But he was too empty.

'Tom wanted him named after you,' she said.

*Did you, Laura?* he wondered. Aloud: 'What are you going to do now?'

'I'll find something.'

He made himself glance at her. The sunset burned on the willow leaves above and on her face, which was now turned toward the infant he could not see. 'Come back to Nakamura,' he said.

'No. Anywhere else.'

'You always loved the mountains,' he groped. 'We—'

'No.' She met his eyes. 'It isn't you, Dad. Never you. But Jimmy is not going to grow up a soldier.' She hesitated. 'I'm sure some of the Espers will keep going, on a new basis, but with the same goals. I think we should join them. He ought to believe

T—c

in something different from what killed his father, and work for it to become real. Don't you agree?'

Mackenzie climbed to his feet against Earth's hard pull. 'I don't know,' he said. 'Never was a thinker. . . . Can I see him?'

'Oh, Dad—'

He went over and looked down at the small sleeping form. 'If you marry again,' he said, 'and have a daughter, would you call her for her mother?' He saw Laura's head bend downward and her hands clench. Quickly he said, 'I'll go now. I'd like to visit you some more, tomorrow or sometime, if you'll have me.'

Then she came to his arms and wept. He stroked her hair and murmured, as he had done when she was a child. 'You do want to return to the mountains, don't you? They're your country too, your people, where you belong.'

'Y-you'll never know how much I want to.'

'Then why not?' he cried.

His daughter straightened herself. 'I can't,' she said. 'Your war is ended. Mine has just begun.'

Because he had trained that will, he could only say, 'I hope you win it.'

'Perhaps in a thousand years—' She could not continue.

Night had fallen when he left her. Power was still out in the city, so the street lamps were dark and the stars stood forth above all roofs. The squad that waited to accompany their colonel to barracks looked wolfish by lantern light. They saluted him and rode at his back, rifles ready for trouble; but there was only the iron sound of horseshoes.

# TURNING POINT

'PLEASE, mister, could I have a cracker for my oontatherium?'

Not exactly the words you would expect at an instant when history changes course and the universe can never again be what it was. *The die is cast; In this sign conquer; It is not fit that you should sit here any longer; We hold these truths to be self-evident; The Italian navigator has landed in the New World; Dear God, the thing works!* – no man with any imagination can recall those, or others like them, and not have a coldness run along his spine. But as for what little Mierna first said to us, on that island half a thousand light-years from home . . .

The star is catalogued AGC 4256836, a K2 dwarf in Cassiopeia. Our ship was making a standard preliminary survey of that region, and had come upon mystery enough – how easily Earthsiders forget that every planet is a complete world! – but nothing extraordinary in this fantastic cosmos. The Traders had noted places that seemed worth further investigation; so had the Federals; the lists were not quite identical.

After a year, vessel and men were equally jaded. We needed a set-down, to spend a few weeks refitting and recuperating before the long swing homeward. There is an art to finding such a spot. You visit whatever nearby suns look suitable. If you come on a planet whose gross physical characteristics are terrestroid, you check the biological details – very, very carefully, but since the operation is largely automated it goes pretty fast – and make contact with the autochthones, if any. Primitives are preferred. That's not because of military danger, as some think. The Federals insist that the natives have no objection to strangers camping on their land, while the Traders don't see how anyone, civilized or not, that hasn't discovered atomic energy can be a menace. It's only that primitives are less apt to ask complicated questions and otherwise make a nuisance of themselves. Spacemen rejoice that worlds with machine civilizations are rare.

Well, Joril looked ideal. The second planet of that sun with more water than Earth, it offered a mild climate everywhere. The

67

biochemistry was so like our own that we could eat native foods, and there didn't seem to be any germs that UX-2 couldn't handle. Seas, forests, meadows made us feel right at home, yet the countless differences from earth lent a fairyland glamour. The indigenes were savages, that is, they depended on hunting, fishing and gathering for their whole food supply. So we assumed there were thousands of little cultures and picked the one that appeared most advanced: not that aerial observation indicated much difference.

Those people lived in neat, exquisitely decorated villages along the western seaboard of the largest continent, with woods and hills behind them. Contact went smoothly. Our semanticians had a good deal of trouble with the language, but the villagers started picking up English right away. Their hospitality was lavish whenever we called on them, but they stayed out of our camp except for the conducted tours we gave and other such invitations. With one vast, happy sigh, we settled down.

But from the first there were certain disturbing symptoms. Granted they had humanlike throats and palates, we hadn't expected the autochthones to speak flawless English within a couple of weeks. Every one of them. Obviously they could have learned still faster if we'd taught them systematically. We followed the usual practice and christened the planet 'Joril' after what we thought was the local word for 'earth' – and then found that 'Joril' meant 'Earth,' capitalized, and the people had an excellent heliocentric astronomy. Though they were too polite to press themselves on us, they weren't merely accepting us as something inexplicable; curiosity was afire in them, and given half a chance they *did* ask the most complicated questions.

Once the initial rush of establishing ourselves was over and we had time to think, it became plain that we'd stumbled on something worth much further study. First we needed to check on some other areas and make sure this Dannicar culture wasn't a freak. After all, the neolithic Mayas had been good astronomers; the ferro-agricultural Greeks had developed a high and sophisticated philosophy. Looking over the maps we'd made from orbit, Captain Barlow chose a large island about 700 kilometers due west. A gravboat was outfitted and five men went aboard.

Pilot: Jacques Lejeune. Engineer: me. Federal militechnic representative: Commander Ernest Baldinger, Space Force of the Solar Peace Authority. Federal civil government representative: Walter Vaughan. Trader agent: Don Haraszthy. He and Vaughan were the principals, but the rest of us were skilled in the multiple jobs of planetography. You have to be, on a foreign world months from home or help.

We made the aerial crossing soon after sunrise, so we'd have a full eighteen hours of daylight. I remember how beautiful the ocean looked below us, like one great bowl of metal, silver where the sun struck, cobalt and green copper beyond. Then the island came over the world's edge, darkly forested, crimson-splashed by stands of gigantic red blossoms. Lejeune picked out an open spot in the woods, about two kilometers from a village that stood on a wide bay, and landed us with a whoop and a holler. He's a fireball pilot.

'Well—' Haraszthy rose to his sheer two meters and stretched till his joints cracked. He was burly to match that height, and his hook-nosed face carried the marks of old battles. Most Traders are tough, pragmatic extroverts; they have to be, just as Federal civils have to be the opposite. It makes for conflict, though. 'Let's hike.'

'Not so fast,' Vaughan said: a thin young man with an intense gaze. 'That tribe has never seen or heard of our kind. If they noticed us land, they may be in a panic.'

'So we go jolly them out of it,' Haraszthy shrugged.

'Our whole party? Are you serious?' Commander Baldinger asked. He reflected a bit. 'Yes, I suppose you are. But I'm responsible now. Lejeune and Cathcart, stand by here. We others will proceed to the village.'

'Just like that?' Vaughan protested.

'You know a better way?' Haraszthy answered.

'As a matter of fact—' But nobody listened. The government operates on some elaborate theories, and Vaughan was still too new in Survey to understand how often theory has to give way. We were impatient to go outside, and I regretted not being sent along to town. Of course, someone had to stay, ready to pull out our emissaries if serious trouble developed.

We emerged into long grass and a breeze that smelled of nothing so much as cinnamon. Trees rustled overhead, against a deep blue sky; the reddish sunlight spilled across purple wildflowers and bronze-colored insect wings. I drew a savoring breath before going around with Lejeune to make sure our landing gear was properly set. We were all lightly clad; Baldinger carried a blast rifle and Haraszthy a radiocom big enough to contact Dannicar, but both seemed ludicrously inappropriate.

'I envy the Jorillians,' I remarked.

'In a way,' Lejeune said. 'Though perhaps their environment is too good. What stimulus have they to advance further?'

'Why should they want to?'

'They don't, consciously, my old. But every intelligent race is descended from animals that once had a hard struggle to survive, so hard they were forced to evolve brains. There is an instinct for adventure, even in the gentlest herbivorous beings, and sooner or later it must find expression—'

'*Holy jumping Judas!*'

Haraszthy's yell brought Lejeune and me bounding back to that side of the ship. For a moment my reason wobbled. Then I decided the sight wasn't really so strange . . . here.

A girl was emerging from the woods. She was about the equivalent of a Terrestrial five-year-old, I estimated. Less than a meter tall (the Jorillians average more short and slender than we), she had the big head of her species to make her look still more elfin. Long blondish hair, round ears, delicate features that were quite humanoid except for the high forehead and huge violet eyes added to the charm. Her brown-skinned body was clad only in a white loincloth. One four-fingered hand waved cheerily at us. The other carried a leash. And at the opposite end of that leash was a grasshopper the size of a hippopotamus.

No, not a grasshopper, I saw as she danced toward us. The head looked similar, but the four walking legs were short and stout, and several others mere boneless appendages. The gaudy hide was skin, not chitin. I saw that the creature breathed with lungs, too. Nonetheless it was a startling monster; and it drooled.

'Insular genus,' Vaughan said. 'Undoubtedly harmless, or she wouldn't— But a child, coming so casually—!'

Baldinger grinned and lowered his rifle. 'What the hell,' he said, 'to a kid everything's equally wonderful. This is a break for our side. She'll give us a good recommendation to her elders.'

The little girl (damn it, I will call her that) walked to within a meter of Haraszthy, turned those big eyes up and up till they met his piratical face, and trilled with an irresistible smile:

'Please, mister, could I have a cracker for my oontatherium?'

I don't quite remember the next few minutes. They were confused. Eventually we found ourselves, the whole five, walking down a sun-speckled woodland path. The girl skipped beside us, chattering like a xylophone. The monster lumbered behind, chewing messily on what we had given it. When the light struck those compound eyes I thought of a jewel chest.

'My name is Mierna,' the girl said, 'and my father makes things out of wood, I don't know what that's called in English, please tell me, oh, carpentry, thank you, you're a nice man. My father thinks a lot. My mother makes songs. They are very pretty songs. She sent me out to get some sweet grass for a borning couch, because her assistant wife is going to born a baby soon, but when I saw you come down just the way Pengwil told, I knew I should say hello instead and take you to Taori. That's our village. We have *twenty-five houses*. And sheds and a Thinking Hall that's bigger than the one in Riru. Pengwil said crackers are awful tasty. Could I have one too?'

Haraszthy obliged in a numb fashion. Vaughan shook himself and fairly snapped, 'How do you know our language?'

'Why, everybody does in Taori. Since Pengwil came and taught us. That was three days ago. We've been hoping and hoping you would come. They'll be so jealous in Riru! But we'll let them visit if they ask us nicely.'

'Pengwil ... a Dannicarian name, all right,' Baldinger muttered. 'But they never heard of this island till I showed them our map. And they couldn't cross the ocean in those dugouts of theirs! It's against the prevailing winds, and square sails—'

'Oh, Pengwil's boat can sail right into the wind,' Mierna laughed. 'I saw him myself, he took everybody for rides, and now my father's making a boat like that too, only better.'

'Why did Pengwil come here?' Vaughan asked.

'To see what there was. He's from a place called Folat. They have such funny names in Dannicar, and they dress funny too, don't they, mister?'

'Folat ... yes, I remember, a community a ways north of our camp,' Baldinger said.

'But savages don't strike off into an unknown ocean for, for curiosity,' I stammered.

'These do,' Haraszthy grunted. I could almost see the relays clicking in his blocky head. There were tremendous commercial possibilities here, foods and textiles and especially the dazzling artwork. In exchange—

'No!' Vaughan exclaimed. 'I know what you're thinking, Trader Haraszthy, and you are not going to bring machines here.'

The big man bridled. 'Says who?'

'Says me, by virtue of the authority vested in me. And I'm sure the Council will confirm my decision.' In that soft air Vaughan was sweating. 'We don't dare!'

'What's a Council?' Mierna asked. A shade of trouble crossed her face. She edged close to the bulk of her animal.

In spite of everything, I had to pat her head and murmur, 'Nothing you need worry about, sweetheart.' To get her mind, and my own, off vague fears: 'Why do you call this fellow an oontatherium? That can't be his real name.'

'Oh, no.' She forgot her worries at once. 'He's a yao and his real name is, well, it means Big-Feet-Buggy-Eyes-Top-Man-Underneath-And-Over. That's what I named him. He's mine and he's lovely.' She tugged at an antenna. The monster actually purred. 'But Pengwil told us about something called an oont you have at your home, that's hairy and scary and carries things and drools like a yao, so I thought that would be a nice English name. Isn't it?'

'Very,' I said weakly.

'What is this oont business?' Vaughan demanded.

Haraszthy ran a hand through his hair. 'Well,' he said, 'you know I like Kipling, and I read some of his poems to some natives one night at a party. The one about the oont, the camel, yeah, I guess that must have been among 'em. They sure enjoyed Kipling.'

'And had the poem letter-perfect after one hearing, and passed it unchanged up and down the coast, and now it's crossed the sea and taken hold,' Vaughan choked.

'Who explained that therium is a root meaning "mammal"?' I asked. Nobody knew, but doubtless one of our naturalists had casually mentioned it. So five-year-old Mierna had gotten the term from a wandering sailor and applied it with absolute correctness: never mind feelers and insectoidal eyes, the yao was a true mammal.

After a while we emerged in a cleared strip fronting on the bay. Against its glitter stood the village, peak-roofed houses of wood and thatch, a different style from Dannicar's but every bit as pleasant and well-kept. Outrigger canoes were drawn up on the beach, where fishnets hung to dry. Anchored some way beyond was another boat. The curved, gaily painted hull, twin steering oars, mat sails and leather tackle were like nothing on our poor overmechanized Earth; but she was sloop-rigged, and evidently a deep keel made it impossible to run her ashore.

'I thought so,' Baldinger said in an uneven voice. 'Pengwil went ahead and invented tacking. That's an efficient design. He could cross the water in a week or less.'

'He invented navigation too,' Lejeune pointed out.

The villagers, who had not seen us descend, now dropped their occupations – cooking, cleaning, weaving, potting, the numberless jobs of the primitive – to come on the run. All were dressed as simply as Mierna. Despite large heads, which were not grotesquely big, odd hands and ears, slightly different body proportions, the women were good to look on: too good, after a year's celibacy. The beardless, long-haired men were likewise handsome, and both sexes were graceful as cats.

They didn't shout or crowd. Only one exuberant horn sounded, down on the beach. Mierna ran to a grizzled male, seized him by the hand, and tugged him forward. 'This is my father,' she crowed. 'Isn't he wonderful? And he thinks a lot. The name he's using right now, that's Sarato. I liked his last name better.'

'One wearies of the same word,' Sarato laughed. 'Welcome, Earthfolk. You do us great . . . *lula* . . . pardon, I lack the term. You raise us high by this visit.' His handshake – Pengwil must have told him about that custom – was hard, and his eyes met ours respectfully but unawed.

The Dannicarian communities turned what little government they needed over to specialists, chosen on the basis of some tests we hadn't yet comprehended. But these people didn't seem to draw even that much class distinction. We were introduced to everybody by occupation: hunter, fisher, musician, prophet (I think that is what *nonalo* means), and so on. There was the same absence of taboo here as we had noticed in Dannicar, but an equally elaborate code of manners – which they realized we could not be expected to observe.

Pengwil, a strongly built youth in the tunic of his own culture, greeted us. It was no coincidence that he'd arrived at the same spot as we. Taori lay almost exactly west of his home area, and had the best anchorage on these shores. He was bursting with desire to show off his boat. I obliged him, swimming out and climbing aboard. 'A fine job,' I said with entire honesty. 'I have a suggestion, though. For sailing along coasts, you don't need a fixed keel.' I described a centerboard. 'Then you can ground her.'

'Yes, Sarato thought of that after he had seen my work. He has started one of such pattern already. He wants to do away with the steering oars also, and have a flat piece of wood turn at the back end. Is that right?'

'Yes,' I said after a strangled moment.

'It seemed so to me.' Pengwil smiled. 'The push of water can be split in two parts like the push of air. Your Mister Ishihara told me about splitting and rejoining forces. That was what gave me the idea for a boat like this.'

We swam back and put our clothes on again. The village was abustle, preparing a feast for us. Pengwil joined them. I stayed behind, walking the beach, too restless to sit. Staring out across the waters and breathing an ocean smell that was almost like Earth's, I thought strange thoughts. They were broken off by Mierna. She skipped toward me, dragging a small wagon.

'Hello, Mister Cathcart!' she cried. 'I have to gather seaweed for flavor. Do you want to help me?'

'Sure,' I said.

She made a face. 'I'm glad to be here. Father and Kuaya and a lot of the others, they're asking Mister Lejeune about ma-the-*matics*. I'm not old enough to like functions. I'd like to hear Mister Haraszthy tell about Earth, but he's talking alone in a house with his friends. Will you tell me about Earth? Can I go there someday?'

I mumbled something. She began to bundle leafy strands that had washed ashore. 'I didn't used to like this job,' she said. 'I had to go back and forth so many times. They wouldn't let me use my oontatherium because he gets buckety when his feet are wet. I told them I could make him shoes, but they said no. Now it's fun anyway, with this, this, what do you call it?'

'A wagon. You haven't had such a thing before?'

'No, never, just drags with runners. Pengwil told us about wheels. He saw the Earthfolk use them. Carpenter Huanna started putting wheels on the drags right away. We only have a few so far.'

I looked at the device, carved in wood and bone, a frieze of processional figures around the sides. The wheels weren't simply attached to axles. With permission, I took the cover off one and

saw a ring of hard-shelled spherical nuts. As far as I knew, nobody had explained ball bearings to Pengwil.

'I've been thinking and thinking,' Mierna said. 'If we made a
great big wagon, then an oontatherium could pull it, couldn't
he? Only we have to have a good way for tying the oontatherium
on, so he doesn't get hurt and you can guide him. I've thinked
. . . thought of a real nice way.' She stooped and drew lines in
the sand. The harness ought to work.

With a full load, we went back among the houses. I lost myself in admiration of the carved pillars and panels. Sarato
emerged from Lejeune's discussion of group theory (the natives
had already developed that, so the talk was a mere comparison
of approaches) to show me his obsidian-edged tools. He said
the coast dwellers traded inland for the material, and spoke of
getting steel from us. Or might we be so incredibly kind as to
explain how metal was taken from the earth?

The banquet, music, dances, pantomimes, conversation, all
was as gorgeous as expected, or more so. I trust the happy pills
we humans took kept us from making too grim an impres-
sion. But we disappointed our hosts by declining an offer to
spend the night. They guided us back by torch-glow, singing the
whole distance, on a twelve-tone scale with some of the damned-
est harmony I have ever come across. When we reached the
boat they turned homeward again. Mierna was at the tail of the
parade. She stood a long time in the coppery light of the single
great moon, waving to us.

Baldinger set out glasses and a bottle of Irish. 'Okay,' he said.
'Those pills have worn off by now, but we need an equivalent.'

'Hoo, yes!' Haraszthy grabbed the bottle.

'I wonder what their wine will be like, when they invent that?'
Lejeune mused.

'Be still!' Vaughan said. 'They aren't going to.'

We stared at him. He sat shivering with tension, under the
cold fluoroluminance in that bleak little cabin.

'What the devil do you mean?' Haraszthy demanded at last.
'If they can make wine half as well as they do everything else,
it'll go for ten credits a liter on Earth.'

'Don't you understand?' Vaughan cried. 'We can't deal with
them. We have to get off this planet and— Oh, God, why did
we have to find the damned thing?' He groped for a glass.

'Well,' I sighed, 'we always knew, those of us who bothered to think about the question, that someday we were bound to meet a race like this. Man ... what is man that Thou art mindful of him?'

'This is probably an older star than Sol,' Baldinger nodded. 'Less massive, so it stays longer on the main sequence.'

'There needn't be much difference in planetary age,' I said. 'A million years, half a million, whatever the figure is, hell, that doesn't mean a thing in astronomy or geology. In the development of an intelligent race, though—'

'But they're *savages*!' Haraszthy protested.

'Most of the races we've found are,' I reminded him. 'Man was too, for most of his existence. Civilization is a freak. It doesn't come natural. Started on Earth, I'm told, because the Middle East dried out as the glaciers receded and something had to be done for a living when the game got scarce. And scientific, machine civilization, that's a still more unusual accident. Why should the Jorillians have gone beyond an Upper Paleolithic technology? They never needed to.'

'Why do they have the brains they do, if they're in the stone age?' Haraszthy argued.

'Why did we, in our own stone age?' I countered. 'It wasn't necessary for survival. Java man, Peking man, and the low-browed rest, they'd been doing all right. But evidently evolution, intraspecies competition, sexual selection ... whatever increases intelligence in the first place continues to force it upward, if some new factor like machinery doesn't interfere. A bright Jorillian has more prestige, rises higher in life, gets more mates and children, and so it goes. But this is an easy environment, at least in the present geological epoch. The natives don't even seem to have wars, which would stimulate technology. Thus far they've had little occasion to use those tremendous minds for anything but art, philosophy, and social experimentation.'

'What is their average IQ?' Lejeune whispered.

'Meaningless,' Vaughan said dully. 'Beyond 180 or so, the scale breaks down. How can you measure an intelligence so much greater than your own?'

There was a stillness. I heard the forest sough in the night around us.

'Yes,' Baldinger ruminated, 'I always realized that our betters must exist. Didn't expect we'd run into them in my own lifetime, however. Not in this microscopic sliver of the galaxy that we've explored. And . . . well, I always imagined the Elders having machines, science, space travel.'

'They will,' I said.

'If we go away—' Lejeune began.

'Too late,' I said. 'We've already given them this shiny new toy, science. If we abandon them, they'll come looking for us in a couple of hundred years. At most.'

Haraszthy's fist crashed on the table. 'Why leave?' he roared. 'What the hell are you scared of? I doubt the population of this whole planet is ten million. There are fifteen billion humans in the Solar System and the colonies! So a Jorillian can outthink me. So what? Plenty of guys can do that already, and it don't bother me as long as we can do business.'

Baldinger shook his head. His face might have been cast in iron. 'Matters aren't that simple. The question is what race is going to dominate this arm of the galaxy.'

'Is it so horrible if the Jorillians do?' Lejeune asked softly.

'Perhaps not. They seem pretty decent. But—' Baldinger straightened in his chair. 'I'm not going to be anybody's domestic animal. I want my planet to decide her own destiny.'

That was the unalterable fact. We sat weighing it for a long and wordless time.

The hypothetical superbeings had always seemed comfortably far off. We hadn't encountered them, or they us. Therefore they couldn't live anywhere near. Therefore they probably never would interfere in the affairs of this remote galactic fringe where we dwell. But a planet only months distance from Earth; a species whose average member was a genius and whose geniuses were not understandable by us: bursting from their world, swarming through space, vigorous, eager, jumping in a decade to accomplishments that would take us a century – if we ever succeeded – how could they help but destroy our painfully built civilization? We'd scrap it ourselves, as the primitives of our old days had scrapped their own rich cultures in the overwhelming face of Western society. Our sons would laugh at our shoddy triumphs, go forth to join the high Jorillian adventure, and come back spirit-broken by failure, to build some feeble imitation of an alien way of life and fester in their hopelessness. And so would every other thinking species, unless the Jorillians were merciful enough to leave them alone.

Which the Jorillians probably would be. But who wants that kind of mercy?

I looked upon horror. Only Vaughan had the courage to voice the thing:

'There are planets under technological blockade, you know. Cultures too dangerous to allow modern weapons, let alone spaceships. Joril can be interdicted.'

'They'll invent the stuff for themselves, now they've gotten the idea,' Baldinger said.

Vaughan's mouth twitched downward. 'Not if the only two regions that have seen us are destroyed.'

'Good God!' Haraszthy leaped to his feet.

'Sit down!' Baldinger rapped.

Haraszthy spoke an obscenity. His face was ablaze. The rest of us sat in a chill sweat.

'You've called *me* unscrupulous,' the Trader snarled. 'Take that suggestion back to the hell it came from, Vaughan, or I'll kick out your brains.'

I thought of nuclear fire vomiting skyward, and a wisp of gas that had been Mierna, and said, 'No.'

'The alternative,' Vaughan said, staring at the bulkhead across from him, 'is to do nothing until the sterilization of the entire planet has become necessary.'

Lejeune shook his head in anguish. 'Wrong, wrong, wrong. There can be too great a price for survival.'

'But for our children's survival? Their liberty? Their pride and—and—'

'What sort of pride can they take in themselves, once they know the truth?' Haraszthy interrupted. He reached down, grabbed Vaughan's shirt front, and hauled the man up by sheer strength. His broken features glared three centimeters from the Federal's. 'I'll tell you what we're going to do,' he said. 'We're going to trade, and teach, and xenologize, and fraternize, the same as with any other people whose salt we've eaten. And take our chances like men!'

'Let him go,' Baldinger commanded. Haraszthy knotted a fist. 'If you strike him, I'll brig you and prefer charges at home. Let him go, I said!'

Haraszthy opened his grasp. Vaughan tumbled to the deck. Haraszthy sat down, buried his head in his hands, and struggled not to sob.

Baldinger refilled our glasses. 'Well, gentlemen,' he said, 'it looks like an impasse. We're damned if we do and damned if we don't, and I lay odds no Jorillian talks in such tired clichés.'

'They could give us so much,' Lejeune pleaded.

'Give!' Vaughan climbed erect and stood trembling before us. 'That's p-p-precisely the trouble. They'd give it! If they could, even. It wouldn't be ours. We probably couldn't understand their work, or use it, or . . . It wouldn't be ours, I say!'

Haraszthy stiffened. He sat like stone for an entire minute before he raised his face and whooped aloud.

*'Why not?'*

Blessed be whisky. I actually slept a few hours before dawn. But the light, stealing in through the ports, woke me then and I couldn't get back to sleep. At last I rose, took the drop-shaft down, and went outside.

The land lay still. Stars were paling, but the east held as yet only a rush of ruddiness. Through the cool air I heard the first bird-flutings from the dark forest mass around me. I kicked off my shoes and went barefoot in wet grass.

Somehow it was not surprising that Mierna should come at that moment, leading her oontatherium. She let go the leash and ran to me. 'Hi, Mister Cathcart! I hoped a lot somebody would be up. I haven't had any breakfast.'

'We'll have to see about that.' I swung her in the air till she squealed. 'And then maybe take a little flyaround in this boat. Would you like that?'

'Oooh!' Her eyes grew round. I set her down. She needed a while longer before she dared ask, 'Clear to Earth?'

'No, not that far, I'm afraid. Earth is quite a ways off.'

'Maybe someday? Please?'

'Someday, I'm quite sure, my dear. And not so terribly long until then, either.'

'I'm going to Earth, I'm going to Earth, I'm going to Earth.' She hugged the oontatherium. 'Will you miss me awfully, Big-Feet-Buggy-Eyes-Top-Man-Underneath-And-Over? Don't drool so sad. Maybe you can come too. Can he, Mister Cathcart? He's a very nice oontatherium, honest he is, and he does so love crackers.'

'Well, perhaps, perhaps not,' I said. 'But you'll go, if you wish. I promise you. Anybody on this whole planet who wants to will go to Earth.'

*As most of them will. I'm certain our idea will be accepted by the Council. The only possible one. If you can't lick 'em ... get 'em to jine you.*

I rumpled Mierna's hair. *In a way, sweetheart, what a dirty trick to play on you! Take you straight from the wilderness to a huge and complicated civilization. Dazzle you with all the tricks and gadgets and ideas we have, not because we're better but simply because we've been at it a little longer than you. Scatter your ten million among our fifteen billion. Of course you'll fall for it. You can't help yourselves. When you realize what's happening, you won't be able to stop, you'll be hooked. I don't think you'll even be able to resent it.*

*You'll be assimilated, Mierna. You'll become an Earth girl. Naturally, you'll grow up to be one of our leaders. You'll contribute tremendous things to our civilization, and be rewarded accordingly. But the whole point is, it will be our civilization. Mine ... and yours.*

*I wonder if you'll ever miss the forest, though, and the little houses by the bay, and the boats and songs and old, old stories, yes, and your darling oontatherium. I know the empty planet will miss you, Mierna. So will I.*

'Come on,' I said. 'Let's go build us that breakfast.'

THE ringing cut like a buzz saw. For a moment Wister denied it. He was riding a white horse whose mane and tail were flames, the great muscles surged between his legs, wind roared and whipped about him, smelling of summer meadows. *Brrrng!* Bees droned through clover. The wind had a tinge of Julie's hair, a sunny odor, but a sharp clean whiff of rocket fuel strengthened as it thrust against him. The horse made one enormous bound and left Earth. Meadows dwindled, the sky darkened until it was an infinitely deep Bonestell blue, and the stars of space glittered forth. *Brrrng!* The horse said with his father's voice, — That's the Big Dipper, which they used to call King Charles' Wain, but long ago it was Odin's *Brrrng!* and at night *Brrrng!* Jupiter far cold mysterious *Brrrng!* Saturn Pluto Andromeda *Brrrng!* outward upward upward *brrrng!* up *up* UP WHETHER YOU LIKE IT OR NOT BRRRNG BRRRNG BRRRNG!

The blackness confused him. At this time of year the sun rose before his alarm went off. Wister flailed his arms blindly, batting away the evil fragments which his dream had become. Florence stirred beside him, muttered herself awake, and sank back into sleep as Wister got control. She snored a little.

The clock face glowed with a small hour. Damnation, that wasn't the alarm, it was the phone. *Brrrng!* Wister swung out of bed. The floor was cool under his bare feet. It relieved the stickiness of his skin a little. He'd been sweating like a pig, though the night wasn't hot so early in summer.

'Okay, okay, okay,' he grumbled automatically, felt his way into the hall and switched on the light. It struck at his eyes as the phone did at his ears. He squinted against it and picked up the receiver. Still only partly active, his mind conjured forth horrible reasons for a night call and his pulse flapped. 'Hello?'

'Dick?' Charlie Huang's voice relieved him of deaths in his sister's family and imminent nuclear attack. 'Sorry, but you've got to get down here soonest. The whole bunch of us, in fact. *Yankee*'s wrecked.'

'Huh?'

'Meteor strike.'

'Can't be! The odds—'

'It had to happen sometime, didn't it? So it happened early in the space flight game, instead of a hundred years from now. I'll fill you in when you arrive. The boys escaped in their ditching capsule. Nothing else was left. They're stuck in orbit around the Moon.'

Wister shook his head violently, trying to clear it. None of this made sense. Even if a ship was hulled by a meteorite, or by a dozen meteorites, you didn't abandon it. You slapped patches over the holes and started repair work on whatever machinery was damaged. Didn't you?

Maybe not. This was the first such accident on record.

There was a click in the receiver. His boss had hung up, doubtless to call someone else. Wister groped on into the kitchen. Make haste slowly, he told himself. Nothing much could be done till the entire gang was assembled, which would take over an hour. Meanwhile he could best stoke his brain with coffee. When young he had always awakened refreshed, set to go, but in recent years he roused slow and gluey-eyed.

*Now cut that out,* he scolded. *Thirty-four is not old.*

The kitchen looked even more dismal than usual. Ordinarily Jim was up with him, chattering away sixty to the dozen while he made breakfast for them; and sunlight rioted in the flowerbeds just outside. This morning he had no distraction from yesterday's dirty dishes. He washed the coffeepot with some difficulty – the sink was full too – and set it to work while he went into the bathroom.

Stripped, he regarded himself for an instant of distaste. He was still fairly slender, but his efforts to keep in shape didn't entirely cope with the effects of a desk job. Slowly potbelly and pudding thighs overtook him. For the $x$th time he resolved to put in an hour a day at the local gym, knew he wouldn't keep the resolution, and swore wearily.

When the shower struck him with hot needles, his bloodstream began moving at a normal pace. It carried the remaining fog out of his head. Briefly he was shocked at himself, worried about his waistline while Cy Enwright and Phil Cohn and Bruno Fellini spun through the shadows behind the Moon. *My God, what am I going to say to their people?* He turned off the water, stepped from the tub, and toweled with quick harsh motions. *I won't say a word. I'll be too busy getting them back home alive.*

*How?*

He returned to the bedroom, switched on the light and dressed. Florence didn't stir. Her face sagged in sleep, as her body did awake, an unhealthy color. She was still snoring. Somehow the knowledge of three men who were his friends, caged among the cold stars, raised a tenderness in Wister. It wasn't Flo's doing that she stopped being the sun and surf and moonglade girl he married, after Jim was born. Some damned glandular change that the doctors couldn't pin down, too subtle for them . . . He stooped and brushed his lips across hers. Her breath was sour.

She'd have to get Jim off to school today. He scribbled a note and tucked it under the alarm clock before he went out to the kitchen. Coffee and a doughnut brought him to full alertness, but he didn't think about the job on hand. That would be useless until he knew just what had happened. Instead he found himself visualizing and remembering the *Yankee* boys.

Big, soft-spoken Cy Enright, Col. USAF Reserve, but you couldn't tell it from his manner. His wife outshone him when you first met them, he seemed only background for her beauty and vivacity – till you got to know them well, then it dawned on you that most of what she was had its source in him, dry wit and calm philosophy and the steel backbone that made her able to laugh with her friends while he was away in space. The other two described themselves as career civilians, though Phil Cohn had served in the Southeast Asia guerrillas some years ago. He was small and dark and quick-moving, a trifle on the bookish side and a nut about Mozart, but also a football fan and hell on wheels at the poker table. This summer he was going to get married and present his mother with the grandchildren she'd been pestering him for. Bruno Fellini, the youngest and handsomest of NASA's stable, wasn't interested in marriage – just women. There had been a couple of hilarious times when the public relations boys must scuttle around like toads in a pot, hushing up affairs that would spoil the Image. Bruno didn't give a damn. He knew perfectly well he was too adroit a rocket pilot to be fired. But loud sports shirt, cocky gait, bad puns, and all, he was the kind of guy who brought flowers when invited to dinner and would hand his bottom buck to anyone that needed it.

*And then there's me,* Wister thought. *We get along pretty well, we four. Yakking, bowling, partying, borrowing tools and books and maybe five till payday, now and then getting drunk together ... yeh, we talk about buying a fifty-foot cruiser one of these years and bumming around the Caribbean or the Mediterranean ... odd how close people become after they've shared such trivia long enough.*

*Those three men have never said or hinted or thought that I'm any less than them, because I turned groundling while they went to Mars and back. Never once.*

He rose from the table. Impulsively, he ducked back along the hall, into Jim's room. The boy still slept with Boo, though the bear's fur was long worn off and little remained of its face except a silly grin. Otherwise the room held the normal clutter of an eight-year-old, and Wister didn't worry too much about him any more. Jim had almost stopped having nightmares, and was now growing at a satisfactory rate. Wister bent close above the tangled head. *Funny,* he thought, *what a warm clean smell children have. They lose it at adolescence. I wonder how come?*

For some reason he was reminded of Julie Quist. He'd almost married her, a dozen years ago in Michigan. But another man, older and with better technique, had cut in on the romance. Only afterward did Wister come to believe that he could probably have gotten her anyhow, if he'd made a real try. But he was young and bitter and— Oh, well.

He straightened from Jim's bed. A picture of a spaceship blasting off caught his eye. He'd hoped the kid actually would stick by every small boy's dream and go in for a NASA career. 'My son the astronaut.' So why not? 'My son the first human being to walk on Titan beneath ringed Saturn.' Thinking of the *Yankee,* Wister was suddenly not quite sure. A coldness touched him; his fists closed together. There had been deaths in space before today, some of them pretty nasty. But Cy and Phil and Bruno were the men with whom he would like sometime to sail the route of Odysseus.

Quickly he turned on his heel, went down the hall and out the front door, shrugging into his topcoat. The eastern sky had turned pale and the suburban street lay clear to the eye, empty, altogether silent except for a dry rustle of palm fronds in a breeze. Westward there still dwelt gloom and a scattering of stars. The Moon was down. Wister was glad of that. He would not have been able to look on it without a shudder.

He got into his car, growled the engine while he lit his first cigarette, and started off. It was pleasant driving this early, at least, with no traffic jam to buck. Though he liked the neighborhood he lived in, he often wondered if it was worth the commuting. Ninety minutes a day made seven and a half hours a week, fifteen complete days a year, gone from his life with nothing to show for their passage but a stomach ulcer. . . . He turned onto the coast highway and opened up the car.

His forebrain began to worry the problem of what had happened, out there in space. *Yankee* had been on a fairly routine mission, part of a series of tests and shakedown flights before starting for Venus. While it circled the Moon, some data were gathered, of course, for the different breeds of scientists to chew on. But nothing very new. All right, so it had taken a meteorite beating, improbable though that was in the emptiness yonder. But then why had it been abandoned? And especially in a solar flare season?

Wister tried to suppress his barren speculations. He'd need a well-rested mind when he actually began work. He made himself watch sunrise, huge and silvery across the ocean, and recall days on those wide beaches when he walked hand in hand with Florence and told her everything he was going to do in space. He'd figured there was an excellent chance of his being tapped for the Mars expedition – well, damn it, there had been; he'd not transferred from the astronautical corps to the ground offices at anyone's request but his own— He realized he had gripped the steering wheel so hard that his fingers hurt and had tramped the gas pedal down to the floorboard. 'Stop that, you idiot!' he barked aloud. 'What good are you to anyone if you smash up?' Shaken, he eased off the pressures.

After a while the sprawling complex of Base came over the low horizon at him. An Aeolus three-stager towered in a gantry, stark against heaven. It was scheduled for a Lunar supply mission next week. Wister had already dismissed a passing thought, that it might be used to save the *Yankee* men instead. Countdown couldn't be advanced more than forty-eight hours or so, and that wasn't enough.

The guard waved him past without inspection. The young face was strained. *He knows,* Wister realized. *The whole layout here will know as soon as people arrive for work. Then the*

*whole planet. If we can pull off a rescue, with the world's eyes on
us, we'll all be set for at least one advancement in grade, and—
But those are my friends up there!*

The parking lot was still almost deserted. Wister jumped from
his car and jogtrotted to the front door of Thimk Hall, as everyone had lately been calling the computer-full building that
housed Orbital Command. Inside, the corridor was unpeopled,
a cavern that went on and on like something in a bad dream, clattering beneath his shoes. He was panting a little when he reached
Charlie Huang's office.

It was blue with smoke. The boss was there, of course, pacing
tiger-fashion. Harry Mowitz, the chief computerman, sat drum-
ming his nails on a chair arm. Bill Delarue, head of communications, perched on the desk. He kept shifting his position. Half
a dozen subordinates hovered unhappily by the far wall.

Huang spun about as Wister came in. 'Ah,' he snapped. 'There
you are. What the devil kept you so long?'

'Are they still alive?' Wister retorted.

'I hope to Christ so. But they've passed behind the Moon, out
of radio reach. Camp Apollo will try to raise them when they
come back around in half an hour. Hawaii's standing by too.'

'Oh, so you've got their orbit?'

'Well, no. Not exactly. But their last regular message said
they were about to assume it, and of course we know how they
planned to park in relation to the *Gal*. That was an hour before
they got hit.'

Wister considered the situation. *Galileo*, the unmanned
Euratom research satellite, was currently circling the Moon in
a four-hour orbit, its instruments telemetering some astrophysi-
cal observations and recording others for analysis the next time it
was brought down to Camp Apollo. *Yankee* was supposed to take
up a path of slightly less radius in the same plane. Radar and
laser transmissions, back and forth between ship and satellite,
would provide data from which the exact shape of the Moon
could be more accurately calculated than hitherto. There was
close cooperation between the American and West European
space programs. ... Yes, Enwright's boys would have been en-
gaged in terminal maneuvers, jockeying themselves into the
right position, when the smash came.

'I have an idea how they got hulled,' Mowitz offered. 'Space
can't be quite as hollow as we believed. We knew that none of

the charted rock storms are anywhere close. But what do we know about meteorites traveling outside the ecliptic plane? They'd zip by Earth too fast to be observed, if no one was looking for them especially.'

'What happened, though?' Wister demanded. His mouth was dry. He went to the water cooler and tapped a Dixie cupful. 'Why leave the ship, even if the rocks made scrap iron out of it?'

'The ship caught fire,' Delarue said.

'What?' Wister didn't think he had heard correctly. 'In space?'

'Yeah,' Huang said. 'Their last message – short-range 'cast on the only radio left, but Camp Apollo monitored it – uh, here's a copy— "Struck by large meteorites. Fire swept through ship. Forced to escape in ditching capsule. *Yankee*. Over."' He raised almond eyes loaded with misery. 'They didn't have a hell of a lot of time, it seems. I imagine only their being in spacesuits saved them. While I was on my own way here, Apollo sent us a new item. Somebody there got a telescopic glimpse, the last few seconds. Said the ship was one long flame. Then it exploded.'

'Oh.' Wister took out another cigarette. Blindly staring before him, he populated the wall with engineering diagrams and differential equations. The answer appeared. 'I see what must've happened. The combustion chamber and tanks were hit. The fuel and liquid oxy got together and ignited—'

'Impossible,' Delarue said. 'The moment anything like that occurred, rocket blast would cease. Obviously! Then you'd be in free fall, and everybody knows you can't have a fire without weight to give a pressure-temperature gradient.'

'You sure can, pal,' Wister told him, 'if colloidal drops of fuel and lox are scattered through the entire hull. Call it a prolonged explosion rather than a fire if you want to. I agree the free fall effect would damp the speed of the reaction; but by the same token, the ship would be ablaze for a few minutes. Then an unpunctured fuel tank blew up, and that was that.'

'But how'd your mixture get dissipated through the ship in the first place? What formed the colloids?'

'Supersonic energy. A meteorite of a few pounds' mass, zipping through a hull filled with air, would generate the granddaddy of all sonic booms. You use supersonics to homogenize milk, don't you?' Wister shrugged. 'If you knows a better 'ole, go to it. But I think a detailed mathematical analysis will bear me out.'

He was not unconscious of their respectful gaze upon him as he lit his cigarette. Orbital Command was damn glad to have an ex-space pilot on its staff, with everything that that implied in the way of training, practical experience, and an ability to grasp the curious ways that natural law can operate beyond Earth's sky. He had long felt sure that he'd get the section when Charlie Huang moved on up the bureaucratic ladder. The suggestion he had just made wouldn't hurt that prospect any. It would influence the design of *Yankee*'s successor.

To hell with that! There must be a way to get them down! 'What's the solar flare prediction?' he asked.

'Uncertain as usual,' Huang said. 'Solar meteorology has a long way to go before it's an exact science. However, we all know this is a bad season, and the last report predicted considerable disturbances within sixty hours. That's about forty-eight hours from this moment.'

Silence fell on the room and pressed inward. There was no need to review the facts, but they streamed idiotically through Wister's consciousness anyhow. A flare on the sun emitted a stream of protons. Since the *Yankee* had been intended for the Venus expedition, it had been equipped with Swanberg screen generators, whose magnetohydrodynamic forces were adequate to deflect any such bombardment. But a ditching capsule was nothing except a thin metal shell tucked into the ship's nose. The interior was heavily padded, there were seats and a radio and tools and cables and such oddments. If a vessel coming in through the atmosphere should fail – it had happened to a Russian job once, when the inflatable gliding surfaces ripped open – the pilot was supposed to use an ocean for his landing pad. A small explosive charge would spung the capsule loose from the ship, and it would float about with the crew until someone arrived to pick them up.

It was not meant for space. Under ideal conditions, it would keep three men alive in the void as long as their air held out: four days, Wister estimated, knowing what part of the vessel's supply was stored there. The intrinsic shielding was poor, but would serve for that length of time – unless radiation got very heavy. Which it would when the sun flared.

Four days max, then, to get them to safety. But more likely two days, or less, because of solar weather. No American craft could be readied on such short notice. But . . .

'Euratom,' Wister said.

'You mean, have they got anything which could get upstairs in a hurry?' Huang asked. 'I checked with Geneva, and the answer is no.'

'Well, the Russkies!'

'Gail's put Washington onto that,' Huang said quietly. 'They're trying to get hold of Karpovitch in person.'

Wister bit his lip, embarrassed, and stubbed out his cigarette.

A junior computerman cleared his throat and inquired, 'Pardon me, but why can't *Galileo* pick them up? I mean, it's remote-controlled, and fueled for a Lunar landing, and passes quite near the capsule at conjunction.'

'And has a net mass of about two tons,' Wister explained, 'which three men in spacesuits would increase by something like 30 percent. Not to mention the uneven distribution of their mass on the shell, which'd royally louse up control and require continual correction blasts. The rocket motor hasn't that much reserve. In fact, *Galileo* carries almost no spare fuel.'

'Why not?' said the young man indignantly.

'Because it lands and takes off from the Moon. Do you know what fuel and lox cost per gallon, after you've shipped 'em from Earth to Camp Apollo? It'll actually be cheaper for Euratom to lose an occasional unmanned job for lack of emergency tanks, than to tote so much extra mass around *and* replace the liquid every few weeks because of boiloff.'

'Dick knows,' Huang said. 'He's our local expert on the subject. Was on the team which inspected the *Gal* last year, after G.E. built it for Euratom. He worked with our own similar project before that, between the time he left the astronautical corps and came here to Orbital.'

'I see,' said the young man.

Wister smiled reminiscently. Those had been two great weeks in Europe. He'd intended to wander about afterward on the Continent. Leave of absence was easy to arrange. But Flo fell sick again at that time. Nothing too serious. It never was. However, her poor tattered nerves went completely to pieces when she was ill, and without his father around, Jim would bear the brunt of it ... just when he was starting to overcome his bedwetting and nightmares and—

And this had nothing to do with three men in a shell hurtling around the Moon.

Another couple of subordinates arrived. Huang nodded. 'That makes a full enough complement,' he said. 'Take over, Harry. Prepare your team to compute whatever needs computing. The orbit first, I suppose, as soon as we get a fix and a Doppler reading.'

'Check.' Mowitz beckoned to his staff. They moved out the door and down the hall in a silent, shuffling herd.

Delarue rose. 'I'd better get on to my own section,' he said.

'Why, they're already standing by, aren't they?' Huang answered. 'They don't need you.'

'Yeah, but I need them,' Delarue muttered between his teeth. 'I can't sit here and do nothing!' He left at a quick, jerky pace.

Alone in the office, Huang and his second-in-command stared at each other. The tobacco haze stung their eyes. The morning sunlight on the parking lot outside was indecently bright.

'Do you really think the Russians will help?' Wister asked after a while, merely to break the silence.

'Oh, yes, if they can,' Huang said. 'Propaganda kudos for them, isn't it, if they bail out the Americans. Besides, they're human too, whatever you think of their government.'

'But are they able? Have they got anything that close to go, right now?'

'Who knows?'

The silence came back. It must be very still in the capsule, Wister thought, remembering his own past missions. Locked in their spacesuits, jammed so close together they could hardly move, the three men would hear little except their breath and heartbeat, see little except a few chill points of blaze in the one tiny port. They could talk to each other by helmet set, of course; but what do you say to the one beside you as you fall helpless over the night side of the Moon? What do you say down on Earth?

A buzzer sounded. Huang started so violently that he knocked an ashtray off his desk. Cigarette butts spilled halfway across the floor. He stabbed the intercom button. 'Yes, what is it?' Wister realized that they were both on their feet, crouched over the black box. His back between the shoulder blades ached with tension.

A woman's voice, from Delarue's team, said, not quite steadily: 'Contact has been made with the capsule, sir, via Camp Apollo and Hawaii. We can plug you in directly if you wish.'

'Yes, yes, what do you think I wish?' Huang yelled. The intercom clicked and hummed. It crashed upon Wister that he had nothing to say to the men in space. Not one damn thing.

Static crackled from the speaker. Faint and distorted, wavering along the edge of audibility, there came: 'Enwright speaking. Hello, hello, are you there, Charlie?'

'Yes—' Huang stared across the box at Wister. 'Take over, Dick,' he mumbled.

'Are you okay?' Wister heard someone ask with his throat. He remembered he must wait: two and a half seconds while the beam crossed nothingness and came back. Nearly half a million miles, with atmospherics and Doppler effect and the dry hiss of the stars to battle along the way. The tiny, unreal voice said:

'Yeah, I think so, except Phil seems to have ruptured his eardrums. That was a lulu of a detonation. We barely made it to the capsule and sprung her free. Everything worked fine, though.' A hesitation. 'So far.'

'What – uh – air? Temperature? $CO_2$ control?'

'We're still alive,' Enwright said bleakly.

'And we . . . we're figuring how to get you down.' Wister had to swallow a couple of times before he could continue. 'We're looking for a vehicle.'

Whining stillness again, until another tone said: 'Bruno speaking. Don't hand us that guff, Dick. You know there isn't any standby. You were a spaceman too.'

*Once,* Wister thought.

'The best thing you can do is get Cy's wife and Phil's girl on the line,' Fellini said. What might have been a chuckle sounded from the black box. 'Me, I'm lucky. I haven't got anyone who makes that much difference.'

*And I've got someone who makes too much difference,* Wister thought; *so I had to quit space, and the sun will warm my skin while it kills you. So I'm even luckier, oh, yes.*

'Stow the dramatics, Bruno,' Enwright said. Cohn, sealed in deafness, must needs hold his mouth. 'They're doing all they can at Base. This is what we collect flight pay for. Dick, what can we do ourselves? I know you're taking observations to figure our orbit, but is there anything else you might need data on?'

'I . . . I can't imagine— What do you see through your port?' Wister asked, as if words could hold off death.

'M-m-m . . . we're tumbling, naturally, so the stars waltz by

in the craziest way. I've timed our rotational velocity as 2.3
r.p.m., though precession louses up my figuring some. Whoops,
I just glimpsed the dawn line of the Moon. Mountains like teeth,
shadows halfway across a gray plain, Judas, what a graveyard!
– hold it – had to cover my face there, a sunbeam . . . I see a piece
of wreckage trailing along, in almost the same orbit as us. A
double tank – yeah compressed air, as far's I can make out the
color code in this damned shifty light. The main air tank. Seems
intact. Must be, come to think of it, or the gas gushing out
would've pushed it into a radically different orbit. The rest of the
ship is scattered from hell to breakfast.'

'Wait a minute,' Wister chattered. 'You have flexible cable,
I know. Two miles' worth isn't it? Why don't you go outside,
jump the jet across, and make fast to that tank? Pull your capsule alongside it?'

'Why I guess we can. 'Druther wait till we're back in the Lunar
shadow cone though. It's awfully hot and bright out there. Not
that we couldn't stand the heat. We can even take a few hours
of radiation outside this shell, at the level my meter's registering.
But frankly, we're uncomfortable aplenty as it is.'

'Sure, that's okay. Wait for shade.'

'Why do the job at all, though? We certainly can't land on a
jet of compressed air!'

'Oh, no, no. But extend your breathing time—'

Fellini's laughter rattled. 'We've got enough here to last us till
the sun flares,' he said.

Wister's nails dug into his palms. 'Anything may help,' he
said. 'I can't imagine how, in this case. Probably it's no use.
But you can't afford to pass up any bets.' Savagely: 'You're
dead, you know, unless one of those few bets pays off.'

'Dick!' Huang cried. 'That was uncalled for.'

Static jeered. Then Enwright's ghost-voice said: 'He's right,
Charlie. We'll secure that tank as soon as we get behind the Moon
again. It won't drift too far from us in a couple of hours.'

'It'll alter your orbit some. Must have more total mass than you
and your capsule do. The momentum exchange—' Huang
slumped. 'Never mind. We can recommute. Okay.'

The speaker hummed and sputtered.

'What else do you want to know?' Enwright asked.

'I can't think of anything,' Huang sighed.

'We'll sign off, then. That is . . . till you put us in touch with our people.'

'Sure. As soon as possible. Meanwhile, uh, uh, would you like some music?'

'No, thanks. Not with reception like this, eh, Bruno?'

'I think I would, if you've got some classic jazz,' Fellini said. 'None of the current slop, though.'

'Oh, well, I can stand it,' Enwright said. 'Thanks for everything, Earth and Apollo. *Au'voir.* Over and out.'

The voice died. Presently the intercom stopped crackling. Delarue came on: 'We'll hold a monitor on them, of course. Say, want I should arrange that music? I've got his kind of tapes at home. Jelly Roll Morton and so forth.'

'Sure,' Huang said. 'Fine.' He punched for Mowitz's section. 'Harry? How're you coming on that orbit?'

'We're processing the data now. Ought to have the elements for you inside fifteen minutes.'

'No hurry, I'm afraid. Especially since you'll have to recalculate next time around. They're going to attach to an extraneous mass. But carry on.' Huang turned the instrument off and rose to his feet. Suddenly he looked old. 'Can you hold the fort for a while?' he asked.

'Me?' Wister replied, startled. 'Why, I suppose— But what—'

'Somebody's got to notify those women and arrange a hook-up.'

Because he knew that Huang knew it, Wister must needs say: 'I'm a personal friend of all concerned, Charlie. I can do that.'

His relief was unabashed when the other said, 'No. I've no right to delegate the hard ones. It'll be a little easier for me to tell 'em anyhow, a comparative stranger. And—' Huang paused. 'You're better qualified to handle this desk in this kind of situation than I am. I'm only an orbits man.'

He went out. Wister sat down in his place and stared through the window. *All right,* he told himself, *now what?*

*Now the death watch, that's what,* he answered. *I'd better see about some transportation for Flo to go shopping. I'll be stuck here till it's over.* (*Why won't she learn to drive? She may not be very strong, but she isn't paralyzed. Could it be my fault? Maybe I should have been tougher with her when— Or maybe not. How can I tell? Too late now.*) *The hell with expense. I'm sick of begging favors from the whole neighborhood. Let her take taxis.* (*I shouldn't have to worry about expense with my salary, even if I don't get flight pay any more. But doctor bills, and a cleaning woman three times a week, and——) Stop that whimpering! You're alive, at least!*

Then the intercom buzzed and he forgot about it. Gail Jackman's voice said: 'Mr. Garth calling from Washington. Can you take the message?'

'Sure can!' He snatched the phone. 'Hello, Richard Wister speaking, Mr. Huang had to go out, he left me in charge.'

'Tom Garth,' said NASA's liaison with the State Department. 'We got the word from Moscow.'

'Yes? Can they?'

'No. I'm sorry. Karpovitch talked to me himself. He said they can raise a *Gagarin*-class ship inside a week, but I told him that was no use. Right?'

'Uh-huh. We're closer to go than that ourselves.'

'No hope, then?'

'We're trying to think of something.'

'Better call a conference. We'll hold a branstorming session here and let you know what we come up with. This could give us all a black eye, propaganda-wise.'

Wister became unable to bandy clichés. 'I'd better hang up,' he said. 'Plenty to get organized here, you know. Thanks for calling. So long.' He clashed the receiver down.

His ulcer stabbed him. Wincing, he pushed the intercom button. 'Gail, could you promote me some crackers and milk?'

'Yes, with pleasure,' said Huang's secretary.

'Uh ... get yourself something too, if you want. I daresay you didn't have a chance for breakfast either. Frankly, I'd like someone to talk to. Help me forget for a minute how useless I am.'

'I understand,' she said gently. 'I'll send an office boy across the highway. Tam's should be open by now.'

He waited, stewing over the emptiness within and without, until Gail entered carrying a tray. Then his heart lifted a trifle. She was pretty – not spectacular, but pleasant to look on, intelligent, cheerful, and uncommitted. Sometimes Wister daydreamed about having an affair with her. It wasn't as if that would deprive Florence of anything she cared about any longer. But since Gail knew he was married, he had never quite figured out how to make the initial move. As she set the food on the desk, sunlight running along her burnished hair and striking through a thin blouse, he wondered if perhaps the intimacy of this moment— No, he was only supposed to think about Cy, Phil and Bruno, wasn't he? Nonetheless he made a ceremony of seating her, and they exchanged smiles.

'Thank'ee, Sir Walter,' she said.

'Raleigh, 'tis a pleasure.' Bitterness surged in him. 'Excuse me. I know I'm being sophomoric. But what can we do?'

She regarded him gravely. 'You're taking this hard, aren't you?'

'Yes,' he said, quite sincere, though not unaware of the dramatic possibilities in his role. 'Aren't we all? Those are us in that capsule.'

She shook her head, 'You're a man. But a woman thinks differently. Oh, of course I pity them, and I'll bawl as soon as I go off duty. Yet I keep thanking God it isn't my man up there.'

Wister gulped at his milk. 'Don't get me wrong,' he said. 'I'm no hero or any such foolish thing. But I'd give – what? An eye or a hand – for a chance to save them.'

'I think you mean that literally,' she murmured.

'I do.' He couldn't remain in his chair, jumped up, walked to the window and stared out at the bland blind sky. 'What makes it especially tough is having been a pilot myself. I know what it's like for them. Suffocating hot, each time the sun beats on the shell. Clothes plastered to your skin with sweat, that runs into your eyes and stings, but you can't rub them, and you itch but can't scratch, and whenever you notice your own stench you gag. You're a bit sick anyway from the tumbling of the shell. It doesn't give much weight, but the gradient is so steep that every time you move the weight shifts, your middle ear protests, and you feel nauseated. And that breaks down your mental defenses. The instincts of a trapped animal yell louder and louder. You sit there waiting for the sun to spew out your death—' He realized what he was saying. 'Pardon me.'

'Go on,' she said. Tears blurred her eyes.

'Furthermore,' he said, 'I can imagine myself all too clearly, outward bound to rescue them. Piloting's a more cerebral thing, though. Push that button, pull that lever, set that wheel; a problem in mathematics, really, which you act out too busy to be afraid or uncomfortable. *Doing* something, before heaven, instead of—'

He stopped. For a very long time he stood altogether motion-less.

'What's the matter?' Gail rose, half frightened.

Wister turned about. His eyes raked her without seeing. He spoke in a stranger's tone. 'Put me through to Geneva.'

'Why—'

'Jansen in Geneva. Head of the Euratom space project. I want to talk to him.' Wister ripped open a drawer, found Huang's slide rule, sat down and reached for the handbooks on the desk. He had forgotten she existed.

*'Steady as she goes.'*

The satellite drifted nearer, an ungainly spindle, tiny across the miles, against the cold, curdled Milky Way. The sun, hammering on Enwright's back, struck its surface. Hard splinters of light rebounded to his eyes. He slitted them and made himself ignore the discomfort. Overtaking the *Galileo* on its slightly smaller orbit, the *Yankee* capsule headed toward the darkness behind the Moon. That pocked gibbous shape loomed enormous to the right. His heart thuttered.

*'N-no ... wait ... reduce speed a few feet per second more.'*

The satellite's clustered rocket tubes blasted momentarily in opposition to the course. A white cloud, tinged with fire-streaks, billowed ahead, expanded, and whiffed to nothing. *Galileo* fell a couple of miles closer to the Moon. Actually, some velocity was gained thereby since the Lunar gravitational pull grew stronger. But relative to the capsule, speed was lost. And there would be a shorter distance to jump, Enwright gauged.

*'Okay, I'm off.'*

He crouched on his toes, where spaceboots lacked the slight stickiness that otherwise held him to the hull. His legs straightened and he soared free. The cable unreeled behind him. Moving at about a dozen feet per second, he took several minutes to go from capsule to satellite. The gap started to widen as he neared, for the orbits were not yet identical. But Enwright had a spaceman's sense of vectors. He had led his target as a hunter leads a duck, and passed within yards. A short blast from the air bottle in his harness corrected the remaining error. The bulky shape, bristling with robotic instruments, swelled before him. He twisted about, somehow acrobatic in his spacesuit, and hit feet first. The slight shock traveled through his spine to rattle his jaws. Changing rotations dizzied him. He made fast.

Turning, with one hand to shade the sunside of his helmet, he saw the capsule and the other men who clung to it. Hastily he secured a bight of the cable to a sturdy-looking bracket, then braced himself and began hauling.

Cohn and Felinni toiled at their end. Slowly the two masses moved together, until at last they bumped in contact. The spin characteristics of the system grew utterly mad. Enwright plugged his radio back into the capsule's transmitter. '*Okay so far. We're all in one piece now. But is there still fuel enough?*'

'*Oh, yes. The* Gal *didn't have to shed much velocity. We're about to lose contact again, you know. Think you'll be ready by the time you come back around to our side?*'

'*Roger. Over and out.*'

The sun fell behind the Moon's ragged shoulder. Bailey's Beads flashed momentarily, then only a wing of soft coronal light was to be seen. It set also. But the crowding stars gave sufficient illumination, and the coolness was a blessing. Their spacesuits were barely able to keep the men going under full sunlight. The chill of the shadow cone meant little for the brief time they were in it; their own hard-working bodies replaced radiated heat.

Hard-working indeed. They had two hours to dismount the capsule's radio transceiver and fix it securely on the *Galileo*; unship the huge air tank from the capsule; lash it even more strongly to the satellite; release the capsule itself, no longer needed to drift free; and tie themselves around *Galileo*'s circumference in such a way as to cause minimum unbalance.

'*Think we'll make it, Cy? Be honest, now.*'

'*How can I tell? But we haven't much to lose, have we?*'

'*I'll answer that question when we're down.*'

The sun struck them with such cruelty that they wondered if flare radiation had begun to sleet through their bodies. Voices entered their helmets.

'*Base to* Yankee Gal. *We've nailed you on our radar. Are you prepared to go?*'

'*Hope so. But don't you want to compute our new orbit first?*'

'*Why? You'll be leaving it right away, and in a totally unpredictable fashion.*'

'*True. I'm not thinking straight any more. Lord, but I'm tired!*'

T—E

'Nothing that some bed rest and a pretty nurse won't cure. Your roentgen background is still tolerable. But the solar meteorologists now expect a flare within five or six hours, so let's get you down fast. Just a minute while I settle myself.'

'Dick, how come you're controlling Galileo? Wouldn't one of the Europeans have more experience?'

'Ordinarily, yes. I'm not doing this for fun. But the trouble is, the handling characteristics must have been radically changed by the added masses. Jansen strongly recommended we use a man with some seat-of-the-pants background as well as a knowledge of this particular telecontrol system. Well, I did pilot some awful boltbuckets, not too many years ago. And the control room here at Base is practically the same as the one in the Midi. G.E. built 'em both, you know. I . . . think I've familiarized myself with Euratom's operating codes, while I waited for you.'

'I know you have, Dick.'

'If I should crash you— No!'

'You won't.'

'Okay, then, let's go. First we have to reorient your main axis. Get it tangential to orbit. Hang on! Over.' The clumsy mass spouted and slewed about. 'Whew! My instruments say you're lined up. But the whole damned system wants to hunt. Crack that barrel fast!'

Enwright reached across to the tank beside him. The main release valve had already been loosened. It turned readily. He felt a surge of thrust as the air poured out. The deep-throated roar vibrated his bones.

In a few minutes the great container was exhausted. Enwright, Fellini, and Cohn worked frantically to release it. The light, flexible cable had strength comparable to steel, and deceleration pressure had tightened every knot. Panting, cursing minutes fled while tools hung at belts worked away. Freed, tank and satellite moved ponderously apart under the force of rotation.

'Yankee Gal to Base. We're clear. Repeat, we're clear. Over.'

'Base to Yankee Gal. As near as we can gauge, you've lost virtually all orbital velocity and are falling fast. There's a wee bit of forward speed to kill, but then—'

Thrust and thrum awoke where fire-tongues wavered. The satellite tilted about, obedient to pulses sent across a quarter-million miles, but awkward, crazily awobble. The Moon's disc grew at a terrifying rate. Deceleration gravities pulled blood from men's nostrils. A whirlpool sucked consciousness downward.

Dust flew up from the Lunar land, driven by the rocket stormwind. *Galileo* inched through sudden night. Radar felt ahead, signaled altitude to the operator; but where he sat at the board on Earth, his knowledge was more than a second behind the truth.

Somehow he balanced the forces. A yard above ground, the satellite hung with zero velocity. A little fuel was left, but he cut the motors rather than tempt fate. A yard is not far to fall under Lunar gravity. Even so, *Galileo*'s weight crumpled the tail assembly like paper. But the shell did not topple, it did not topple.

Slowly the dust settled. The sun, near the horizon, flung long rays over a scored and barren plain. Three shapes, lashed to the wreck, stirred and called each other's names.

'*Base* to Yankee Gal. *Base* to Yankee Gal. *Come in. Do you read us? Are you all right? Come in, for mercy's sake!*'

'*We . . . ugh . . . Bruno, Phil – Yes. We're pretty much okay. A couple of broken bones, I think, but no serious bleeding, so what the hell. You even put us down in the shadow of a crag.*'

'*You're a bit southwest of the Riphaeans. One minute, please— Yes, they have an exact fix on you. A hopper has already left Camp Apollo. You'll be in the hospital inside three hours.*'

'*Thanks for our lives, Dick.* . . . '*As the shadow of a great rock in a weary land—*' '

Wister let go the controls as if the skeleton had dissolved from him. He sagged back in his chair, hardly noticing those who crowded near and shouted.

Gail Jackman dropped the cloth with which she had mopped his face as he worked. It was drenched. She sank to the floor, hugged her knees, and burst into tears.

Huang pushed through the mob with a fifth of Scotch. Wister drank deep. A measure of strength returned. He got up, hunkered down, and patted Gail on the shoulder. 'Why, everything's fine now,' he whispered.

'I'm sorry,' she gulped. 'It was so— How did you do it? I'd heard there wasn't enough fuel to do it. I couldn't understand what you were trying, b-b-but there wasn't time to ask. . . . The way you sat there – somebody had to—'

Wister blinked. 'Oh, that,' he said tonelessly. There were too mucking many people around. 'Dumb luck. The big air tank.

Mass nearly equal to the capsule plus men. That much expanding gas, heated by the sun, should be able to kill most of the satellite's orbital velocity. In a four-hour track around the Moon that's, uh, about eight-tenths mile per second. Which is over 50 percent of escape velocity, or 35 percent of the total speed it has to shed for a soft landing. With 35 percent of the work done almost free, there should be enough fuel to set down a 20 percent greater mass, even allowing for the extra maneuvers necessary. Shouldn't there be? Dumb luck.'

He straightened and shuffled from the room, Huang clearing a path for him.

'Can I have a few days' rest?' he croaked when they were alone in the hall.

'Take a month if you want. I'll get somebody to drive you home now.' Huang shivered. 'I'm still too wrung out to· do it myself.'

Somebody had hung Wister's coat in his office. As he entered to get it, the phone rang on his desk. He laid the receiver to his ear. Florence's voice said, 'Dick? I've been trying and trying to get hold of you. Did everything work out good?'

'Yes,' he said.

'That's wonderful,' she said politely. 'Darling, I'm so sorry, but I didn't hear the alarm. You remember you left a note for me to get Jimmy off to school? Well, I slept right through the alarm and woke up feeling so terrible that—'

'Never mind,' he said. 'I'll be home in a little while.'

# EPILOGUE

His name was a set of radio pulses. Converted into equivalent sound waves, it would have been an ugly squawk; so because he, like any consciousness, was the center of his own coordinate system, let him be called Zero.

He was out hunting that day. Energy reserves were low in the cave. That other who may be called One – being the most important dweller in Zero's universe – had not complained. But there was no need to. He also felt a dwindling potential. Accumulators grew abundantly in their neighborhood, but an undue amount of such cells must be processed to recharge One while she was creating. Motiles had more concentrated energy. And, of course, they were more highly organized. Entire parts could be taken from the body of a motile, needing little or no reshaping for One to use. Zero himself, though the demands on his functioning were much less, wanted a more easily assimilated charge than the accumulators provided.

In short, they both needed a change of diet.

Game did not come near the cave any more. The past hundred years had taught that it was unsafe. Eventually, Zero knew, he would have to move. But the thought of helping One through mile upon mile, steep, overgrown, and dangerous, made him delay. Surely he could still find large motiles within a few days' radius of his present home. With One's help he fastened a carrier rack on his shoulders, took weapons in hand, and set forth.

That was near sunset. The sky was still light when he came on spoor: broken earthcrystals not yet healed, slabs cut from several boles, a trace of lubricant. Tuning his receptors to the highest sensitivity, he checked all the bands commonly made noisy by motiles. He caught a low-amplitude conversation between two persons a hundred miles distant, borne this far by some freak of atmospherics; closer by he sensed the impulses of small scuttering things, not worth chasing; a flier jetted overhead and filled his perception briefly with static. But no vibration

of the big one. It must have passed this way days ago and now
be out of receptor-shot.

Well, he could follow the trail, and catch up with the clumsy
sawyer in time. It was undoubtedly a sawyer – he knew these
signs – and therefore worth a protracted hunt. He ran a quick
check on himself. Every part seemed in good order. He set
into motion, a long stride which must eventually overhaul anything on treads.

Twilight ended. A nearly full moon rose over the hills like a
tiny cold lens. Night vapors glowed in masses and streamers
against a purple-black sky where stars glittered in the optical
spectrum and which hummed and sang in the radio range. The
forest sheened with alloy, flashed with icy speckles of silicate.
A wind blew through the radiation-absorber plates overhead,
setting them to ringing against each other; a burrower whirred, a
grubber crunched through lacy crystals, a river brawled chill and
loud down a ravine toward the valley below.

As he proceeded, weaving among trunks and girders and
jointed rods with the ease of long practice, Zero paid most attention to his radio receptors. There was something strange in the
upper communication frequencies, tonight, an occasional brief
note ... set of notes, voice, drone, like nothing he had heard
before or heard tell of. ... But the world was a mystery. No one
had been past the ocean to the west or the mountains to the east.
Finally Zero stopped listening and concentrated on tracking his
prey. That was difficult, with his optical sensors largely nulli-
fied by the darkness, and he moved slowly. Once he tapped lubricant from a cylinder growth and once he thinned his acids with
a drink of water. Several times he felt polarization in his energy
cells and stopped for a while to let it clear away: he rested.

Dawn paled the sky over distant snowpeaks, and gradually
turned red. Vapors rolled up the slopes from the valley, tasting
of damp and sulfide. Zero could see the trail again, and began
to move eagerly.

Then the strangeness returned – louder.

Zero slid to a crouch. His lattice swiveled upward. Yes, the
pulses did come from above. They continued to strengthen. Soon
he could identify them as akin to the radio noise associated with
the functioning of a motile. But they did not sense like any type
he knew. And there was something else, a harsh flickering overtone, as if he also caught leakage from the edge of a modu-

lated short-wave beam—

The sound struck him.

At first it was the thinnest of whistles, high and cold above the dawn clouds. But within seconds it grew to a roar that shook the earth, reverberated from the mountains, and belled absorber plates until the whole forest rang. Zero's head became an echo chamber; the racket seemed to slam his brain from side to side. He turned dazzled, horrified sensors heavenward. And he saw the thing descending.

For a moment, crazily, he thought it was a flier. It had the long spindle-shaped body and the airfins. But no flier had ever come down on a tail of multicolored flame. No flier blocked off such a monstrous portion of sky. When the thing must be two miles away!

He felt the destruction as it landed, shattered frames, melted earthcrystals, a little burrower crushed in its den, like a wave of anguish through the forest. He hurled himself flat on the ground and hung on to sanity with all four hands. The silence which followed, when the monster had settled in place, was like a final thunderclap.

Slowly Zero raised his head. His perceptions cleared. An arc of sun peered over the sierra. It was somehow outrageous that the sun should rise as if nothing had happened. The forest remained still, hardly so much as a radio hum to be sensed. The last echoes flew fading between the hills.

A measure of resolution: this was no time to be careful of his own existence. Zero poured full current into his transmitter. '*Alarm, alarm! All persons receiving, prepare to relay. Alarm!*'

Forty miles thence, the person who may as well be called Two answered, increasing output intensity the whole time: 'Is that you, Zero? I noticed something peculiar in the direction of your establishment. What is the matter?'

Zero did not reply at once. Others were coming in, a surge of voices in his head, from mountaintops and hills and lowlands, huts and tents and caves, hunters, miners, growers, searakers, quarriers, toolmakers, suddenly become a unity. But he was flashing at his own home: 'Stay inside, One. Conserve energy. I am unharmed, I will be cautious, keep hidden and stand by for my return.'

'Silence!' called a stridency which all recognized as coming from Hundred. He was the oldest of them, he had probably

gone through a total of half a dozen bodies. Irreversible polarization had slowed his thinking a little, taken the edge off, but the
wisdom of his age remained and he presided over their coun-
cils. 'Zero, report what you have observed.'

The hunter hesitated. 'That is not easy. I am at—' He described the location. ('Ah, yes,' murmured Fifty-Six, 'near that
large galena lick.') 'The thing somewhat resembles a flier, but
enormous, a hundred feet long or more. It came down about two
miles north of here on an incandescent jet and is now quiet. I
thought I overheard a beamed signal. If so, the cry was like nothing any motile ever made.

'In these parts,' Hundred added shrewdly. 'But the thing must
have come from far away. Does it look dangerous?'

'Its jet is destructive,' Zero said, 'but nothing that size, with
such relatively narrow fins, could glide about. Which makes me
doubt it is a predator.'

'Lure accumulators,' said Eight.

'Eh? What about them?' asked Hundred.

'Well, if lure accumulators can emit signals powerful enough
to take control of any small motile which comes near and make
it enter their grinders, perhaps this thing has a similar ability.
Then, judging from its size, its lure must have tremendous
range and close up could overpower large motiles. Including
even persons?'

Something like a shiver moved along the communication
band.

'It is probably just a grazer,' said Three. 'If so—' His overt
signal trailed off, but the thought continued in all their partly
linked minds: *A motile that big! Megawatt-hours in its energy
cells. Hundreds or thousands of usable parts. Tons of metal.
Hundred, did your great-grandcreator recall any such game,
fabulous millennia ago?*

*No.*

*If it is dangerous, it must be destroyed or driven off. If not,
it must be divided among us. In either case: attacked!*

Hundred rapped the decision forth. 'All male persons take
weapons and proceed to rendezvous at Broken Glade above the
Coppertaste River. Zero, stalk as close as seems feasible, observe
what you can, but keep silence unless something quite unfore-
seeable occurs. When we are gathered, you can describe details
on which we may base a specific plan. Hasten!'

The voices toned away in Zero's receptor circuits. He was alone again.

The sun cleared the peaks and slanted long rays between the forest frames. Accumulators turned the black faces of their absorber plates toward it and drank thirstily of radiation. The mists dissipated, leaving boles and girders ashine with moisture. A breeze tinkled the silicate growths underfoot. For a moment Zero was astonishingly conscious of beauty. The wish that One could be here beside him, and the thought that soon he might be fused metal under the monster's breath, sharpened the morning's brightness.

Purpose congealed in him. Further down was a turmoil of frank greed. In all the decades since his activation there had been no such feast as this quarry should provide. Swiftly, he prepared himself. First he considered his ordinary weapons. The wire noose would never hold the monster, nor did he think the iron hammer would smash delicate moving parts (it did not seem to have any), or the steel bolts from his crossbow pierce a thin plate to short out a crucial circuit. But the clawed, spear-headed pry bar might be of use. He kept it in one hand while two others unfastened the fourth and laid it with his extra armament in the carrier rack. Thereupon they deftly hooked his cutting torch in its place. No one used this artificial device except for necessary work, or to finish off a big motile whose cells could replace the tremendous energy expended by the flame, or in cases of dire need. But if the monster attacked him, that would surely constitute dire need. His only immediate intention was to spy on it.

Rising, he stalked among shadows and sun reflections, his camouflage-painted body nearly invisible. Such motiles as sensed him fled or grew very still. Not even the greater slasher was as feared a predator as a hunting person. So it had been since that ancient day when some forgotten savage genius made the first crude spark gap and electricity was tamed.

Zero was about halfway to his goal, moving slower and more carefully with each step, when he perceived the newcomers.

He stopped dead. Wind clanked the branches above him, drowning out any other sound. But his electronic sensors told him of ... two ... three moving shapes, headed from the monster. And their emission was as alien as its own.

In a different way. Zero stood for a long time straining to

sense and to understand what he sensed. The energy output of the three was small, hardly detectable even this close; a burrower or skitterer used more power to move itself. The output felt peculiar, too, not really like a motile's: too simple, as if a mere one or two circuits oscillated. Flat, cold, activityless. But the signal output, on the other hand – it *must* be signal, that radio chatter – why, that was a shout. The things made such an uproar that receptors tuned at minimum could pick them up five miles away. As if they did not know about game, predators, enemies.

Or as if they did not care.

A while more Zero paused. The eeriness of this advent sent a tingle through him. It might be said he was gathering courage. In the end he gripped his pry bar more tightly and struck off after the three.

They were soon plain to his optical and radar senses among the tall growths. He went stock-still behind a frame and watched. Amazement shocked his very mind into silence. He had assumed, from their energy level, that the things were small. But they stood more than half as big as he did! And yet each of them had only one motor, operating at a level barely sufficient to move a person's arm. That could not be their power source. But what was?

Thought returned to him. He studied their outlandishness in some detail. They were shaped not altogether unlike himself, though two-armed, hunchbacked, and featureless. Totally unlike the monster, but unquestionably associated with it. No doubt it had sent them forth as spy eyes, like those employed by a box-roller. Certain persons had been trying for the last century or so to develop, from domesticated motiles, similar assistants for hunting persons. Yes, a thing as big and awkward as the monster might well need auxiliaries.

Was the monster then indeed a predator? Or even – the idea went like a lightning flash through Zero's entire circuitry – a thinker? Like a person? He struggled to make sense of the modulated signals between the three bipeds. No, he could not. But—

Wait!

Zero's lattice swung frantically back and forth. He could not shake off the truth. That last signal had come from the monster, hidden by a mile of forest. From the monster to the bipeds. And were they answering?

The bipeds were headed south. At the rate they were going, they might easily come upon traces of habitation, and follow those traces to the cave where One was, long before Hundred's males had gathered at Broken Glade.

The monster would know about One.

Decision came. Zero opened his transmitter to full output, but broadcast rather than beamed in any degree. He would give no clue where those were whom he called, 'Attention, attention! Tune in on me: direct sensory linkage. I am about to attempt capture of these motiles.'

Hundred looked through his optics, listened with his receptors, and exclaimed, 'No, wait, you must not betray our existence before we are ready to act.'

'The monster will soon learn of our existence in any event,' Zero answered. 'The forest is full of old campsites, broken tools, traps, chipped stones, slag heaps. At present I should have the advantage of surprise. If I fail and am destroyed, that ought still to provide you with considerable data. Stand alert!'

He plunged from behind the girders.

The three had gone past. They sensed him and spun about. He heard a jagged modulation of their signal output. A reply barked back, lower in frequency. The voice of the monster? There was no time to wonder about that. Slow and clumsy though they were, the bipeds had gotten into motion. The central one snatched a tube slung across its back. Pounding toward them, through shattering crystals and clangorous branches, Zero thought, *I have not yet made any overtly hostile move, but*— The tube flashed and roared.

An impact sent Zero staggering aside. He went to one knee. Ripped circuits overwhelmed him with destruction signals. As the pain throbbed toward extinction, his head cleared enough to see that half his upper left arm was blown off.

The tube was held steady on him. He rose. The knowledge of his danger flared in him. A second biped had its arms around the third, which was tugging a smaller object from a sheath.

Zero discharged full power through his effectors. Blurred to view by speed, he flung himself to one side while his remaining left hand threw the pry bar. It went meteorlike across a shaft of sunlight and struck the tube. The tube was pulled from the biped's grasp, slammed to the ground and buckled.

Instantly Zero was upon the three of them. He had already identified their communication system, a transmitter and antenna actually outside the skin! His one right hand smashed across a biped's back, tearing the radio set loose. His torch spat with precision. Fused, the communicator of a second biped went dead.

The third one tried to escape. Zero caught it in four strides, plucked off its antenna, and carried it wildly kicking under one arm while he chased the other two. When he had caught the second, the first stood its ground and battered forlornly at him with its hands. He lashed them all together with his wire rope. As a precaution, he emptied the carrier rack of the one which had shot him. Those thin objects might be dangerous even with the tube that had launched them broken. He stuffed the bipeds into his own carrier.

For a moment, then, he lingered. The forest held little sonic noise except the wind in the accumulators. But the radio spectrum clamored. The monster howled; Zero's own broadcast rolled between sky and mountainside, from person to person and so relayed across the land.

'No more talk now,' he finished his report. 'I do not want the monster to track me. I have prevented these auxiliaries from communicating with it. Now I shall take them to my cave for study. I hope to present some useful data at the rendezvous.'

'This may frighten the monster off,' Seventy-Two said.

'So much the better,' Hundred answered.

'In that case,' Zero said, 'I will at least have brought back something from my hunt.'

He snapped off his transmission and faded into the forest shadows.

### 2

The boat had departed from the spaceship on a mere whisper of jets. Machinery inboard hummed, clicked, murmured, sucked in exhausted air and blew out renewed; busied itself with matters of warmth and light, computation and propulsion. But it made no more than a foundation for silence.

Hugh Darkington stared out the forward port. As the boat curved away from the mother ship's orbit, the great hull gleamed across his sky — fell astern and rapidly dwindled until lost to view. The stars which it had hidden sprang forth, icy-sharp points of glitter against an overwhelming blackness.

They didn't seem different to him. They were, of course. From Earth's surface the constellations would be wholly alien. But in space so many stars were visible that they made one chaos, at least to Darkington's eyes. Captain Thurshaw had pointed out to him, from the ship's bridge, that the Milky Way had a new shape, this bend was missing and that bay had not been there three billion years ago. To Darkington it remained words. He was a biologist and had never paid much attention to astronomy. In the first numbness of loss and isolation, he could think of nothing which mattered less than the exact form of the Milky Way.

Still the boat spiraled inward. Now the moon drifted across his view. In those eons since the *Traveler* left home, Luna had retreated from Earth: not as far as might have been predicted, because (they said) Bering Straits had vanished with every other remembered place; but nonetheless, now it was only a tarnished farthing. Through the ship's telescopes it had looked like itself. Some new mountains, craters, and maria, some thermal erosion of old features, but Thurshaw could identify much of what he once knew. It was grotesque that the moon should endure when everything else had changed.

Even the sun. Observed through a dimmer screen, the solar disc was bloated and glaring. Not so much in absolute terms, perhaps. Earth had moved a little closer, as the friction of interplanetary dust and gas took a millennial toll. The sun itself had grown a little bigger and hotter, as nuclear reactions intensified. In three billion years such things became noticeable even on the cosmic scale. To a living organism they totaled doomsday.

Darkington cursed under his breath and clenched a fist till the skin stretched taut. He was a thin man, long-faced, sharp-featured, his brown hair prematurely sprinkled with gray. His memories included beautiful spires above an Oxford quad, wonder seen through a microscope, a sailboat beating into the wind off Nantucket, which blew spray and a sound of gulls and church bells at him, comradeship bent over a chessboard or hoisting beer steins, forests hazy and ablaze with Indian summer: and all these things were dead. The shock had worn off, the hundred men and women aboard the *Traveler* could function again, but home had been amputated from their lives and the stump hurt.

Frederika Ruys laid her own hand on his and squeezed a little. Muscle by muscle he untensed himself, until he could twitch a smile in response to hers. 'After all,' she said, 'we knew we'd be gone a long time. That we might well never come back.'

'But we'd have been on a living planet,' he mumbled.

'So we can still find us one,' declared Sam Kuroki from his seat at the pilot console. 'There're no less than six G-type stars within fifty light-years.'

'It won't be the same,' Darkington protested.

'No,' said Frederika. 'In a way, though, won't it be more? We, the last humans in the universe, starting the race over again?'

There was no coyness in her manner. She wasn't much to look at, plump, plain, with straight yellow hair and too wide a mouth. But such details had ceased to matter since the ship ended time acceleration. Frederika Ruys was a brave soul and a skilled engineer. Darkington felt incredibly lucky that she had picked him.

'Maybe we aren't the last, anyhow,' Kuroki said. His flat features broke in one of his frequent grins; he faced immensity with a sparrow's cockiness. 'Ought to've been other colonies than ours planted, oughtn't there? Of course, by now their descendants 'ud be bald-headed dwarfs who sit around thinking in calculus.'

'I doubt that,' Darkington sighed. 'If humans had survived anywhere else in the galaxy, don't you think they would at least have come back and . . . and reseeded this with life? The mother planet?' He drew a shaken breath. They had threshed this out a hundred times or more while the *Traveler* orbited about unrecognizable Earth, but they could not keep from saying the obvious again and again, as a man must keep touching a wound on his body. 'No, I think the war really did begin soon after we left. The world situation was all set to explode.'

That was why the *Traveler* had been built, and even more why it had departed in such haste, his mind went on. Fifty couples scrambling off to settle on Tau Ceti II before the missiles were unleashed. Oh, yes, officially they were a scientific team, and one of the big foundations had paid for the enterprise. But in fact, as everyone knew, the hope was to insure that a fragment of civilization would be saved, and someday return to help rebuild. (Even Panasia admitted that a total war would throw history back a hundred years; Western governments were less optimistic.) Tension had mounted so horribly fast in the final months that no time was taken for a really careful check of the field drive. So new and little understood an engine ought to have had scores of test flights before starting out under full power. But ... well ... next year might be too late. And exploratory ships *had* visited the nearer stars, moving just under the speed of light, their crews experiencing only a few weeks of transit time. Why not the *Traveler*?

'The absolute war?' Frederika said, as she had done so often already. 'Fought until the whole world was sterile? No. I won't believe it.'

'Not in that simple and clean-cut a way,' Darkington conceded. 'Probably the war did end with a nominal victor: but he was more depopulated and devastated than anyone had dared expect. Too impoverished to reconstruct, or even to maintain what little physical plant survived. A downward spiral into the Dark Ages.'

'M-m-m, I dunno,' Kuroki argued. 'There were a lot of machines around. Automation, especially. Like those self-re-producing, sun-powered, mineral-collecting sea rafts. And a lot of other self-maintaining gadgets. I don't see why industry couldn't be revived on such a base.'

'Radioactivity would have been everywhere,' Darkington pointed out. 'Its long-range effect on ecology ... Oh, yes, the process may have taken centuries, as first one species changed or died, and then another dependent on it, and then more. But how could the human survivors recreate technology when biology was distintegrating around them?' He shook himself and stiffened his back, ashamed of his self-pity a minute ago, looking horror flatly in the face. 'That's my guess. I could be wrong, but it seems to fit the facts. We'll never know for certain, I suppose.'

Earth rolled into sight. The planetary disc was still edged with blueness darkening toward black. Clouds still trailed fleecy above shining oceans; they gleamed upon the darkness near the terminator as they caught the first light before sunrise. Earth was forever fair.

But the continental shapes were new, speckled with hard points of reflection upon black and ochre where once they had been softly green and brown. There were no polar caps; sea level temperatures ranged from eighty to two hundred degrees Fahrenheit. No free oxygen remained: the atmosphere was nitrogen, its oxides, ammonia, hydrogen sulfide, sulfur dioxide, carbon dioxide, and steam. Spectroscopes had found no trace of chlorophyll or any other complex organic compound. The ground cover, dimly glimpsed through clouds, was metallic.

This was no longer Earth. There was no good reason why the *Traveler* should send a boat and three highly unexpendable humans down to look at its lifelessness. But no one had suggested leaving the Solar System without such a final visit. Darkington remembered being taken to see his grandmother when she was dead. He was twelve years old and had loved her. It was not her in the box, that strange unmeaningful mask, but where then was she?

'Well, whatever happened seemed to be three billion years in the past,' Kuroki said, a little too loudly. 'Forget it. We got troubles of our own.'

Frederika's eyes had not left the planet. 'We can't ever forget, Sam,' she said. 'We'll always wonder and hope – they, the children at least – hope that it didn't happen to them too cruelly.' Darkington started in surprise as she went on murmuring, very low, oblivious of the men:

'*to tell you of the ending of the day.*
*And you will see her tallness with surprise,*
*and looking into gentle, shadowed eyes*
*protest: it's not that late; you have to stay*

*awake a minute more, just one, to play*
*with yonder ball. But nonetheless you rise*
*so they won't hear her say, "A baby cries,*
*but you are big. Put all your toys away."*

'*She lets you have a shabby bear in bed,*
*though frankly doubting that you two can go*
*through dream-shared living rooms or wingless flight.*
*She tucks the blankets close beneath your head*
*and smooths your hair and kisses you, and so*
*goes out, turns off the light. "Good night. Sleep tight."* '

Kuroki glanced around at her. The plaid shirt wrinkled across his wide shoulders. 'Pomes yet,' he said. 'Who wrote that?'

'Hugh,' said Frederika. 'Didn't you know he published poetry?

Quite a bit. I admired his work long before I met him.'

Darkington flushed. Her interest was flattering, but he regarded *Then Death Will Come* as a juvenile effort.

However, his embarrassment pulled him out of sadness. (On the surface. Down beneath, it would always be there, in every one of them. He hoped they would not pass too much of it on to their children. Let us not weep eternally for Zion.) Leaning forward, he looked at the planet with an interest that mounted as the approach curve took them around the globe. He hoped for a few answers to a hell of a lot of questions.

For one thing, why, in three billion years, had life not re-evolved? Radioactivity must have disappeared in a few centuries at most. The conditions of primordial Earth would have returned. Or would they? What had been lacking this time around?

He woke from his brown study with a jerk as Kuroki said, 'Well, I reckon we can steepen our trajectory a bit.' A surprising interval had passed. The pilot touched controls and the mild acceleration increased. The terrestrial disc, already enormous, swelled with terrifying velocity, as if tumbling down upon them.

Then, subtly, it was no longer to one side or above, but was beneath; and it was no longer a thing among the stars but the convex floor of bowl-shaped creation. The jets blasted more strongly. Kuroki's jaws clenched till knots of muscle stood forth. His hands danced like a pianist's.

He was less the master of the boat, Darkington knew, than its helper. So many tons, coming down through atmospheric turbulence at such a velocity, groping with radar for a safe landing spot, could not be handled by organic brain and nerves. The boat's central director – essentially a computer whose input came from the instruments and whose efferent impulses went directly to the controls – performed the basic operations. Its task was fantastically complex: very nearly as difficult as the job of guiding the muscles when a man walks. Kuroki's fingers told the boat, 'Go that way,' but the director could overrule him.

'I think we'll settle among those hills.' The pilot had to shout now, as the jets blasted stronger. 'Want to come down just east of the sunrise line, so we'll have a full day ahead of us, and yonder's the most promising spot in this region. The lowlands look too boggy.'

Darkington nodded and glanced at Frederika. She smiled

T—F

and made a thumbs-up sign. He leaned over, straining against his safety harness, and brushed his lips across hers. She colored with a pleasure that he found oddly moving. Someday, on another planet – that possibly hadn't been born when they left Earth—

He had voiced his fears to her, that the engine would go awry again when they started into deep space, and once more propel them through time, uncontrollably until fuel was exhausted. A full charge in the tanks was equivalent to three billion years, plus or minus several million; or so the physicists aboard had estimated. In six billion A.D. might not the sun be so swollen as to engulf them when they emerged?

She had rapped him across the knuckles with her slide rule and said no, you damned biologist, but you'll have to take my word for it because you haven't got the math. I've studied it as far as differential equations, he said. She grinned and answered that then he'd never had a math course. It seemed, she said, that time acceleration was readily explained by the same theory which underlay the field drive. In fact, the effect had been demonstrated in laboratory experiments. Oh, yes, I know about that, he said; reactive thrust is rotated through a fourth dimension and gets applied along the temporal rather than a spatial axis. You do not know a thing about it, she said, as your own words have just proved. But never mind. What happened to us was that a faulty manifold generated the t-acceleration effect in our engine. Now we've torn everything down and rebuilt from scratch. We know it'll work right. The tanks are recharged. The ship's ecosystem is in good order. Any time we want, we can take off for a younger sun, and travel fifty light-years without growing more than a few months older. After which, seeing no one else was around, she sought his arms; and that was more comforting than her words.

*A last good-bye to Grandmother Earth,* he thought. *Then we can start the life over again that we got from her.*

The thrust upon him mounted. Toward the end he lay in his chair, now become a couch, and concentrated on breathing.

They reached ground.

Silence rang in their ears for a long while. Kuroki was the first to move. He unstrapped his short body and snapped his chair back upright. One hand unhooked the radio microphone, another punched buttons. 'Boat calling *Traveler*,' he intoned.

'We're okay so far. Come in, *Traveler*. Hello, hello.'

Darkington freed himself, stiffly, his flesh athrob, and helped Frederika rise. She leaned on him a minute. 'Earth,' she said. Gulping: 'Will you look out of the port first, dearest? I find I'm not brave enough.'

He realized with a shock that none of them had yet glanced at the landscape. Convulsively, he made the gesture.

He stood motionless for so long that finally she raised her head and stared for herself.

### 3

They did not realize the full strangeness before they donned spacesuits and went outside. Then, saying very little, they wandered about looking and feeling. Their brains were slow to develop the gestalts which would allow them really to see what surrounded them. A confused mass of detail could not be held in the memory, the underlying form could not be abstracted from raw sense impressions. A tree is a tree, anywhere and any-when, no matter how intricate its branching or how oddly shaped its leaves and blossoms. But what is a—

—thick shaft of gray metal, planted in the sand, central to a labyrinthine skeleton of straight and curved girders, between which run still more enigmatic structures embodying helices and toruses and Möbius strips and less familiar geometrical ele-ments; the entire thing some fifty feet tall; flaunting at the top several hundred thin metal plates whose black sides are turned toward the sun?

When you have reached the point of being able to describe it even this crudely, then you *have* apprehended it.

Eventually Darkington saw that the basic structure was re-peated, with infinite variation of size and shape, as far as he could see. Some specimens tall and slender, some low and broad, they dominated the hillside. The deeper reaches were made gloomy by their overhang, but sun speckles flew piercingly bright within those shadows as the wind shook the mirror faces of the plates. That same wind made a noise of clanking and clash-ing and far-off deep booming, mile after metal mile.

There was no soil, only sand, rusty red and yellow. But out-side the circle which had been devastated by the boat's jets, Darkington found the earth carpeted with prismatic growths, a few inches high, seemingly rooted in the ground. He broke one off for closer examination and saw tiny crystals, endlessly repeated, in some transparent siliceous material: like snowflakes and spiderwebs of glass. It sparkled so brightly, making so many rainbows, that he couldn't well study the interior. He could barely make out at the center a dark clump of ... wires, coils, transistors? *No,* he told himself, *don't be silly.* He gave it to Frederika, who exclaimed at its beauty.

He himself walked across an open stretch, hoping for a view even vaguely familiar. Where the hillside dropped too sharply to support anything but the crystals – they made it one dazzle of diamonds – he saw eroded contours, the remote white sword of a waterfall, strewn boulders and a few crags like worn-out obelisks. The land rolled away into blue distances; a snow-capped mountain range guarded the eastern horizon. The sky overhead was darker than in his day, faintly greenish blue, full of clouds. He couldn't look near the fierce big sun.

Kuroki joined him. 'What d'you think, Hugh?' the pilot asked.

'I hardly dare say. You?'

'Hell, I can't think with that bloody boiler factory clattering at me.' Kuroki grimaced behind his faceplate. 'Turn off your sonic mike and let's talk by radio.'

Darkington agreed. Without amplification, the noise reached him through his insulated helmet as a far-off tolling. 'We can take it for granted,' he said, 'that none of this is accidental. No minerals could simply crystallize out like this.'

'Don't look manufactured to me, though.'

'Well,' said Darkington, 'you wouldn't expect them to turn out their products in anything like a human machine shop.'

'Them?'

'Whoever ... whatever ... made this. For whatever purpose.'

Kuroki whistled. 'I was afraid you'd say something like that. But we didn't see a trace of – cities, roads, anything – from orbit. I know the cloudiness made seeing pretty bad, but we couldn't have missed the signs of a civilization able to produce stuff on this scale.'

'Why not? If the civilization isn't remotely like anything we've ever imagined?'

Frederika approached, leaving a cartful of instruments behind. 'The low and medium frequency radio spectrum is crawling,' she reported. 'You never heard so many assorted hoots, buzzes, whirrs, squeals, and whines in your life.'

'We picked up an occasional bit of radio racket while in orbit,' Kuroki nodded. 'Didn't think much about it then.'

'Just noise,' Frederika said hastily. 'Not varied enough to be any kind of, of communication. But I wonder what's doing it?'

'Oscillators,' Darkington said. 'Incidental radiation from a variety of – oh, hell, I'll speak plainly – machines.'

'But—' Her hand stole toward his. Glove grasped glove. She wet her lips. 'No, Hugh, this is absurd. How could any one be capable of making ... what we see ... and not have detected us in orbit and – and done something about us?'

Darkington shrugged. The gesture was lost in his armor. 'Maybe they're biding their time. Maybe they aren't here at the moment. The whole planet could be an automated factory, you know. Like those ocean mineral harvesters we had in our time' – it hurt to say that – 'which Sam mentioned on the way down. Somebody may come around periodically and collect the production.'

'Where do they come from?' asked Kuroki in a rough tone.

'I don't know, I tell you. Let's stop making wild guesses and start gathering data.'

Silence grew between them. The skeleton towers belled. Finally Kuroki nodded. 'Yeah. What say we take a little stroll? We may come on something.'

Nobody mentioned fear. They dared not.

Re-entering the boat, they made the needful arrangements. The *Traveler* would be above the horizon for several hours yet. Captain Thurshaw gave his reluctant consent to an exploration on foot. The idea conflicted with his training, but what did survey doctrine mean under these conditions? The boat's director could keep a radio beam locked on the ship and thus relay communication between Earth and orbit. While Kuroki talked, Darkington and Frederika prepared supplies. Not much was needed. The capacitor pack in each suit held charge enough to power thermostat and air renewer for a hundred hours, and they only planned to be gone for three or four. They loaded two packboards with food, water, and the 'buckets' used for such natural functions as eating, but that was only in case their return should be delayed. The assorted scientific instruments they took were more to the point. Darkington holstered a pistol. When he had finished talking, Kuroki put the long tube of a rocket gun and a rackful of shells on his own back. They closed their helmets anew and stepped out.

'Which way?' Frederika asked.

'Due south,' Darkington said after studying the terrain. 'We'll be following this long ridge, you see. Harder to get lost.' There was little danger of that, with the boat emitting a continuous directional signal. Nonetheless they all had compasses on their wrists and took note of landmarks as they went.

The boat was soon lost to view. They walked among surrealistic rods and frames and spirals, under ringing sheet metal. The crystals crunched beneath their tread and broke sunlight into hot shards of color. But not many rays pushed through the tangle overhead; shadows were dense and restless. Darkington began to recognize unrelated types of structure. They included long, black, seemingly telescopic rods, fringed with thin plates; glassy spheres attached to intricate grids; cables that looped from girder to girder. Frequently a collapsed object was seen crumbling on the ground.

Frederika looked at several disintegrated specimens, examined others in good shape, and said: 'I'd guess the most important material, the commonest, is an aluminum alloy. Though – see here – these fine threads embedded in the core must be copper. And this here is probably manganese steel with a protective coating of . . . um . . . something more inert.'

Darkington peered at the end of a broken strut through a magnifying glass. 'Porous,' he said. 'Good Lord, are these actually capillaries to transport water?'

'I thought a capillary was a hairy bug with lots of legs that turned into a butterfly,' said Kuroki. He ducked an imaginary fist. 'Okay, okay, somebody's got to keep up morale.'

The boat's radio relayed a groan from the monitor aboard the ship. Frederika said patiently, 'No, Sam, the legs don't turn into a butterfly—,' but then she remembered there would never again be bravely colored small wings on Earth and banged a hand against her faceplate as if she had been about to knuckle her eyes.

Darkington was still absorbed in the specimen he held. 'I never heard of a machine this finely constructed,' he declared. 'I thought nothing but a biological system could—'

'Stop! Freeze!'

Kuroki's voice rapped in their earphones. Darkington laid a hand on his pistol butt. Otherwise only his head moved, turning inside the helmet. After a moment he saw the thing too.

It stirred among shadows, behind a squat cylinder topped with the usual black-and-mirror plates. Perhaps three feet long, six or eight inches high . . . It came out into plain view. Darkington glimpsed a slim body and six short legs of articulated dull metal. A latticework swiveled at the front end like a miniature radio-radar beamcaster. Something glinted beadily beneath, twin lenses? Two thin tentacles held a metal silver off one of the great stationary structures. They fed it into an orifice, and sparks shot back upward—

'Holy Moses,' Kuroki whispered.

The thing stopped in its tracks. The front-end lattice swung toward the humans. Then the thing was off, unbelievably fast. In half a second there was nothing to see.

Nobody moved for almost a minute. Finally Frederika clutched Darkington's arm with a little cry. The rigidity left ham and he babbled of experimental robot turtles in the early days of cybernetic research. Very simple gadgets. A motor drove a wheeled platform, steered by a photoelectric unit that approached light sources by which the batteries might be recharged and then, when this was done, became negatively phototropic and sought darkness. An elementary feedback circuit. But the turtles had shown astonishing tenacity, had gone over obstacles or even around. . . .

'That beast there was a good deal more complicated,' she interrupted.

'Certainly, certainly,' Darkington said. 'But—'

'I'll bet it heard Sam talk on the radio, spotted us with radar – or maybe eyes, if those socketed glass things were eyes – and took off.'

'Very possibly, if you must use anthropomorphic language. However—'

'It was eating that strut.' Frederika walked over to the piece of metal which the runner had dropped. She picked it up and came stiffly back with it. 'See, the end has been ground away by a set of coarse emery wheels or something. You couldn't very well eat alloy with teeth like ours. You have to grind it.'

'Hey!' Kuroki objected. 'Let's not go completely off the deep end.'

'What the hell's happened down there?' called the man aboard the *Traveler*.

They resumed walking, in a dreamlike fashion, as they re-counted what they had seen. Frederika concluded: 'Th⸱ ...
this arrangement might conceivably be some kind of aut⸱
factory – chemosynthetic or something – if taken by itsel⸱
not with beasts like that one running loose.'

'Now wait,' Darkington said. 'They could be maintenance robots, you know. Clear away rubbish and wreckage.'

'A science advanced enough to build what we see wouldn't use such a clumsy system of maintenance,' she answered. 'Get off your professional caution, Hugh, and admit what's obvious.'

Before he could reply, his earphones woke with a harsh jabber. He stopped and tried to tune in – it kept fading out, he heard it only in bursts – but the band width was too great. What he did hear sounded like an electronic orchestra gone berserk. Sweat prickled his skin.

When the sound had stopped: 'Okay,' breathed Kuroki, 'you tell me.'

'Could have been a language, I suppose,' said Frederika, dry-throated. 'It wasn't just a few simple oscillations like that stuff on the other frequencies.'

Captain Thurshaw himself spoke from the orbiting ship. 'You better get back to the boat and sit prepared for quick blast-off.'

Darkington found his nerve. 'No, sir. If you please. I mean, uh, if there are intelligences ... if we really do want to contact them ... now's the time. Let's at least make an effort.'

'Well—'

'We'll take you back first, of course, Freddie.'

'Nuts,' said the girl. 'I stay right here.'

Somehow they found themselves pushing on. Once, crossing an open spot where only the crystals stood, they spied something in the air. Through binoculars, it turned out to be a metallic object shaped vaguely like an elongated manta. Apparently it was mostly hollow, upborne by air currents around the fins and propelled at low speed by a gas jet. 'Oh, sure,' Frederika muttered. 'Birds.'

They re-entered the area of tall structures. The sonic amplifiers in their helmets were again tuned high, and the clash of plates in the wind was deafening. Like a suit of armor, Dark-ington thought idiotically. Could be a poem in that. Empty armor on a wild horse, rattling and tossing as it was galloped down an inexplicably deserted city street – symbol of––

The radio impulses that might be communication barked again in their earphones. 'I don't like this,' Thurshaw said from the sky. 'You're dealing with too many unknowns at once. Return to the boat and we'll discuss further plans.'

They continued walking in the same direction, mechanically. *We don't seem out of place here ourselves, in this stiff cold forest,* Darkington, thought. *My God, let's turn around. Let's assert our dignity as organic beings. We aren't mounted on rails!*

'That's an order,' Thurshaw stated.

'Very well, sir,' Kuroki said. 'And, uh, thanks.'

The sound of running halted them. They whirled. Frederika screamed.

'What's the matter?' Thurshaw shouted: 'What's the matter?' The unknown language ripped across his angry helplessness.

Kuroki yanked his rocket gun loose and put the weapon to his shoulder. 'Wait!' Darkington yelled. But he grabbed at his own pistol. The oncomer rushed in a shower of crystal splinters, whipping rods and loops aside. Its gigantic weight shuddered in the ground.

Time slowed for Darkington, he had minutes or hours to tug at his gun, hear Frederika call his name, see Kuroki take aim and fire. The shape was mountainous before him. Nine feet tall, he estimated in a far-off portion of his rocking brain, three yards of biped four-armed monstrosity, head horned with radio lattice, eyes that threw back sunlight in a blank glitter, grinder orifice and–– The rocket exploded. The thing lurched and half fell. One arm was in ruins.

'Ha!' Kuroki slipped a fresh shell into his gun. 'Stay where you are, you!'

Frederika, wildly embracing Darkington, found time to gasp, 'Sam, maybe it wasn't going to do any harm,' and Kuroki snapped, 'Maybe it was. Too goddam big to take chances with.' Then everything smashed.

Suddenly the gun was knocked spinning by a hurled iron bar they hadn't even noticed. And the giant was among them. A swat across Kuroki's back shattered his radio and dashed him to earth. Flame spat and Frederika's voice was cut short in Darkington's receivers.

He pelted off, his pistol uselessly barking. 'Run, Freddie!' he bawled into his sonic microphone. 'I'll try and––' The

machine picked him up. The pistol fell from his gr[e]
moment later, Thurshaw's horrified oaths were gone: Darkin[g]
ton's radio antenna had been plucked out by the roots. Frederika
tried to escape, but she was snatched up just as effortlessly.
Kuroki, back on his feet, stood where he was and struck with
ludicrous fists. It didn't take long to secure him either. Hog-
tied, stuffed into a rack on the shoulders of the giant, the three
humans were borne off southward.

4

At first Zero almost ran. The monster must have known
where its auxiliaries were and something of what had happened
to them. Now that contact was broken, it might send forth others
to look for them, better armed. Or it might even come itself,
roaring and burning through the forest. Zero fled.

Only the monster's voice, raggedly calling for its lost members, pursued him. After a few miles he crouched in a rod
clump and strained his receptors. Nothing was visible but thickly
growing accumulators and bare sky. The monster had ceased to
shout. Though it still emitted an unmodulated signal, distance
had dwindled this until the surrounding soft radio noise had
almost obliterated that hum.

The units Zero had captured were making considerable sound-
wave radiation. If not simply the result of malfunction in their
damaged mechanism, it must be produced by some auxiliary
system which they had switched on through interior controls.
Zero's sound receptors were not sensitive enough to tell him
whether the emission was modulated. Nor did he care. Certain
low forms of motile were known to have well-developed sonic
parts, but anything so limited in range was useless to him except
as a warning of occurrences immediately at hand. A person
needed many square miles to support himself. How could there
be a community of persons without the effortless ability to talk
across trans-horizon distances?

Irrelevantly, for the first time in his century and half of
existence, Zero realized how few persons he had ever observed
with his own direct optics. How few he had touched. Now and
then, for this or that purpose, several might get together. A
bride's male kin assisted her on her journey to the groom's dwell-
ing. Individuals met to exchange the products of their labor.

But still – this rally of all functional males at Broken Glade, to hunt the monster, would be the greatest assemblage in tradition. Yet not even Hundred had grasped is uniqueness.

For persons were always communicating. Not only practical questions were discussed. In fact, now that Zero thought about it, such problems were the least part of discourse. The major part was ritual, or friendly conversation, or art. Zero had seldom met Seven as a physical entity, but the decades in which they criticized each other's poetry had made them intimate. The abstract tone constructions of Ninety-six, the narratives of Eighty, the speculations about space and time of Fifty-nine – such things belonged to all.

Direct sensory linkage, when the entire output of the body was used to modulate the communication band, reduced still further the need for physical contact. Zero had never stood on the seashore himself. But he had shared consciousness with Fourteen, who lived there. He had perceived the slow inward movement of waves, their susurrus, the salt in the air; he had experienced the smearing of grease over his skin to protect it from corrosion, drawing an aquamotile from a net and feasting. For those hours, he and the searaker had been one. Afterward he had shown Fourteen the upland forest. . . .

*What am I waiting for?* Consciousness of his here-and-now jarred back into Zero. The monster had not pursued. The units on his back had grown quiescent. But he was still a long way from home. He rose and started off again, less rapidly but with more care to obliterate his traces.

As the hours passed, his interior sensors warned him increasingly of a need for replenishment. About midday he stopped and unloaded his three prizes. They were feebly squirming and one of them had worked an arm loose. Rather than lash them tight again, he released their limbs and secured them by passing the rope in successive loops around their middle and a tall stump, then welding everything fast with his torch.

That energy drain left him ravenous. He scouted the forest in a jittery spiral until he found some accumulators of the calathi-form sort. A quick slash with his pry bar exposed their spongy interiors, rich with energy storage cells and mineral salts. They were not very satisfying eaten unprocessed, but he was too empty to care. With urgency blunted, he could search more slowly and thoroughly. Thus he found the traces of a burrow, dug into the sand, and came upon a female digger. She was heavy with a half-completed new specimen and he caught her easily. This too would have been better if treated with heat and acid, but even raw the materials tasted good in his grinder.

Now to get something for One. Though she, better than he, could slow down her functioning when nourishment was scarce, a state of coma while the monster was abroad could be dangerous. After hunting for another hour, Zero had the good luck to start a rotor. It crashed off among the rods and crystals, faster than he could run, but he put a crossbow bolt through its hub. Dismembered and packed into his carrier, it made an immensely cheering burden.

He returned to his prizes. Moving quietly in comparison to the windy clatter of the forest, he came upon them unobserved. They had quit attempting to escape – he saw the wire was shiny where they had tried to saw it on a sharp rock – and were busy with other tasks. One of them had removed a box-like object from its back and inserted its head(?) and arms through gasketed holes. A second was just removing a similar box from its lower section. The third had plugged a flexible tube from a bottle into its face.

Zero approached. 'Let me inspect those,' he said, before thinking how ridiculous it was to address them. They shrank away from him. He caught the one with the bottle and unplugged the tube. Some liquid ran out. Zero extended his chemical sensor and tasted cautiously. Water. Very pure. He did not recall ever having encountered water so free of dissolved minerals.

Thoughtfully, he released the unit. It stoppered the tube. So, Zero reflected, they required water like him, and carried a supply with them. That was natural; they (or, rather, the monster they served) could not know where the local springs and streams were. But why did they suck through a tube? Did they lack a proper liquid-ingestion orifice? Evidently. The small hole in the head. into which the tube had fitted, had automatically closed as the nipple was withdrawn.

The other two had removed their boxes. Zero studied these and their contents. There were fragments of mushy material in both, vaguely similar to normal body sludge. Nourishment or waste? Why such a clumsy system? It was as if the interior mechanism must be absolutely protected from contact with the environment.

He gave the boxes back and looked more thoroughly at their users. They were not quite so awkward as they seemed at first. The humps on their backs were detachable carriers like his. Some of the objects dangling at their waist or strapped to their arms must also be tools. (Not weapons or means or escape, else they would have used them before now. Specialized artificial attachments, then, analogous to a torch or a surgical ratchet.) The basic bipedal shape was smoother than his own, nearly featureless except for limb joints. The head was somewhat more complicated, though less so than a person's. Upon the cylindrical foundation grew various parts, including the sound-wave generators which babbled as he stood there watching. The face was a glassy plate, behind which moved ... what? Some kind of jointed, partly flexible mechanism.

There was no longer any possibility of radio communication with – or through – them. Zero made a few experimental gestures, but the units merely stirred about. Two of them embraced. The third waved its arms and made sonic yelps. All at once it squatted and drew geometrical shapes in the sand, very much like the courtship figures drawn by a male dune-runner.

So ... they not only had mechanical autonomy, like the spy eyes of a boxroller, but were capable of some independent behavior. They were more than simple remote-control limbs and sensors of the monster. Most probably they were domesticated motiles.

But if so, then the monster race had modified their type even more profoundly than the person race had modified the type of its own tamed motiles down in the lowlands. These bipeds were comically weak in proportion to size; they lacked grinders and liquid-ingestion orifices; they used sonics to a degree that argued their radio abilities were primitive; they required ancillary apparatus; in short, they were not functional by themselves. Only the care and shelter furnished by their masters allowed them to remain long in existence.

*But what are the masters? Even the monster may well be only another motile. Certainly it appeared to lack limbs. The masters may be persons like us, come from beyond the sea or the mountain with skills and powers transcending our own.*

*But then what do they want? Why have they not tried to communicate with us? Have they come to take our land away?*

The question was jolting. Zero got hastily into motion. With his rack loaded, he had no room for his prizes. Besides, being crammed into it for hours was doubtless harmful to them; they moved a good deal more strongly now, after a rest, than when he first took them out. He simply left them tied together, cut the wire loose from the stump, and kept that end in one hand. Since he continued to exercise due caution about leaving a trail, he did not move too fast for them to keep up. From time to time they would stagger and lean on each other for support – apparently their energy cells polarized more quickly than his – but he found they could continue if he let them pause a while, lie down, use their curious artifacts.

The day passed. At this time of year, not long past the vernal equinox, the sun was up for about twenty hours. After dark, Zero's captives began stumbling and groping. He confirmed by direct sense perception that they had no radar. If they ever did, that part had been wrecked with their communicators. After some thought, he fashioned a rough seat from a toppled bole and nudged them to sit upon it. Thus he carried them in two hands. They made no attempt to escape, emitted few sounds, obviously they were exhausted. But to his surprise, they began to stir about and radiate sonics when he finally reached home and set them down. He welded the end of their rope to an iron block he kept for emergencies.

Part of him reflected that their mechanism must be very strange indeed, maybe so strange that they would not prove ingestible. Obviously their cells went to such extremes of polarization that they became comatose, which a person only did in emergencies. To them, such deactivation appeared to be normal, and they roused spontaneously.

He dismissed speculation. One's anxious voice had been rushing over him while he worked. 'What has happened? You are hurt! Come closer, let me see, oh, your poor arm! Oh, my dear!'

'Nothing serious,' he reassured her. 'I shot a rotor. Prepare yourself a meal before troubling about me.'

He lowered himself to the cave floor beside her great beautiful bulk. The glow globes, cultivated on the rough stone walls, shed luster on her skin and on the graceful tool tendrils that curled forth to embrace him. His chemical sensor brought him a hint of solvents and lubricants, an essence of femaleness. The cave mouth was black with night, save where one star gleamed bright and somehow sinister above the hills. The forest groaned and tolled. But here he had light and her touch upon his body. He was home.

She unshipped the rack from his shoulders but made no motion toward the food-processing cauldron. Most of her tools and all her attention were on his damaged arm. 'We must replace everything below the elbow,' she decided; and, as a modulation: 'Zero, you brave clever adored fool, why did you hazard yourself like that? Do you not understand, even yet, without you my world would be rust?'

'I am sorry ... to take so much from the new one,' he apologized.

'No matter. Feed me some more nice large rotors like this and I will soon replace the loss, and finish all the rest too.' Her mirth fluttered toward shyness. 'I want the new one activated soon myself, you know, so we can start another.'

The memory of that moment last year, when his body pattern flowed in currents and magnetic fields through hers, when the two patterns heterodyned and deep within her the first crystallization took place, glowed in him. Sensory linkage was a wan thing by comparison.

What they did together now had a kindred intimacy. When she had removed the ruined forearm and he had thrust the stump into her repair orifice, a thousand fine interior tendrils enfolded it, scanning, relaying, and controlling. Once again, more subtly than in reproduction, the electro-chemical-mechanical systems of One and Zero unified. The process was not consciously controllable; it was a female function; One was at this moment no different from the most primitive motile joined to her damaged mate in a lightless burrow.

It took time. The new person which her body was creating within itself was, of course, full size and, as it happened, not far from completion. (Had the case been otherwise, Zero would have had to wait until the new one did in fact possess a well-developed arm.) But it was not yet activated; its most delicate and critical synaptic pathways were still only half-finished, gradually crystallizing out of solution. A part could not lightly nor roughly be removed.

But in the end, One's functions performed the task. Slowly, almost reluctantly, Zero withdrew his new hand. His mind and hers remained intertwined a while longer. At last, with a shaky little overtone of humor, she exclaimed, 'Well, how do your fingers wiggle? Is everything good? Then let us eat. I am famished!'

Zero helped her prepare the rotor for consumption. They threw the damaged forearm into the cauldron too. While they processed and shared the meal, he recounted his experiences. She had shown no curiosity about the three bipeds. Like most females, she lacked any great interest in the world beyond her home, and had merely assumed they were some new kind of wild motile. As he talked, the happiness died in her. 'Oh, no,' she said, 'you are not going out to fight the lightning breather, are you?'

'Yes, we must.' He knew what image terrified her, himself smashed beyond hope of reconstruction, and added in haste: 'If we leave it free, no tradition or instinct knows what it may do. But surely, at the very least so large a thing will cause extensive damage. Even if it is only a grazer, its appetite will destroy untold acres of accumulators; and it may be a predator. On the other hand, if we destroy it, what a hoard of nourishment! Your share and mine will enable us to produce a dozen new persons. The energy will let me range for hundreds of miles, thus gaining still more food and goods for us.'

'If the thing can be assimilated,' she said doubtfully. 'It could be full of hydrofluoric acid or something, like a touch-me-not.'

'Yes, yes. For that matter, the flier may be the property of intelligent beings: which does not necessarily mean we will not destroy and consume it. I intend to find out about that aspect right now. If the monster's auxiliaries are ingestible, the monster itself is almost sure to be.'

'But if not— Zero, be careful!'

'I will. For your sake also.' He stroked her and felt an answering vibration. It would have been pleasant to sit thus all night, but he must soon be on his way to rendezvous. And first he must dissect at least one specimen. He took up his pry bar and approached the three units.

5

Darkington awoke from a nightmare-ridden half-sleep when he was dumped on the cave floor. He reached for Frederika and she came to him. For a space there was nothing but their murmuring.

Eventually they crouched on the sand and looked about. The giant that captured them had welded the free end of the wire rope to an immovable chunk of raw iron. Darkington was attached at that side, then the girl, and Kuroki on the outer end. They had about four feet of slack from one to the next. Nothing in the kit remaining to them would cut those strands.

'Limestone cave, I guess, Kuroki croaked. Behind the faceplate he was gaunt, bristly, and sunken-eyed. Frederika didn't look much better. They might not have survived the trip here if the robot hadn't carried them the last few hours. Nonetheless an odd, dry clarity possessed Darkington's brain. He could observe and think as well as if he had been safe on shipboard. His body was one enormous ache, but he ignored that and focused on comprehending what had happened.

Here near the entrance, the cave was about twenty feet high and rather more wide. A hundred feet deeper inward, it narrowed and ended. That area was used for storage: a junk shop of mechanical and electronic parts, together with roughly fashioned metal and stone tools that looked almost homelike. The walls were overgrown with thin wires that sprouted scores of small crystalline globes. These gave off a cool white light that made the darkness outside appear the more elemental.

'Yes, a cave in a sheer hillside,' said Frederika. 'I saw that much. I kept more or less conscious all the way here, trying to keep track of our route. Not that that's likely to do us much good, is it?' She hugged her knees. 'I've got to sleep soon – oh, but I have to sleep!'

'We got to get in touch.' Kuroki's voice rose. (Thank heaven and some ages-dead engineer that sound mikes and earphones could be switched on by shoving your chin against the right button! With talk cut off, no recourse would have remained but to slip quietly into madness.) 'God damn it, I tried to show that tin nightmare we're intelligent. I drew diagrams and—' He checked himself. 'Well, probably its builders don't monitor it. We'll have another go when they show up.'

'Let's admit the plain facts, Sam,' Frederika said tonelessly. 'There aren't any builders. There never were any.'

'Oh, no.' The pilot gave Darkington a beggar's look. 'You're the biologist, Hugh. Do you believe that?'

Darkington bit his lip. 'I'm afraid she's right.'

Frederika's laugh barked at them. 'Do you know what that

big machine is, there in the middle of the cave? The one the robot is fooling around with? I'll tell you. His wife!' She broke off. Laughter echoed too horribly in their helmets.

Darkington gazed in that direction. The second object had little in common with the biped shape, being low and wide – twice the bulk – and mounted on eight short legs which must lend very little speed or agility. A radio lattice, optical lenses, and arms (two, not four) were similar to the biped's. But numerous additional limbs were long goosenecks terminating in specialized appendages. Sleek blued metal covered most of the body.

And yet, the way those two moved—

'I think you may be right about that also,' Darkington said at last.

Kuroki beat the ground with his fist and swore. 'Sorry, Freddie,' he gulped. 'But won't you, for God's sake, explain what you're getting at? This mess wouldn't be so bad if it made some sense.'

'We can only guess,' Darkington said.

'Well, guess, then!'

'Robot evolution,' Frederika said. 'After man was gone, the machines that were left began to evolve.'

'No,' said Kuroki, 'that's nuts. Impossible!'

'I think what we've seen would be impossible any other way,' Darkington said. 'Metallic life couldn't arise spontaneously. Only carbon atoms make the long hookups needed for the chemical storage of biological information. But electronic storage is equally feasible. And ... before the *Traveler* departed ... self-reproducing machines were already in existence.'

'I think the sea rafts must have been the important ones.' Frederika spoke like someone in dream. Her eyes were fixed wide and unblinking on the two robots. 'Remember? They were essentially motorized floating boxes, containing metallurgic processing plants and powered by solar batteries. They took dissolved minerals out of sea water, magnesium, uranium, whatever a particular raft was designed for. When it had a full cargo, it went to a point on shore where a depot received its load. Once empty, it returned to open waters for more. It had an inertial navigation device, as well as electronic sensors and various homeostatic systems, so it could cope with the normal vicissitudes of its environment.

'And it had electronic templates which bore full information on its own design. They controlled mechanisms aboard, which made any spare part that might be needed. Those same mechanisms also kept producing and assembling complete duplicate rafts. The first such outfit cost hundreds of millions of dollars to manufacture, let alone the preliminary research and development. But once made, it needed no further investment. Production and expansion didn't cost anyone a cent.

'And after man was gone from Earth . . . all life had vanished . . . the sea rafts were still there, patiently bringing their cargoes to crumbling docks on barren shores, year after year after meaningless year—'

She shook herself. The motion was violent enough to be seen in armor. 'Go on, Hugh,' she said, her tone turned harsh. 'If you can.'

'I don't know any details,' he began cautiously. 'You should tell me how mutation was possible to a machine. But if the templates were actually magnetic recordings on wire or tape, I expect that hard radiation would affect them, as it affects an organic gene. And for a while there was certainly plenty of hard radiation around. The rafts started making imperfect duplicates. Most were badly designed and, uh, foundered. Some, though, had advantages. For instance, they stopped going to shore and hanging about for decades waiting to be unloaded. Eventually some raft was made which had the first primitive ability to get metal from a richer source than the ocean: namely, from other rafts. Through hundreds of millions of years, an ecology developed. We might as well call it an ecology. The land was reconquered. Wholly new *types* of machine proliferated. Until today, well, what we've seen.'

'But where's the energy come from?' Kuroki demanded.

'The sun, I suppose. By now, the original solar battery must be immensely refined. I'd make a guess at dielectric storage on the molecular level, in specialized units – call them cells – which may even be of microscopic size. Of course, productivity per acre must be a good deal lower than it was in our day. Alloys aren't as labile as amino acids. But that's offset to a large extent by their greater durability. And, as you can see in this cave, by interchangeability.'

'Huh?'

'Sure. Look at those spare parts stacked in the rear. Some will no doubt be processed, analogously to our eating and digesting food. But others are probably being kept for use as such. Suppose you could take whole organs from animals you killed and install them in yourself to replace whatever was wearing out. I rather imagine that's common on today's Earth. The 'black box' principle was designed into most machines in our own century. It would be inherited.'

'Where's the metal come from in the first place?'

'From lower types of machine. Ultimately from sessile types that break down ores, manufacture the basic alloys, and concentrate more dielectric energy than they use. Analogous to vegetation. I daresay the, uh, metabolism involves powerful reagents. Sulfuric and nitric acids in glass-lined compartments must be the least of them. I doubt if there are any equivalent of microbes, but the ecology seems to manage quite well without. It's a grosser form of existence than ours. But it works. It works.'

'Even sex.' Frederika giggled a little crazily.

Darkington squeezed her gauntleted hand until she grew calmer. 'Well,' he said, 'quite probably in the more complex machines, reproduction has become the speciality of one form while the other specializes in strength and agility. I daresay there are corresponding psychological differences.'

'Psychological?' Kuroki bridled. 'Wait a minute! I know there is – was – a lot of loose talk about computers being electronic brains and such rot, but—'

'Call the phenomenon what you like,' Darkington shrugged. 'But the robot uses tools which are made, not grown. The problem is how to convince it that *we* think.'

'Can't it see?' Frederika exclaimed. 'We use tools too. Sam drew mathematical pictures. What more does it want?'

'I don't know enough about this world to even guess,' Darkington said tiredly. 'But I suppose . . . well . . . we might once have seen a trained ape doing all sorts of elaborate things, without ever assuming it was more than an ape. No matter how odd it looked.'

'Or maybe the robot just doesn't give a damn,' Kuroki said.

'There were people who wouldn't have.'

'If Hugh's guess about the "black box" is right,' Frederika added slowly, 'then the robot race must have evolved as hunters, instead of hunting being invented rather late in their evolution. As if men had descended from tigers instead of simians. How much psychological difference would that make?'

No one replied. She leaned forlornly against Darkington. Kuroki turned his eyes from them, perhaps less out of tact than loneliness. His girl was several thousand miles away, straight up, with no means for him to call her and say good-by.

Thurshaw had warned the insistent volunteers for this expedition that there would be no rescue. He had incurred sufficient guilt in letting three people – three percent of the human race – risk themselves. If anything untoward happened, the *Traveler* would linger a while in hopes the boat could somehow return. But in the end the *Traveler* would head for the stars. Kuroki's girl would have to get another father for the boy she might name Sam.

*I wish to hell Freddie were up there with her,* Darkington thought. *Or do I? Isn't that simply what I'm supposed to wish? God! Cut that out. Start planning!*

His brain spun like wheels in winter mud. What to do, what to do, what to do? His pistol was gone, so were Kuroki's rockets, nothing remained but a few tools and instruments. At the back of the cave there were probably stored some weapons with which a man could put up a moment's fight. (Only a moment, against iron and lightning; but that would end the present, ultimate horror, of sitting in your own fear-stink until the monster approached or the air-renewal batteries grew exhausted and you strangled.) The noose welded around his waist, ending in a ton of iron, choked off any such dreams. They must communicate, somehow, anyhow, plead, threaten, promise, wheedle. But the monster hadn't cared about the Pythagorean theorem diagrammed in sand. What next, then? How did you say 'I am alive' to something that was not alive?

Though what was aliveness? Were proteins inherently and unescapably part of any living creature? If the ancient sea rafts had been nothing except complicated machines, at what point of further complication had their descendants come to life? *Now stop that, you're a biologist, you know perfectly well that any such question is empirically empty, and anyhow it has nothing to do with preserving the continuity of certain protein chemistries which are irrationally much loved.*

'I think it talks by radio.' Kuroki's slow voice sounded oddly through the thudding in Darkington's head. 'It probably hasn't got any notion that sound waves might carry talk. Maybe it's even deaf. Ears wouldn't be any too useful in that rattletrap jungle. And our own radios are busted.' He began to fumble in the girl's pack. 'I'm not feeling you up, Freddie. Your space-suit isn't exactly my type. But I think I could cobble together one working set from the pieces of our three, if I can borrow some small tools and instruments. Once we make systematic noises on its talk band, the robot might get interested in trying to savvy us.'

'Sam,' she said faintly, 'for that idea you can feel me up all you want.'

'I'll take a rain check.' He could actually chuckle, Darkington heard. 'I'm sweaty enough in this damn suit to pass for a rain-storm just by myself.'

He began to lay out the job. Darkington, unable to help, ashamed that he had not thought of anything, turned attention back to the robots. They were coupled together, ignoring him.

Frederika dozed off. How slowly the night went. But Earth was old, rotating as wearily as . . . as himself . . . He slept.

A gasp awoke him.

The monster stood above them. Tall, tall, higher than the sky, it bestrode their awareness and looked down with blank eyes upon Kuroki's pitiful, barely begun work. One hand was still a torch and another hand had been replaced, it was invulnerable and soulless as a god. For an instant Darkington's half-aroused self groveled before it.

Then the torch spat, slashed the wire rope across, and Kuroki was pulled free.

Frederika cried out. 'Sam!'

'Not . . . so eager . . . pal,' the pilot choked in the robot's arms. 'I'm glad you like me, but, ugh . . . careful!'

With a free hand, the robot twisted experimentally at Kuroki's left leg. The suit joints turned. Kuroki shrieked. Darkington thought he heard the leg bones leave their sockets.

'No! You filthy machine!' He plunged forward. The rope stopped him cold. Frederika covered her faceplate and begged Kuroki to be dead.

He wasn't, yet. He wasn't even unconscious. He kept on screaming as the robot used a prying tool to drag the leg off his armor. Leakseal compound flowed from between the fabric layers and preserved the air in the rest of his suit.

The robot dropped him and sprang back, frantically fanning

itself. A whiff of oxygen, Darkington realized amidst the red and black disintegration of his sanity. Oxygen was nearly as reactive as fluorine, and there had been no free oxygen on Earth since— Kuroki's agony jerked toward silence.

The robot reapproached with care, squatted above him, poked at the exposed flesh, tore loose a chunk for examination and flung it aside. The metal off a joint seemed better approved.

Darkington's universe roared and exploded. He lunged again. close to Kuroki and wept. The biologist himself was even nearer. He could have touched the robot as well as the body. Instead, though, he retreated, mumbling and mewing.

The robot had clearly learned a lesson from the gas, but was just as clearly determined to go on with the investigation. It stood up, moved a cautious distance away, and jetted a thin, intensely blue flame from its torch hand. Kuroki's corpse was divided across the middle.

Darkington's universe roared and exploded. He lunged again. The rope between him and Frederika was pulled across the fire-beam. The strands parted like smoke.

The robot pounced at him, ran into the oxygen gushing from Kuroki's armor, and lurched back. Darkington grabbed the section of rope that joined him to the block. The torch was too bright to look at. If he touched its flame, that was the end of him too. But there was no chance to think about such matters. Blindly and animally, he pulled his leash across the cutting jet.

He was free.

'Get out, Freddie!' he coughed, and ran straight toward the robot. No use trying to run from a thing that could overtake him in three strides. The torch had stopped spitting fire, but the giant moved in a wobbly, uncertain fashion, still dazed by the oxygen. By pain? Savagely, in the last spark of awareness, Darkington hoped so. *'Get out, Freddie!'*

The robot staggered in pursuit of him. He dodged around the other machine, the big one that they had called female. To the back of the cave. A weapon to fight with, gaining a moment where Frederika might escape. An extra pry bar lay on the floor. He snatched it and whirled. The huge painted shape was almost upon him.

He dodged. Hands clashed together just above his helmet. He pelted back to the middle of the cave. The female machine was edging into a corner. But slow, awkward—

Darkington scrambled on top of it.

An arm reached from below to pluck him off. He snarled and struck with the pry bar. The noise rang in the cave. The arm sagged, dented. This octopod had nothing like the biped's strength. Its tool tendrils, even more frail, curled away from him.

The male robot loomed close. Darkington smashed his weapon down on the radio lattice at his feet. It crumpled. He brandished the bar and howled senselessly, 'Stand back, there! One step more and I'll give her the works! I'll kill her!

The robot stopped. Monstrous it bulked, an engine that could tear apart a man and his armor, and raised its torch hand.

'Oh, no,' Darkington rasped. He opened a bleeder valve on his suit, kneeling so the oxygen would flow across the front end of the thing on which he rode. Sensors ought to be more vulnerable than skin. He couldn't hear if the she-robot screamed as Kuroki had done. That would be on the radio band. But when he gestured the male back, it obeyed.

'Get the idea?' he panted, not as communication but as hatred. 'You can split my suit open with your flame gun, but my air will pour all over this contraption here. Maybe you could knock me off her by throwing something, but at the first sign of any such move on your part, I'll open my bleeder valve again. She'll at least get a heavy dose of oxy. And meanwhile I'll punch the sharp end of this rod through one of those lenses. Understand? Well, then stay where you are, machine!'

The robot froze.

Frederika came near. She had slipped the loop of cable joining her to Kuroki off what was left of his torso. The light shimmered on her faceplate so Darkington couldn't see through, and her voice was strained out of recognition. 'Hugh, oh, Hugh!'

'Head back to the boat,' he ordered. Rationality was returning to him.

'Without you? No.'

'Listen, this is not the place for grandstand heroics. Your first duty is to become a mother. But what I hope for, personally, is that you can return in the boat and fetch me. You're no pilot, but they can instruct you by radio from the ship if she's above the horizon. The general director does most of the work in any event. You land here, and I can probably negotiate a retreat for for myself.'

'But – but – the robot needed something like twenty hours to bring us here. And it knew the way better than I do. I'll have to go by compass and guess, mostly. Of course, I won't stop as often as it did. No more than I have to. But still – say twenty hours for me – you can't hold out that long!'

'I can damn well try,' he said. 'You got any better ideas?'

'All right, then. Good-by, Hugh. No, I mean so long. I love you.'

He grunted some kind of answer, but didn't see her go. He had to keep watching the robot.

6

'Zero!' his female called, just once, when the unit sprang upon ⌐er back. She clawed at it. The pry bar smashed across her arm. He felt the pain-surge within her sensors, broadcast through her communicator, like a crossbow bolt in his body.

Wildly, he charged. The enemy unit crashed the bar down on One's lattice. She shrilled in anguish. Affected by the damage that crippled her radar, her communicator tone grew suddenly, hideously different. Zero slammed himself to a halt.

Her sobbing, his own name blindly repeated, overwhelmed the burning in him where the corrosive gas had flowed. He focused his torch to a narrow beam and took careful aim.

The unit knelt, fumbling with its free hand. One screamed again, louder. Her tendrils flailed about. Numbly, Zero let his torch arm droop. The unit rose and poised its weapon above her lenses. A single strong thrust downward through the glass could reach her brain. The unit gestured him back. He obeyed.

'Help,' One cried. Zero could not look at the wreckage of her face. There was no escaping her distorted voice. 'Help, Zero. It hurts so much.'

'Hold fast,' he called in his uselessness. 'I cannot do anything. Not now. The thing is full of poison. That is what you received.' He managed to examine his own interior perceptions. 'The pain will abate in a minute . . . from such a small amount. But if you got a large dose— I do not know. It might prove totally destructive. Or the biped might do ultimate mechanical damage before I could prevent it. Hold fast, One mine. Until I think of something.'

'I am afraid,' she rattled. 'For the new one.'

'Hold fast,' he implored. 'If that unit does you any further harm, I will destroy it slowly. I expect it realizes as much.'

The other functional biped came near. It exchanged a few ululations with the first, turned and went quickly from the cave. 'It must be going back to the flying monster,' said One. The words dragged from her, now and then she whimpered as her perceptions of damage intensified, but she could reason again. 'Will it bring the monster here?'

'I cannot give chase,' said Zero unnecessarily. 'But—' He gathered his energy. A shout blasted from his communicator. '*Alarm, alarm! All persons receiving, prepare to relay. Alarm!*'

Voice flashed in his head, near and far, and it was as if they poured strength into him. He and One were not alone in a night cave, a scuttling horror on her back and the taste of poison only slowly fading. Their whole community was here.

He reported the situation in a few phrases. 'You have been rash,' Hundred said, shaken. 'May there be no further penalties for your actions.'

'What else would you have had him do?' defended Seven. 'We cannot deal randomly with a thing as powerful as the monster. Zero took upon himself the hazards of gathering information. Which he has succeeded in, too.'

'Proving the danger is greater than we imagined,' shuddered Sixteen.

'Well, that is a valuable datum.'

'The problem now is, what shall we do?' Hundred interrupted. 'Slow though you say it is, I expect the auxiliary that escaped can find the monster long before we can rendezvous and get up into the hills.'

'Until it does, though, it cannot communicate, its radio being disabled,' Zero said. 'So the monster will presumably remain where it is, ignorant of events. I suggest that those persons who are anywhere near this neighborhood strike out directly toward that area. They can try to head off the biped.'

'You can certainly capture it in a few minutes,' Hundred said.

'I cannot leave this place.'

'Yes, you can. The thing that has seized your female will not logically do anything more to her, unprovoked, lest she lose her present hostage value.'

'How do you know?' Zero retorted. 'In fact, I believe if I captured its companion, this unit would immediately attack One.

What hope does it have except in the escape of the other, that may bring rescue?'

'Hope is a curious word to use in connection with an elaborated spy eye,' Seven said.

'If it is,' Zero said. 'Their actions suggest to me that these bipeds are more than unthinking domesticated motiles.'

'Let be!' Hundred said. 'There is scant time to waste. We may not risk the entire community for the sake of a single member. Zero, go fetch back that biped.'

Unmodulated radio buzzed in the night. Finally Zero said, 'No.' One's undamaged hand reached toward him, but she was too far away for them to touch each other. Nor could she caress him with radar.

'We will soon have you whole again,' he murmured to her. She did not answer, with the community listening.

Hundred surrendered, having existed long enough to recognize unbendable negation. 'Those who are sufficiently near the monster to reach it before dawn, report,' he directed. When they had finished – about thirty all told – he said, 'Very well, proceed there. Wherever feasible, direct your course to intercept the probable path of the escaped unit. If you capture, it, inform us at once. The rest of us will rendezvous as planned.'

One by one the voices died out in the night, until only Hundred, who was responsible, and Seven, who was a friend, were in contact with Zero. 'How are you now, One?' Seven asked gently.

'I function somewhat,' she said in a tired, uneven tone. 'It is strange to be radar blind. I keep thinking that heavy objects are about to crash into me. When I turn my optics that way, there isn't anything.' She paused. 'The new one stirred a little bit now. A motor impulse pathway must have been completed. Be careful, Zero,' she begged. 'We have already taken an arm tonight.'

'I cannot understand your description of the bipeds' interior,' Hundred said practically. 'Soft, porous material soaked in sticky red liquid; acrid vapors— How do they *work*? Where is the mechanism?'

'They are perhaps not functional at all,' Seven proposed. 'They may be purely artificial devices, powered by chemical action.'

'Yet they act intelligently,' Zero argued. 'If the monster – or the monster's masters – do not have them under direct control – and certainly there is no radio involved—'

'There may be other means than radio to monitor an auxiliary,' Seven said. 'We know so little, we persons.'

'In that case,' Zero answered, 'the monster has known about this cave all the time. It is watching me at this moment, through the optics of that thing on One's back.'

'We must assume otherwise,' Hundred said.

'I do,' Zero said. 'I act in the belief that these bipeds are out of contact with the flier. But if nevertheless they perform as they have been doing, then they certainly have independent function, including at least a degree of intelligence.' A thought crashed through him, so stunning that he could not declare it at once. Finally: 'They may be the monster's masters! It may be the auxiliary, they the persons!'

'No, no, that is impossible,' Hundred groaned. Seven's temporary acceptance was quicker; he had always been able to leap from side to side of a discussion. He flashed:

'Let us assume that in some unheard-of fashion, these small entities are indeed the domesticators, or even the builders, of that flying thing. Can we negotiate with them?'

'Not after what has happened,' Zero said bleakly. He was thinking less about what he had done to them than what they had done to One.

Seven continued 'I doubt it myself, on philosophical grounds. They are too alien. Their very functioning is deadly: the destruction wrought by their flier, the poison under their skins. Eventually, a degree of mutual comprehension may be achieved. But that will be a slow and painful process. Our first responsibility is to our own form of existence. Therefore we must unmistakably get the upper hand, before we even try to talk with them.' In quick excitement, he added, 'And I think we can.'

Zero and Hundred meshed their intellects with his. The scheme grew like precipitation in a supersaturated pond. Slow and feeble, the strangers were only formidable by virtue of highly developed artifacts (or, possibly, domesticated motiles of radically modified type): the flier, the tube which had blown off Zero's arm, and other hypothetical weapons. But armament unused is no threat. If the flier could be immobilized—

Of course, presumably there were other dwarf bipeds inside it. Their voices had been heard yesterday. But Zero's trip here had proven that they lacked adequate nighttime senses. Well, grant them radar when in an undamaged condition. Radar can be confused, if one knows how.

Hundred's orders sprang forth across miles to the mountaineers now converging on the flier: 'Cut the heaviest accumulator strands you can find in the forest. Twist them into cables. Under cover of darkness, radar window, and distraction objects, surround the monster. We believe now that it may not be sentient, only a flier. Weld your cables fast to deeply founded boles. Then, swiftly, loop them around the base of the flier. Tie it down!'

'No,' said Twenty-nine, aghast. 'We cannot weld the cables to its skin. It would annihilate us with one jetblast. We would have to make nooses first and—'

'So make the nooses,' Zero said. 'The monster is not a perfectly tapered spindle. The jets bulge out at the base. Slip the nooses around the body just above the jets. I hardly think it can rise then, without tearing its own tubes out.'

'Easy for you to say, Zero, safe in your cave.'

'If you knew what I would give to have matters otherwise—'

Abashed, the hunters yielded. Their mission was not really so dangerous. The nooses – two should be ample if the cable was heavy – could be laid in a broad circle around the area which the jets had flattened and devastated. They could be drawn tight from afar, and would probably slip upward by themselves, coming to rest just above the tubes, where the body of the flier was narrowest. If a cable did get stuck on something, someone would have to dash close and free it. A snort of jetfire during those few seconds would destroy him. But quite probably the flier, or its masters, could be kept from noticing him.

'And when we do have the monster leashed, what then?' asked Twenty-nine.

'We will do what seems indicated,' Hundred said. 'If the aliens do not seem to be reaching a satisfactory understanding with us – if we begin to entertain any doubts – we can erect trebuchets and batter the flier to pieces.'

'That might be best,' said Zero, with a revengeful look at One's rider.

'Proceed as ordered,' said Hundred.

'But what about us?' Zero asked. 'One and myself?'

'I shall come to you,' Seven said. 'If nothing else, we can

stand watch and watch. You mentioned that the aliens polarize more easily than we do. We can wait until it drops from exhaustion.'

'Good,' said Zero. Hope lifted in him as if breaking through a shell. 'Did you hear, One? We need only wait.'

'Pain,' she whispered. Then, resolutely: 'I can minimize energy consumption. Comatose, I will not sense anything. ...' He felt how she fought down terror, and guessed what frightened her: the idea that she might never be roused. 'I will be guarding you all the time,' he said. 'You and the new one.'

'I wish I could touch you, Zero—' Her radiation dimmed, second by second. Once or twice consciousness returned, kicked upward by fear; static gasped in Zero's perception; but she slipped again into blackness.

When she was quite inert, he stood staring at the unit on her. No, the entity. Somewhere behind that glass and horrible tissue, a brain peered back at him. He ventured to move an arm. The thing jerked its weapon aloft. It seemed indeed to have guessed that the optics were her most vulnerable spot. With immense care, Zero let his arm fall again. The entity jittered about, incapable of his own repose. Good. Let it drain its energy the faster.

He settled into his own thoughts. Hours wore away. The alien paced on One's broad back, sat down, sprang up again, slapped first one hand and then another against its body, made long noises that might possibly be intended to fight off coma. Sometimes it plugged the water tube into its face. Frequently Zero saw what looked like a good chance to catch it off guard – with a sudden rush and a flailing blow, or an object snatched off the floor and thrown, or even a snap shot with his torch – but he decided not to take the hazard. Time was his ally.

Besides, now that his initial rage had abated, he began to hope he might capture the entity undamaged. Much more could be learned from a functional specimen than from the thing which lay dismembered near the iron block. Faugh, the gases it was giving off! Zero's chemical sensor retracted in disgust.

The first dawnlight grayed the cave mouth.

'We have the flier!' Twenty-nine's exuberant words made Zero leap where he stood. The alien scrambled into motion. When Zero came no closer, it sagged again. 'We drew two cables around its body. No trouble whatsoever. It never stirred. Only made the same radio hum. It still has not moved.'

'I thought—' someone else in his party ventured. 'Not long ago . . . was there not a gibberish signal from above?'

'There might well be other fliers above the clouds,' agreed Hundred from the valley. 'Have a care. Disperse yourselves. Remain under cover. The rest of us will have rendezvoused by early afternoon. At that time we will confer afresh. Meanwhile, report if anything happens. And . . . good work, hunters.'

Twenty-nine offered a brief sensory linkage. Thus Zero saw the place: the cindered blast area, and the upright spindle shining in the first long sunlight, and the cables that ran from its waist to a pair of old and mighty accumulator boles. Yes, the thing was captured for certain. Wind blew over the snowpeaks, set forest to chiming and scattered the little sunrise clouds. He had rarely known his land so beautiful.

The perception faded. He was in his cave again. Seven called: 'I am getting close now, Zero. Shall I enter?'

'No, best not. You might alarm the alien into violence. I have watched its movements the whole night. They grow more slow and irregular each hour. It must be near collapse. Suppose you wait just outside. When I believe it to be comatose, I will have you enter. If it does not react to the sight of you, we will know it has lost consciousness.'

'If it is conscious,' mused Seven. 'Despite our previous discussion, I cannot bring myself to believe quite seriously that these are anything but motiles or artifacts. Very ingenious and complex, to be sure . . . but aware, like a person?'

The unit made a long series of sonic noises. They were much weaker than hitherto. Zero allowed satisfaction to wax in him. Nevertheless, he would not have experienced this past night again for any profit.

Several hours later, a general alarm yanked his attention back outward. 'The escaped auxiliary has returned! It has entered the flier!'

'What? You did not stop it?' Hundred demanded.

Twenty-nine gave the full report. 'Naturally, after the change of plan, we were too busy weaving cables and otherwise preparing ourselves to beat the forest for the dwarf. After the flier was captured, we dispersed ourselves broadly as ordered. We made nothing like a tight circle around the blasted region. Moreover, our attention was directed at the flier, in case it tried to escape, and at the sky in case there should be more fliers. Various wild motiles were about, which we ignored, and the wind has gotten very loud in the accumulators. Under such circumstances, you will realize that probability actually favored the biped unit passing between us and reaching the open area unobserved.

'When it was first noticed, no person was close enough to reach the flier before it did. It slid a plate aside in one of the jacks which support the flier and pulled a switch. A portal opened in the body above and a ladder was extruded. By that time, a number of us had entered the clearing. The unit scrambled up the ladder. We hesitated, fearing a jetblast. None came. But how could we have predicted that? When at last we did approach, the ladder had been retracted and the portal was closed. I pulled the switch myself but nothing happened. I suppose the biped, once inside, deactivated that control by means of a master switch.'

'Well, at least we know where it is,' Hundred said. 'Disperse again, if you have not already done so. The biped may try to escape, and you do not want to get caught in the jetblast. Are you certain the flier cannot break your cables?'

'Quite certain. Closely observed, the monster – the flier seems to have only a thin skin of light alloy. Nor would I expect it to be strong against the unnatural kind of stresses imposed by our tethers. If it tries to rise, it will pull itself in two.'

'Unless,' said Fourteen as he hastened through valley mists toward Broken Glade, 'some biped emerges with a torch and cuts the cables.'

'Just let it dare!' said Twenty-nine, anxious to redeem his crew's failure.

'It may bring strong weapons,' Zero warned.

'Ten crossbows are cocked and aimed at that portal. If a biped shows itself, we will fill it with whetted steel.'

'I think that will suffice,' Zero said. He looked at the drooping shape upon One. 'They are not very powerful, these things. Ugly, cunning, but weak.'

Almost as if it knew it was being talked about, the unit reeled to its feet and shook the pry bar at him. Even Zero could detect the dullness in its noises. *Another hour,* he thought, *and One will be free.*

Half that time had gone by when Seven remarked from outside, 'I wonder why the builders ... whoever the ultimate intelligences are behind these manifestations ... why have they come?'

'Since they made no attempt to communicate with us,' Zero

said in renewed grimness, 'we must assume their purpose is hostile.'

'And?'

'Teach them to beware of us.'

He felt already the pride of victory. But then the monster spoke.

Up over the mountains rolled the voice, driven by the power which hurled those hundreds of tons through the sky. Roaring and raging through the radio spectrum, louder than lightning, enormous enough to shake down moon and stars, blasted that shout. Twenty-nine and his hunters yelled as the volume smote their receptors. Their cry was lost, drowned, engulfed by the tide which seethed off the mountainsides. Here and there, where some accumulator happened to resonate, blue arcs of flame danced in the forest. Thirty miles distant, Zero and Seven still perceived the noise as a clamor in their heads. Hundred and his followers in the valley stared uneasily toward the ranges. On the seashore, females called, 'What is that? What is that?' and aquamotiles dashed themselves about in the surf.

Seven forgot all caution. He ran into the cave. The enemy thing hardly moved. But neither Zero nor Seven observed that. Both returned to the entrance and gazed outward with terror.

The sky was empty. The forest rang in the breeze. Only that radio roar from beyond the horizon told of anything amiss. 'I did not believe—' stammered Seven. 'I did not expect – a tone that loud—'

Zero, who had One to think about, mustered decisiveness. 'It is not hurting us,' he said. 'I am glad not to be as close as the hunters are, but even they should be able to endure it for a while. We shall see. Come, let us two go back inside. Once we have secured our prisoner—'

The monster began to talk.

No mere outrageous cry this time, but speech. Not words, except occasionally. A few images. But such occurrences were coincidental. The monster spoke in its own language, which was madness.

Seized along every radio receptor channel there was in him, total sensory and mental linkage, Zero became the monster.

DITditditditDAHdit-nulnulnulnul-ditditDAHdah  &  the vector sum: infinitesimals infinitelyadded from nul-to-IN-FINITY, dit – ditdit – DA – ditditditnul(gammacolored chaos,

T—G

*bang* goes a universe scattering stars&planets&bursts-of-fire
BLOCK THAT NEUTRON BLOCK THAT NEUTRON
BLOCK THAT BLOCK THAT BLOCK THAT NEU-
TRON)oneone*** nononul – DATTA – ditditchitterchitter-
chitter burning suns & moons, burning stars & brains, burningburningburning Burning DahditDahditDahdit give me fifty
million logarithms this very microsecond or you will Burn
ditditditdit – DAYADHVAM – DAMYATA

and one long wild logarithmic spiral down spacetime-energy
continuum of potentialgradient Xproduct i,j,k but multiply
Time by the velocity of light in nothingness and the square root
of minus one (two, three, four, five, six CHANGE for duodeci-
mal computation          zzzzzzzzzzz)

buzzzzzzzzzzzZ

intergral over sigma of del cross H d sigma equals one over
c times integral over sigma partial of E with respect to t dot d
sigma but correct for nonsphericalshapentropicoordinatetrans-
formationtop & quantumelectrodynamiccchargelectricalephaselag-
radientemperature rising to burning Burning BURNING

dit-dit-chitterchitterchitter from eyrie to blind gnawer and
back again O help the trunk is burningburningburning THERE-
FORE ANNUL in the name of the seven thunders.

Everything-that-has-been, break up the roots of existence
and strike flat the thick rotundity o' the world RRRIP space-
time across and throw it on the upleaping primordial energy
for now all that was & will be, the very fact that it once *did* exist,
is canceled and torn to pieces and Burning

Burning

Burning

Burning

As the sun fell down the bowl of sky, and the sky cracked open,
and the mountains ran like rivers forming faces that gaped and
jeered, and the moon rose in the west and spat the grisliness of
what he had done at him, Zero ran. Seven did not; could not;
lay by the cave entrance, which was the gate of all horrors and
corruptions, as if turned to salt. And when God descended, still
shouting in His tongue which was madness, His fiery tail melted
Seven to a pool.

Fifty million years later the star called Wormwood ascended
to heaven; and a great silence fell upon the land.

Eventually Zero returned home. He was not surprised to find

that the biped was gone. Of course it had been reclaimed by its Master. But when he saw that One was not touched, he stood mute for a long while indeed.

After he roused her, she – who had been unawake when the world was broken and refashioned – could not understand why he led her outside to pray that they be granted mercy, now and in the hour of their dissolution.

7

Darkington did not regain full consciousness until the boat was in space. Then he pulled himself into the seat beside Frederika. 'How did you do it?' he breathed.

Her attention remained focused on piloting. Even with the help of the director and radio instructions from the ship, it was no easy task for a novice. Absently, she answered, 'I scared the robots away. They'd made the boat fast, you see. With cables too thick to pull apart. I had to go back out and cut them with a torch. But I'd barely gotten inside ahead of the pack. I didn't expect they would let me emerge. So I scared them off. After that, I went out, burned off the cables, and flew to get you.'

'Barely in time,' he shuddered. 'I was about to pass out. I did keel over once I was aboard.' A time went by with only the soft rushing noise of brake jets. 'Okay,' he said, 'I give up. I admit you're beautiful, a marvel of resourcefulness, and I can't guess how you shooed away the enemy. So tell me.'

The director shut off the engine. They floated free. She turned her face, haggard, sweaty, begrimed, and dear, toward him and said diffidently, 'I didn't have any inspiration. Just a guess and nothing to lose. We knew for pretty sure that the robots communicated by radio. I turned the boat's 'caster on full blast, hoping the sheer volume would be too much for them. Then something else occurred to me. If you have a radio transceiver in your head, hooked directly into your nervous system, wouldn't that be sort of like telepathy? I mean, it seems more direct somehow than routing everything we say through a layrnx. Maybe I could confuse them by emitting unfamiliar signals. Not any old signals, of course. They'd be used to natural radio noise. But – well – the boat's general director includes a pretty comlicated computer, carrying out millions of operations per second. Information is conveyed, not noise; but at the same time, it didn't seem to me like information that a bunch of semi-savages could handle.

'Anyhow, there was no harm in trying. I hooked the broadcaster in parallel with the effector circuits, so the computer's output not only controlled the boat as usual but also modulated the radio emission. Then I assigned the computer a good tough problem in celestial navigation, put my armor back on, summoned every ounce of nerve I had, and went outside. Nothing happened. I cut the cables without seeing any trace of the robots. I kept the computer "talking" while I jockeyed the boat over in search of the cave. It must have been working frantically to compensate for my clumsiness; I hate to imagine what its output 'sounded' like. Felt like? Well, when I'd landed, I opened the airlock and, and, and you came inside, and—' Her fists doubled. 'Oh, God, Hugh! How can we tell Sam's girl?'

He didn't answer.

With a final soft impulse, the boat nudged against the ship. As grapnels made fast, the altered spin of the vessels put Earth back in view. Darkington looked at the planet for minutes before he said :

'Good-by. Good luck.'

Frederika wiped her eyes with hands that left streaks of dirt in the tears. 'Do you think we'll ever come back?' she wondered.

'No,' he said. 'It isn't ours any more.'

# THE CRITIQUE OF IMPURE REASON

THE robot entered so quietly, for all his bulk, that Felix Tunny didn't hear. Bent over his desk, the man was first aware of the intruder when a shadow came between him and the fluoroceil. Then a last footfall quivered the floor, a vibration that went through Tunny's chair and into his bones. He whirled, choking on a breath, and saw the blue-black shape like a cliff above him. Eight feet up, the robot's eyes glowed angry crimson in a faceless helmet of a head.

A voice like a great gong reverberated through the office: 'My, but you look silly.'

'What the devil are you doing?' Tunny yelped.

'Wandering about,' said Robot IZK-99 airily. Hither and yon, yon and hither. Observing life. How deliciously right Brochet is!'

'Huh?' said Tunny. The fog of data, estimates, and increasingly frantic calculations was only slowly clearing from his head.

IZK-99 extended an enormous hand to exhibit a book. Tunny read *The Straw and the Bean: a Novel of Modern Youth by Truman Brochet* on the front. The back of the dust jacket was occupied by a colorpic of the author, who had bangs and delicate lips. Deftly, the robot flipped the book open and read aloud:

> 'Worms,' she said, 'that's what they are, worms, that's what we-uns all are, Billy Chile, worms that grew a spine an' a brain way back in the Obscene or the Messyzoic or whenever it was.' Even in her sadnesses Ella Mae must always make her sad little jokes, which saddened me still more on this day of sad rain and dying magnolia blossoms. 'We don't want them,' she said. 'Backbones an' brains, I mean, honey. They make us stiff an' topheavy, so we can't lie down no more an' be jus' nothin' ay-tall but worms.'
>
> 'Take off your clothes,' I yawned.

'What has that got to do with anything?' Tunny asked.

'If you do not understand,' said IZK-99 coldly, 'there is no

149

use in discussing it with you. I recommend that you read Arnold Roach's penetrating critical essay on this book. It appeared in the last issue of *Pierce, Arrow! The Magazine of Penetrating Criticism*. He devotes four pages to analyzing the various levels of meaning in that exchange between Ella Mae and Billy Child.'

'Ooh,' Tunny moaned. 'Isn't it enough I've got a hangover, a job collapsing under me because of you, and a fight with my girl, but you have to mention that rag?'

'How vulgar you are. It comes from watching stereovision.' The robot sat down in a chair, which creaked alarmingly under his weight, crossed his legs and leafed through his book. The other hand lifted a rose to his chemosensor. 'Exquisite,' he murmured.

'You don't imagine I'd sink to reading what they call fiction these days, do you?' Tunny sneered, with a feeble hope of humiliating him into going to work. 'Piddling little experiments in the technique of describing more and more complicated ways to feel sorry for yourself – what kind of entertainment is that for a man?'

'You simply do not appreciate the human condition,' said the robot.

'Hah! Do you think you do, you conceited hunk of animated tin?'

'Yes, I believe so, thanks to my study of the authors, poets, and critics who devote their lives to the exploration and description of Man. Your Miss Forelle is a noble soul. Ever since I looked upon my first copy of that exquisitely sensitive literary quarterly she edits, I have failed to understand what she sees in you. To be sure,' IZK-99 mused, 'the relationship is not unlike that between the nun and the Diesel engine in *Regret For Two Doves*, but still ... At any rate, if Miss Forelle has finally told you to go soak your censored head in expurgated wastes and then put the unprintable thing in an improbable place, I for one heartily approve.'

Tunny, who was no mama's boy – he had worked his way through college as a whale herder and bossed construction gangs on Mars – was so appalled by the robot's language that he could only whisper, 'She did not. She said nothing of the sort.'

'I did not mean it literally,' IZK-99 explained. 'I was only quoting the renunciation scene in *Gently Come Twilight*. By Stichling, you know – almost as sensitive a writer as Brochet.'

Tunny clenched fists and teeth and battled a wild desire to pull the robot apart, plate by plate and transistor by transistor. He couldn't, of course. He was a big blond young man with a homely, candid face; his shoulders strained his blouse and the legs coming out of his shorts were thickly muscular; but robots had steelloy frames and ultrapowered energizers. Besides, though his position as chief estimator gave him considerable authority in Planetary Developments, Inc., the company wouldn't let him destroy a machine which had cost several million dollars. Even when the machine blandly refused to work and spent its time loafing around the plant, reading, brooding, and denouncing the crass bourgeois mentality of the staff.

Slowly, Tunny mastered his temper. He'd recently thought of a new approach to the problem; might as well try it now. He leaned forward. 'Look, Izaak,' he said in the mildest tone he could manage, 'have you ever considered that we need you? That the whole human race needs you?'

'The race needs love, to be sure,' said the robot, 'which I am prepared to offer; but I expect that the usual impossibility of communication will entangle us in the typical ironic loneliness.'

'No, *no*, NO – um – that is, the human race needs those minerals that you can obtain for us. Earth's resources are dwindling. We can get most elements from the sea, but some are in such dilute concentration that it isn't economically feasible to extract them. In particular, there's rhenium. Absolutely vital in alloys and electronic parts that have to stand intense irradiation. It always was scarce, and now it's in such short supply that several key industries are in trouble. But on the Dayside of Mercury—'

'Spare me. I have heard all that *ad nauseam*. What importance have any such dead, impersonal, mass questions, contrasted to the suffering, isolated soul? No, it is useless to argue with me. My mind is made up. For the disastrous consequences of not being able to reach a firm decision, I refer you to the Freudian analyses of *Hamlet*.'

'If you're interested in individuals,' Tunny said, 'you might consider me. I'm almost an ancestor of yours, God help me. I was the one who suggested commissioning a humanoid robot with independent intelligence for the Mercury project. This company's whole program for the next five years is based on having you go. If you don't, I'll be out on my ear. And jobs are none too easy to come by. How's that for a suffering, isolated soul?'

'You are not capable of suffering,' said Izaak. 'You are much too coarse. Now do leave me to my novel.' His glowing eyes returned to the book. He continued sniffing the rose.

Tunny's own gaze went back to the bescribbled papers which littered his desk, the result of days spent trying to calculate some way out of the corner into which Planetary Developments, Inc. had painted itself. There wasn't any way that he could find. The investment in Izaak was too great for a relatively small outfit like this. If the robot didn't get to work, and soon, the company would be well and thoroughly up Dutchman's Creek.

In his desperation Tunny had even looked again into the hoary old idea of remote-controlled mining. No go – not on Mercury's Dayside, where the nearby sun flooded every tele-device with enough heat and radiation to assure fifty percent chance of breakdown in twenty-four hours. It had been rare luck that the rhenium deposits were found at all, by a chemotrac sent from Darkside Base. To mine them, there must be a creature with senses, hands, and intelligence, present on the spot, to make decisions and repair machinery as the need arose. Not a human; no rad screen could long keep a man alive under that solar bombardment. The high-acceleration flight to Darkside, and home again when their hitch was up, in heavily shielded and screened spaceships, gave the base personnel as much exposure as the Industrial Safety Board allowed per lifetime. The miner had to be a robot.

Only the robot refused the task. There was no way, either legal or practical, to make him take it against his will. Tunny laid a hand on his forehead. No wonder he'd worried himself close to the blowup point, until last night he quarreled with Janet and got hyperbolically drunk. Which had solved nothing.

The phone buzzed on his desk. He punched Accept. The face of William Barsch, executive vice-president, leaped into the screen, round, red, and raging.

'*Tunny!*' he bellowed.

'I-yi-yi! – I mean hello, sir.' The engineer offered a weak smile.

'Don't hello me, you glue-brained idiot! When is that robot taking off?'

'Never,' said Izaak. At his electronic reading speed, he had finished the novel and now rose from his chair to look over

Tunny's shoulder.

'You're fired!' Barsch howled. 'Both of you!'

'I hardly consider myself hired in the first place,' Izaak said loftily. 'Your economic threat holds no terrors. My energizer is charged for fifty years of normal use, after which I can finance a recharge by taking a temporary position. It would be interesting to go on the road at that,' he went on thoughtfully, 'like those people in that old book the Library of Congress reprostatted for me. Yes, one might indeed find satori in going, man, going, never mind where, never mind why—'

'You wouldn't find much nowadays,' Tunny retorted. 'Board a transcontinental tube at random, and where does it get you? Wherever its schedule says. The bums aren't seeking enlightenment, they're sitting around on their citizens' credit watching SteeVee.' He wasn't paying much attention to his own words, being too occupied with wondering if Barsch was really serious this time.

'I gather as much,' said Izaak, 'although most contemporary novels and short stories employ more academic settings. What a decadent civilization this is: no poverty, no physical or mental disease, no wars, no revolutions, no beatniks!' His tone grew earnest. 'Please understand me, gentlemen. I bear you no ill will. I despise you, of course, but in the most cordial fashion. It is not fear which keeps me on Earth – I am practically indestructible; not anticipated loneliness – I enjoy being unique; not any prospect of boredom in the usual sense – talent for the work you had in mind is engineered into me. No, it is the absolute insignificance of the job. Beyond the merely animal economic implications, rhenium has no meaning. Truman Brochet would never be aware the project was going on, let alone write a novel about it. Arnold Roach would not even mention it *en passant* in any critical essay on the state of the modern soul as reflected in the major modern novelists. Do you not see my position? Since I was manufactured, of necessity, with creative intelligence and a need to do my work right, I *must* do work I can respect.'

'Such as what?' demanded Barsch.

'When I have read enough to feel that I understand the requirements of literary technique, I shall seek a position on the staff of some quarterly review. Or perhaps I shall teach. I may even try my hand at a subjectively oriented novel.'

'Get out of this plant,' Barsch ordered in a muted scream.

'Very well.'

'No, wait!' cried Tunny. 'Uh ... Mr. Barsch didn't mean that. Stick around, Izaak. Go read a criticism or something.'

'Thank you, I shall.' The robot left the office, huge, gleaming, irresistible, and smelling his rose.

'Who do you think you are, you whelp, countermanding me?' Barsch snarled. 'You're not only fired, I'll see to it that—'

'Please, sir,' Tunny said. 'I know this situation. I should. Been living with it for two weeks now, from its beginning. You may not realize that Izaak hasn't been outside this building since he was activated. Mostly he stays in a room assigned him. He gets his books and magazines and stuff by reprostat from the public libraries, or by pneumo from publishers and dealers. We have to pay him a salary, you know – he's legally a person – and he doesn't need to spend it on anything but reading matter.'

'And you want to keep on giving him free rent and let him stroll around disrupting operations?'

'Well, at least he isn't picking up any further stimuli. At present we can predict his craziness. But let him walk loose in the city for a day or two, with a million totally new impressions blasting on his sensors, and God alone knows what conclusions he'll draw and how he'll react.'

'Hm.' Barsch's complexion lightened a bit. He gnawed his lip a while, then said in a more level voice: 'Okay, Tunny, perhaps you aren't such a total incompetent. This mess may not be entirely your fault, or your girl friend's. Maybe I, or someone, should have issued a stricter directive about what he ought and ought not be exposed to for the first several days after activation.'

*You certainly should have,* Tunny thought, but preserved a tactful silence.

'Nevertheless,' Barsch scowled, 'this fiasco is getting us in worse trouble every day. I've just come from lunch with Henry Lachs, the news magazine publisher. He told me that rumors about the situation have already begun to leak out. He'll sit on the story as long as he can, being a good friend of mine, but that won't be much longer. He can't let *Entropy* be scooped, and someone else is bound to get the story soon.'

'Well, sir, I realize we don't want to be a laughingstock—'

'Worse than that. You know why our competitors haven't planned to tackle that rhenium mine. We had the robot idea first and got the jump on them. Once somebody's actually digging ore, he can get the exclusive franchise. But if they learn what's happened to us ... well, Space Metals already has a humanoid contracted for. Half built, in fact. They intended to use him on Callisto, but Mercury would pay a lot better.'

Tunny nodded sickly.

Barsch's tone dropped to an ominous purr. 'Any ideas yet on how to change that clanking horror's so-called mind?'

'He doesn't clank, sir,' Tunny corrected without forethought.

Barsch turned purple. 'I don't give two squeals in hell whether he clanks or rattles or sings high soprano! I want results! I've got half our engineers busting their brains on the problem. But if you, yourself, personally, aren't the one who solves it, we're going to have a new chief estimator. Understand?' Before Tunny could explain that he understood much too well, the screen blanked.

He buried his face in his hands, but that didn't help either. The trouble was, he liked his job, in spite of drawbacks like Barsch. Also, while he wouldn't starve if he was fired, citizen's credit wasn't enough to support items he'd grown used to, such as a sailboat and a cabin in the Rockies, nor items he hoped to add to the list, such as Janet Forelle. Besides, he dreaded the chronic ennui of the unemployed.

He told himself to stop thinking and get busy on the conundrum – no, that wasn't what he meant either— Oh, fireballs! He was no use at this desk today. Especially remembering the angry words he and Janet had exchanged. He'd probably be no use anywhere until the quarrel was mended. At least a diplomatic mission would clear his head, possibly jolt his mind out of the rut in which it now wearily paced.

'Ooh,' he said, visualizing his brain with a deep circular rut where there tramped a tiny replica of himself, bowed under a load of pig iron and shod with cleats. Hastily, he punched a button on his recep. 'I've got to go out;' he said. 'Tell 'em I'll be back when.'

The building hummed and murmured as he went down the hall. Open doorways showed offices, laboratories, control machines clicking away like Hottentots. Now and then he passed a human technie. Emerging on the fifth-story flange he took a dropshaft down to the third, where the northbound beltway

ran. Gentle gusts blew upward in his face, for there was a gray
February sky overhead and the municipal heating system had to
radiate plenty of ergs. Lake Michigan, glimpsed through soaring
gaily colored skyscrapers, looked the more cold by contrast.
Tunny found a seat on the belt, ignoring the aimlessly riding
mass of people around him, mostly unemployed. He stuffed his
pipe and fumed smoke the whole distance to the University of
Chicapolis.

Once there, he had to transfer several times and make his way
through crowds younger, livelier, and more purposeful than
those off campus. Education, he recalled reading, was the third
largest industry in the world. He did read, whatever Izaak said
– nonfiction, which retained a certain limited popularity;
occasionally a novel, but none more recent than from fifty years
ago. 'I'm not prejudiced against what's being written nowadays,'
he had told Janet. 'I just don't think it should be allowed to ride
in the front ends of streetcars.'

She missed his point, having a very limited acquaintance with
mid-twentieth century American history. 'If your attitude isn't
due to prejudice, that's even worse,' she said. 'Then you are con-
genitally unable to perceive the nuances of modern reality.'

'Bah! I earn my money working with the nuances of modern
reality: systems analyses, stress curves, and spaceship orbits.
That's what ails fiction these days and poetry. There's nothing
left to write about that the belles-lettrists think is important.
The only sociological problem of any magnitude is mass boredom, and you can't squeeze much plot or interest out of that.
So the stuff gets too, too precious for words – and stinks.'

'Felix, you can't say that!'

'Can and do, sweetheart. Naturally, economics enters into
the equation too. On the one hand, for the past hundred years
movies, television, and now SteeVee have been crowding the
printed word out of the public eye. (Hey, what a gorgeous
metaphor!) Apart from some nonfiction magazines, publishing
isn't a commercial enterprise any longer. And on the other hand,
in a society as rich as ours, a limited amount of publishing remains feasible: endowed by universities or foundations or individual vanity or these authors' associations that have sprung up
in the past decade. Only it doesn't try to be popular entertainment, it's abandoned that field entirely to SteeVee and become
nothing but an academic mutual admiration society.'

'Nonsense! Let me show you Scomber's critical essay on Tench. He simply tears the man to pieces.'

'Yeah, I know. One-upmanship is part of the game too. The whole point is, though, that this mental inbreeding – no, not even that: mental – uh, I better skip *that* metaphor – anyhow, it never has and never will produce anything worth the time of a healthy human being.'

'Oh, so I'm not a healthy human being?'

'I didn't mean that. You know I didn't. I only meant, well, you know ... the great literature always was based on wide appeal, Sophocles, Shakespeare, Dickens, Mark Twain—'

But the fat was irretrievably in the fire. One thing led at high speed to another, until Tunny stormed out or was thrown out – he still wasn't sure which – and went to earth in the Whirling Comet Bar.

It wasn't that Janet was stuffy, he reminded himself as he approached the looming mass of the English building. She was cute as a kitten, shared his pleasure in sailboats and square dancing and low-life beer joints and most other things; also, she had brains, and their arguments were usually spirited but great mutual fun. They had dealt with less personal topics than last night's debate, though. Janet, a poet's daughter and a departmental secretary, took her magazine very seriously. He hadn't realized how seriously.

The beltway reached his goal. Tunny knocked out his pipe and stepped across the deceleration strips to the flange. The dropshaft lifted him to the fiftieth floor, where University publications had their offices. There was more human activity here than most places. Writing and editing remained people functions, however thoroughly automated printing and binding were. In spite of his purpose, Tunny walked slowly down the hall, observing with pleasure the earnest young coeds in their brief bright skirts and blouses. With less pleasure he noted the earnest young men. There wasn't much about them to suggest soldierly Aeschylus or roistering Marlowe or seagoing Melville or razzmatazz Mencken; they tended to be pale, long-haired, and ever so concerned with the symbolic import of a deliberately omitted comma.

The door marked *Pierce, Arrow!* opened for him and he entered a small shabby office heaped with papers, books, microspools, and unsold copies of the magazine. Janet sat at the desk behind a manual typer and a stack of galleys. She was small herself, pert, extremely well engineered, with dark wavy hair that fell to her shoulders and big eyes the color of the Gulf Stream. Tunny paused and gulped. His heart began to knock.

'Hi,' he said after a minute.

She looked up. 'What – Felix!'

'I, uh, uh, I'm sorry about yesterday,' he said.

'Oh, darling. Do you think I'm not? I was going to come to you.' She did so, with results that were satisfactory to both parties concerned, however sickening they might have been to an outside observer.

After quite a long while, Tunny found himself in a chair with Janet on his lap. She snuggled against him. He stroked her hair and murmured thoughtfully: 'Well, I suppose the trouble was each suddenly realized how dead set on his own odd quirk the other one is. But we can live with the difference between us, huh?'

'Surely,' Janet sighed. 'And then, too, I didn't stop to think how worried you were, that robot and everything, and the whole miserable business my fault.'

'Lord, no. How could you have predicted what'd happen? If anyone is responsible, I am. I took you there and could have warned you. But I didn't know either. Perhaps nobody would have known. Izaak's kind of robot isn't too well understood as yet. So few have been built, there's so little need for them.'

'I still don't quite grasp the situation. Just because I talked to him for an hour or two – poor creature, he was so eager and enthusiastic – and then sent him some books and—'

'That's precisely it. Izaak had been activated only a few days before. Most of his knowledge was built right into him, so to speak, but there was also the matter of ... well, psychological stabilization. Until the end of the indoctrination course, which is designed to fix his personality in the desired pattern, a humanoid robot is extremely susceptible to new impressions. Like a human baby. Or perhaps a closer analogy would be imprinting in some birds: present a fledgling with almost any object at a certain critical stage in its life, and it'll decide that object is its mother and follow the thing around everywhere. I never imagined, though, that modern literary criticism could affect a robot that way. It seemed so alien to everything he was made for,

What I overlooked, I see now, was the fact that Izaak's fully humanoid. He isn't meant to be programmed, but has a free intelligence. Evidently freer than anyone suspected.'

'Is there no way to cure him,'

'Not that I know of. His builders told me that trying to wipe the synapse patterns would ruin the whole brain. Besides, he doesn't want to be cured, and he has most of the legal rights of a citizen. We can't compel him.'

'I do so wish I could do something. Can this really cost you your job?'

' 'Fraid so. I'll fight to keep it, but—'

'Well,' Janet said, 'we'll still have my salary.'

'Nothing doing. No wife is going to support me.'

'Come, come. How medieval can a man get?'

'Plenty,' he said. She tried to argue, but he stopped her in the most pleasant and effective manner. Some time went by. Eventually, with a small gasp, she looked at the clock.

'Heavens! I'm supposed to be at work this minute. I don't want to get myself fired, do I?' She bounced to her feet, a sight which slightly compensated for her departing his lap, smoothed her hair, kissed him again, and sped out the door.

Tunny remained seated. He didn't want to go anywhere, least of all home. Bachelor apartments were okay in their place, but after a certain point in a man's life they got damn cheerless. He fumbled out his pipe and started it again.

Janet was such a sweet kid, he thought. Bright, too. Her preoccupation with these latter-day word games actually did her credit; she wasn't content to stay in the dusty files of books written centuries ago, and word games were the only ones in town. Given a genuine literary milieu, she might well have accomplished great things, instead of fooling around with – what was the latest guff? Tunny got up and wandered over to her desk. He glanced at the galleys. Something by Arnold Roach.

—the tense, almost fetally contracted structure of this story, exquisitely balanced in the ebb and flow of words forming and dissolving images like the interplay of ripples in water, marks an important new advance in the tradition of Arapaima as modified by the school of Barbel. Nevertheless it is necessary to make the assertion that a flawed tertiary symbolism exists, in that the connotations of the primary word

in the long quotation from Pollack which opens the third
of the eleven cantos into which the story is divided, are not, as
the author thinks, so much negative as—

'Yingle, yingle, yingle,' Tunny muttered. 'And they say
engineers can't write decent English. If I couldn't do better
than that with one cerebral hemisphere tied behind my back,
I'd—'

At which point he stopped cold and stared into space with a
mountingly wild surmise. His jaw fell. So did his pipe. He
didn't notice.

Five minutes later he exploded into action.

Four hours later, her secretarial stint through for the day,
Janet returned to do some more proofreading. As the door
opened, she reeled. The air was nearly unbreathable. Through
a blue haze she could barely see her man, grimy, disheveled,
smoking volcanically, hunched over her typer and slamming
away at the keys.

'What off Earth!' she exclaimed.

'One more minute, sweetheart,' Tunny said. Actually he
spent 11.3 more minutes by the clock, agonizing over his last
few sentences. Then he ripped the sheet out, threw it on a stack
of others, and handed her the mess. 'Read that.'

'When my eyes have stopped smarting,' Janet coughed. She
had turned the air 'fresher on full blast and seated herself on
the edge of a chair to wait. Despite her reply, she took the manuscript. But she read the several thousand words with a puzzle-
ment that grew and grew. At the end, she laid the papers slowly
down and asked, 'Is this some kind of joke?'

'I hope not,' said Tunny fervently.

'But—'

'Your next issue is due out when? In two weeks? Could you
advance publication, and include this?'

'What? No, certainly I can't. That is, darling, I have to
reject so many real pieces merely for lack of space, that it breaks
my heart and ... and I've got obligations to them, they trust
me—'

'So.' Tunny rubbed his chin. 'What do you think of my essay?
As a pure bit of writing.'

'Oh ... hm ... well, it's clear and forceful, but naturally the
technicalities of criticism—'

'Okay. You revise it, working in the necessary poop. Also, choose a suitable collection of your better rejects, enough to make up a nice issue. Those characters will see print after all.' While Janet stared with bewildered though lovely blue eyes, Tunny stabbed out numbers on the phone.

'Yes, I want to talk with Mr. Barsch. No, I don't give a neutrino whether he's in conference or not. You tell him Felix Tunny may have the answer to the robot problem. ... Hello, boss. Look, I've got an idea. Won't even cost very much. Can you get hold of a printing plant tonight? You know, someplace where they can run off a few copies of a small one-shot magazine? ... Sure it's short notice. But didn't you say Henry Lachs is a friend of yours? Well, presume on his friendship—'

Having switched off, Tunny whirled about, grabbed Janet in his arms, and shouted, 'Let's go!'

'Where?' she inquired, not unreasonably.

The pneumo went *Whirr-ping* and tossed several items onto the mail shelf. IZK-99 finished reading *Neo-Babbitt: the Entrepreneur as Futility Symbol in Modern Literature*, crossed his room with one stride, and went swiftly through the envelopes. The usual two or three crank letters and requests for autographs – any fully humanoid robot was news – plus a circular advertising metal polish and ... wait ... a magazine. Clipped to this was a note bearing the letterhead of The Mañana Literary Society. '—new authors' association ... foundation-sponsored quarterly review ... sample copies to a few persons of taste and discrimination whom we feel are potential subscribers ...' The format had a limp dignity, with a plain cover reading:

p
i                          Volume One
p                          Number One
e
t
t
the journal of
analytical criticism

Excited and vastly flattered, IZK-99 read it on the spot, in 148 seconds: so fast that he did a double take and stood for a time lost in astonishment. The magazine's contents had otherwise been standard stuff, but this one long article— Slowly, very carefully, he turned back to it and reread:

THUNDER BEYOND VENUS, by Charles Pilchard,
Wisdom Press (Newer York, 2026), 214 pp., UWF $6.50.
*Reviewed by Pierre Hareng*
*Dept. of English, Miskatonic University*

For many years I have been analyzing, dissecting, and
evaluating with the best of them, and it has indeed been
a noble work. Yet everything has its limits. There comes to
each of us a bump, as Poorboy so poignantly says in *Not Soft
Is the Rock*. Suddenly a new planet swims into our ken, a
new world is opened, a new element is discovered, and we
stand with tools in our hands which are not merely inadequate
to the task, but irrelevant. Like those fortunate readers who
were there at the moment when Joyce invented the stream
of consciousness, when Kafka plunged so gladly into the
symbolism of absolute nightmare, when Falkner delineated
the artistic beauty of the humble corncob, when Durrell abol-
ished the stream of consciousness, we too are suddenly crossing the threshold of revolution.

Charles Pilchard has not hitherto been heard from. The
intimate details of his biography, the demonstration of the
point-by-point relationship of these details to his work, will
furnish material for generations of scholarship. Today,
though, we are confronted with the event itself. For *Thunder
Beyond Venus* is indeed an event, which rocks the mind and
shakes the emotions and yet, at the same time, embodies a touch
so sure, an artistry so consummate, that even Brochet has not
painted a finer miniature.

The superficial skeleton is almost scornfully simple. It is,
indeed, frankly traditional – the Quest motif in modern guise
– dare I say that it could be made into a stereodrama? It is
hard to imagine the sheer courage which was required to use
so radical a form that many may find it incomprehensible.
But in exactly this evocation of the great ghosts of Odysseus,
King Arthur, and Don Juan, the author becomes immediately
able to explore (implicitly; he is never crudely explicit) childhood with as much haunting delicacy as our most skilled
specialists in this type of novel. Yet, unlike them, he is not
confined to a child protagonist. Thus he achieves a feat of
time-binding which for richness of symbolic overtones can well

be matched against Betta's famous use of the stopped clock image in *The Old Man and the Umbrella*. As the hero himself cries, when trapped in that collapsing tunnel which is so much more than the obvious womb/tomb: 'Okay, you stupid planet, you've got me pinched where it hurts, but by heaven, I've had more fun in life than you ever did. And I'll whip you yet!'

The fact that he does then indeed overcome the deadly Venusian environment and goes on to destroy the pirate base and complete the project of making the atmosphere Earthlike (a scheme which an engineer friend tells me is at present being seriously contemplated) is thus made infinitely more than a mechanical victory. It is a closing of the ring: the hero, who begins strong and virile and proud, returns to that condition at the end. The ironic overtones of this are clear enough, but the adroit use of such implements along the way as the pick which serves him variously as tool, weapon, and boathook when he and the heroine must cross the river of lava (to take only one random example from this treasure chest) add both an underscoring and a commentary which must be read repeatedly to be appreciated.

And on and on.

When he had finished, IZK-99 went back and perused the article a third time. Then he punched the phone. 'Public library,' said the woman in the screen.

Tunny entered the office of *Pierce, Arrow!* and stood for a moment watching Janet as she slugged the typer. Her desk was loaded with papers, cigarette butts, and coffee equipment. Dark circles under her eyes bespoke exhaustion. But she plowed gamely on.

'Hi, sweetheart,' he said.

'Oh ... Felix.' She raised her head and blinked. 'Goodness, is it that late?'

'Yeah. Sorry I couldn't get here sooner. How're you doing?'

'All right – I guess – but darling, it's so dreadful.'

'Really?' He came to her, stopped for a kiss, and picked up the reprostat page which she was adapting.

The blaster pointed straight at Jon Dace's chest. Behind its gaping muzzle sneered the mushroom-white face and yellow slit-pupilled eyes of Hark Farkas. 'Don't make a move Earth pig!' the pirate hissed. Jon's broad shoulders stiffened. Fury seized him. His keen eyes flickered about, seeking a possible way out of this death trap—

'M-m-m, yeh, that is pretty ripe,' Tunny admitted. 'Where's it from? Oh, yes, I see. *Far Out Science Fiction*, May 1950. Couldn't you do any better than that?'

'Certainly. Some of those old pulp stories are quite good, if you take them on their own terms.' Janet signaled the coffee-maker to pour two fresh cups. 'But others, ugh! I needed a confrontation scene, though, and this was the first that came to hand. Time's too short to make a thorough search.'

'What've you made of it?' Tunny read her manuscript:

The gun opened a cerberoid mouth at him. Behind it, his enemy's face was white as silent snow, secret snow, where the eyes (those are pearls that were) reflected in miniature the sandstorm that hooted cougar-colored on the horizon.

'Hey, not bad. "Cougar-coloured." I like that.'

There went a hissing: 'Best keep stance, friend-stranger-brother whom I must send before me down the tunnel.' Jon's shoulders stiffened. Slowly, he answered—

'Uh, sweetheart, honest, that cussing would make a bull-dozer blush.'

'How can you have intellectual content without four-letter words?' Janet asked, puzzled.

Tunny shrugged. 'No matter, I suppose. Time's too short, as you say, to polish this thing, and Izaak won't know the difference. Not after such a smörgåsbord of authors and critics as he's been gobbling down .. besides, having so little experience of actual, as opposed to fictional humans.'

'Time's too short to *write* this thing,' Janet corrected, her mouth quirking upward. 'How did you ever find the stuff we're plagiarizing? I'd no idea any such school of fiction had ever existed.'

'I knew about it vaguely, from mention in the nineteenth-and twentieth-century books I've read, but to tell the truth, what I did in this case was ask the Library of Congress to search its microfiles for adventure-story publications of that era and 'stat me a million words' worth.' Tunny sat down and reached for his coffee. 'Whew, I'm bushed!'

'Hard day?' Janet said softly.

'Yeah. Keeping Izaak off my neck was the worst part.'

'How did you stall him?'

'Oh, I had his phone tapped. He called the local library first, for a 'stat. When they didn't have the tape, he called a speciality shop that handles fiction among other things. But at that point I switched him over to a friend of mine, who pretended to be a clerk in the store. This guy told Izaak he'd call Newer York and order a bound copy from the publisher. Since then the poor devil has been chewing his fingernails, or would if a robot were able to, and faunching . . . mainly in my office.'

'Think we can meet his expectations?'

'I dunno. My hope is that this enforced wait will make the prize seem still more valuable. Of course, some more reviews would help. Are you positive you won't run one in *Pierce*?'

'I told you, we're so short of space—'

'I talked to Barsch about that. He'll pay for the additional pages and printing.'

'Hm-m-m . . . literary hoaxes do have an honorable old tradition, don't they? But oh, dear— I just don't know.'

'Barsch has gotten around Henry Lachs,' Tunny insinuated. 'There'll be a review in *Entropy*. You wouldn't want to be scooped by a lousy middlebrow news magazine would you?'

Janet laughed. 'All right, you win. Submit your article and I'll run it.'

'I'll submit to you anytime,' Tunny said. After a while: 'Well, I feel better now. I'll take over here while you catch a nap. Let's see, what pickle did we leave our bold hero in?'

This novel at once vigorous and perceptive . . . the most startling use of physical action to further the development that has been seen since Conrad, and it must be asserted that Conrad painted timidly in comparison to the huge, bold, brilliant, and yet minutely executed splashes on Pilchard's canvas . . . this seminal work, if one will pardon the expression . . . the metrical character of the whole, so subtle that the fact the book is a rigidly structured poem will escape many readers. . . .

          – *Pierce, Arrow!*

Two hundred years ago, in the quiet, tree-shaded town of

Amherst, Mass., spinster poetess Emily Dickinson (1830–86) wrote of the soul:

> Unmoved, she notes the chariot's pausing
> At her low gate;
> Unmoved, an emperor is kneeling
> Upon her mat.

In the brief poem of which these lines are a stanza, she expressed a sense of privacy and quiet independence which afterward vanished from the American scene as thoroughly as Amherst vanished into the Atlantic metropolitan complex.

It may seem strange to compare the shy, genteel lady of Puritan derivation to Charles Pilchard and his explosive, intensely controversial first novel. Yet the connection is there. The *Leitmotif** of *Thunder Beyond Venus* is not the story itself. That story is unique enough, breathtakingly original in its use of physical struggle to depict the dark night of the soul. Some would say almost too breathtaking. Dazzled, the reader may fail to see the many underlying layers of meaning. But Emily Dickinson would understand the aloof, independent soul which animates hero Jon Dace.

Tall (6 ft. 3½ in.), robust (225 lb.), balding Charles Pilchard, 38, himself a fanatical seeker of privacy, has written a master's thesis on Rimbaud but never taught. Instead he has lived for more than ten years on citizen's credit while developing his monumental work. [Cut of Charles Pilchard, captioned, 'No charioteer he.'] Twice married, once divorced, he does not maintain a fixed residence but describes himself, like Jon, as 'Swimming around in the ocean called Man.' He has probed deeply into the abysses of that ocean. Yet he has not emerged with the carping negativism of today's nay-sayers. For although he fully appreciates the human tragedy, Pilchard is in the end a triumphant yea-sayer. . . .

* Borrowed from the operatic works of Richard Wagner (1813–83), Emily Dickinson's stormy German contemporary, this word has come to mean an underlying and recurrent theme.

*– Entropy*

The robot entered so noisily that Felix Tunny heard him halfway down the corridor. The engineer turned from his desk and waited. His fingers gripped his chair arms until the nails turned white.

'Hello, Izaak,' he got out. 'Haven't seen you for a couple of days.'

'No,' said the robot. 'I have been in my room, thinking. And reading.'

'Reading what?'

'*Thunder Beyond Venus*, of course. Over and over. Is anybody reading anything else?' One steel finger tapped the volume. 'You have read it yourself, have you not?' Izaak asked on a challenging note.

'Well, you know how it goes,' Tunny said. 'Things are rather frantic around here, what with the company's plans being disrupted and so forth. I've been meaning to get around to it.'

'Get around to it!' Izaak groaned. 'I suppose eventually you will get around to noticing sunlight and the stars.'

'Why, I thought you were above any such gross physical things,' Tunny said. This was the payoff. His throat was so dry he could hardly talk.

Izaak didn't notice. 'It has proven necessary to make a re-evaluation,' he said. 'This book has opened my eyes as much as it has opened the eyes of the critics who first called my attention to its subtlety, its profundity, its universal significance and intensely individual analysis. Pilchard has written the book of our age, as Homer, Dante, and Tolstoy wrote the books of their own ages. He explores what is meaningful today as well as what is meaningful for all time.'

'Bully for Pilchard.'

'The conquest of space is, as the article in *pipett* showed, also the conquest of self. The microcosm opens on the macrocosm, which reflects and re-reflects the observer. This is the first example of the type of book that will be written and discussed for the next hundred years.'

'Could be.'

'None but an utter oaf would respond to this achievement as tepidly as you,' Izaak snapped. 'I shall be glad to see the last of you.'

'Y-y-you're going away? Where? (Hang on, boy, count-down to zero!)

'Mercury. Please notify Barsch and have my spaceship made ready. I have no desire to delay so important an experience.'

Tunny sagged in his chair. 'By no means,' he whispered. 'Don't waste a minute.'

'I make one condition, that for the entire period of my service you send to me with the cargo ships any other works by Pilchard that may appear, plus the quarterlies to which I subscribe and the other exemplars of the literary mode he has pioneered which I shall order on the basis of reviews I read. They must be transcribed to metal, you realize, because of the heat.'

'Sure, sure. Glad to oblige.'

'When I return,' Izaak crooned, 'I shall be so uniquely qualified to criticize the new novels that some college will doubtless give me a literary quarterly of my own.'

He moved toward the door. 'I must go arrange for *Thunder Beyond Venus* to be transcribed on steelloy,' he said.

'Why not tablets of stone?' Tunny muttered.

'That is not a bad idea. Perhaps I shall.' Izaak went out.

When he was safely gone, Tunny whooped. For a while he danced around his office like a peppered Indian, until he whirled on the phone. Call Barsch and tell him— No, to hell with Barsch. Janet deserved the good news first.

She shared his joy over the screens. Watching her, thinking of their future, brought a more serious mood on Tunny. 'My conscience does hurt me a bit,' he confessed. 'It's going to be a blow to Izaak, out there on Dayside, when his brave new school of literature never appears.'

'Don't be too certain about that,' Janet said. 'In fact— Well I was going to call you today. We're in trouble again, I'm afraid. You know that office and clerk we hired to pretend to be Wisdom Press, in case Izaak tried to check up? She's going frantic. Calls are streaming in. Thousands of people already, furious because they can't find *Thunder Beyond Venus* anywhere. She's handed them a story about an accidental explosion in the warehouse, but— What can we do?'

'Oy.' Tunny sat quiet for a space. His mind flew. 'We did run off some extra copies, didn't we?' he said at length.

'Half a dozen or so. I gave one to Arnold Roach. He simply had to have it, after seeing the other articles. Now he's planning a rave review for *The Pacific Monthly*, with all sorts of sarcastic comments about how *Entropy* missed the whole point of the book. Several more critics I know have begged me at least to lend them my copy.'

Tunny smote the desk with a large fist. 'Only one way out
f this,' he decided. 'Print up a million and stand by to print
nore. I don't just mean tapes for libraries, either. I mean regular,
ound volumes.'

'What?'

'I have a hunch that commercial fiction has been revived as
f this week. Maybe our book is crude, but it does touch some-
hing real, something that people believe in their hearts is im-
ortant. If I'm right, then there's going to be a spate of novels
ike this, and man will make a whopping profit, and some will
ven be genuinely good. ... Lord, Lord,' Tunny said in awe.
We simply don't know our own strength, you and I.'

'Let's get together,' Janet suggested, 'and find out.'

*A selection
of recent
Panther Books
is to be found
in the following
pages*

Tune in to

---

# Panther Crimeband

---

An all-star series
presenting the best in mystery,
detection, and suspense

## THE IPCRESS FILE
Len Deighton 3/6

Never before have you read a spy story like this – a novel of
terrifying originality by an ingenious and idiosyncratic
writer of great talent.

'Something entirely new in spy fiction'
EVENING STANDARD

## FLORENTINE FINISH
Cornelius Hirschberg 3/6

A dazzling thriller involving three murders set against
the fascinating background of the New York diamond trade.

Winner of the Edgar Allan Poe Award of the Mystery Writers
of America.

'The best crime novel of 1964'
BOOKS AND BOOKMEN

## THE RELUCTANT ASSASSIN
Alain Reynaud-Fourton 3/6

Five gangsters meticulously plot a final coup to make
them rich for life – a narcotics job worth a cool million dollars.
Things are going smoothly – to the point where each is getting
ready to pick up his million. Then one of them gets greedy.

## DEATH THE SURE PHYSICIAN
John Wakefield 3/6

A hospital bed is a logical enough place to die; but not as Manuela, a wardmaid at St. Ethelburga's hospital, died. Not so murderously.

'Brilliant'
THE GUARDIAN

'Plenty of clues, passion and general information make this a first-class detective story'
BOOKS AND BOOKMEN

## FLUSH AS MAY
P. M. Hubbard 3/6

A vanishing corpse, a sinister policeman, a famous TV personality, and a quiet English village – where a primitive cult engages in macabre rites!

'If any man ever had the art of making you read on, it is P. M. Hubbard'
TATLER

## THE CHINESE BELL MURDERS
Robert van Gulik 5/–

'A rich new vein of detective fiction'
TIMES LITERARY SUPPLEMENT

'To the old Chinese, Judge Dee was as real as Sherlock Holmes and Mr. van Gulik has had the capital notion of turning three stories of Judge Dee into one long tale. Welcome, welcome, Judge Dee and Mr. van Gulik'
J. B. PRIESTLEY

## THE CHINESE LAKE MURDERS
Robert van Gulik 5/–

'Judge Dee remains the happiest recent addition to detective fiction'
NEW YORK POST

"It is head and shoulders above the day-to-day stuff that comes roaring from the press"
TIME AND TIDE

# ALFIE
## Bill Naughton

Alfie's not really a bad sort. It's just that he's got this insatiable appetite for the opposite sex. 'Birds" are irresistible to him, sort of second nature.
Three in one evening if necessary! And necessary is the right word.

ALFIE has been made into the sensational film starring Michael Caine as Alfie, and his birds Shelley Winters, Millicent Martin, Julia Foster, Jane Asher, Shirley Anne Field, Eleanor Bron, and Vivien Merchant.

**3/6**


# LATE NIGHT ON WATLING STREET
## Bill Naughton

In these brilliant tales Bill Naughton illumines the seamy world of long-distance lorry-drivers, brash publicans, and small-time crooks.
The all-night caff on the Great North Road, the dark doorway of a back-street shop, the grimy streets of the Elephant and Castle – these are the haunts of his characters, portrayed with tender intimacy, deep compassion and robust vitality.

'Dramatic, pungent'
TIMES LITERARY SUPPLEMENT

**3/6**

# DON'T GO AWAY I MIGHT FALL DOWN
## Julian More

Rips the glittering travel-posters off the Côte d'Azur.

*A young Englishman and a French girl play out their half-comic, half-pathetic story and, by the last page, have shown the reader an unforgettable picture of this amazing coast in the off-season, warts and other excrescences and all*
THE SPHERE

3/6


# THE CORRUPTERS
## Dariel Telfer

Tells of the gruesome murder of a pregnant girl and the subsequent scandal and soul-searching in Mesa City, a very average American town. With such best-sellers as *The Caretakers* and *The Guilty Ones* to her credit Dariel Telfer has established herself as the natural heir to the Grace Metallious of *Peyton Place*.

*Makes Sodom and Gomorrah look like Pinky and Perky at play*
SCOTSMAN

5/-

## Famous authors in
## Panther Books

| | |
|---|---|
| Henry Miller | Henry Williamson |
| Norman Mailer | Vladimir Nabokov |
| Maurice Procter | Fernando Henriques |
| Jean-Paul Sartre | John O'Hara |
| Jean Genet | Howard Fast |
| Alan Moorehead | Hubert Monteilhet |
| Nicholas Monsarrat | Julian Mitchell |
| Colin Willock | Agnar Mykle |
| James Jones | Simon Raven |
| Erich Maria Remarque | Marcel Proust |
| Len Deighton | John Rechy |
| Saki | Gore Vidal |
| Jack London | John Barth |
| James Hadley Chase | Alan Williams |
| Georgette Heyer | Bill Naughton |
| Rex Stout | John Horne Burns |
| Isaac Asimov | David Caute |
| Jules Verne | Ivan Turgenev |
| Hans Habe | Colin Wilson |
| Marquis de Sade | H.P. Lovecraft |
| Doris Lessing | Rachel Carson |
| Mary McCarthy | Jerzy Peterkiewicz |
| Edmund Wilson | Curzio Malaparte |